PREACHER'S
HELL

PREACHER'S HELL

WILLIAM W. JOHNSTONE
AND J. A. JOHNSTONE

PINNACLE BOOKS
Kensington Publishing Corp.
kensingtonbooks.com

PINNACLE BOOKS are published by

Kensington Publishing Corp.
900 Third Avenue
New York, NY 10022

All Kensington titles, imprints, and distributed lines are available at special quantity discounts for bulk purchases for sales promotion, premiums, fundraising, and educational or institutional use.

Special book excerpts or customized printings can also be created to fit specific needs. For details, write or phone the office of the Kensington Sales Manager: Kensington Publishing Corp., 900 Third Avenue, New York, NY 10022. Attn. Sales Department. Phone: 1-800-221-2647.

First Pinnacle Books Trade Paperback Printing: March 2026

ISBN: 978-0-7860-5217-2

ISBN: 978-0-7860-5219-6 (eBook)

10 9 8 7 6 5 4 3 2 1

Printed in the United States of America

The authorized representative in the EU for product safety and compliance is eucomply OU, Parnu mnt 139b-14, Apt 123 Tallinn, Berlin 11317, hello@eucompliancepartner.com.

PREACHER'S
HELL

CHAPTER 1

Preacher looped his thumb over the hammer of his rifle and said, "I got a hunch we're walkin' into a trap, boys. I know that's what we figured on, but just to make sure, how do you feel about turnin' around and goin' the other way?"

"Umm," the tall, broad-shouldered Indian standing nearby replied.

"You're absolutely correct, Nighthawk," said the diminutive figure standing between the buckskin-clad frontiersman and the towering Crow warrior. "That would indeed feel as if we were running away, and doing so has always stuck in my craw, shall we say? In the Scriptures, the Book of Lamentations advises us not to flee from trouble but to face it head-on. It's widely believed that the Prophet Jeremiah was the author of Lamentations, and he certainly was one to face his troubles and not run from them. You make a very good point, my friend."

"So what you and Nighthawk are sayin', Audie, is we should go ahead," Preacher drawled with a faint smile on his rugged, beard-stubbled face.

"Indubitably."

The man called Audie stood only a little taller than Preacher's waist. He didn't even come that high on Nighthawk. Despite his small stature, he was wiry and muscular and a fierce fighter when he needed to be.

Generally, though, Audie preferred to outthink trouble if he could. He had spent years as a professor of natural history and philosophy at an Eastern university before turning his back on the academic life to head west and become a mountain man. He had fit in surprisingly well in the untamed mountains, especially after he'd met Nighthawk and the two of them had become inseparable friends.

During their travels, the two of them had encountered Preacher, who was already becoming a legend west of the Mississippi despite being a relatively young man.

Over the years since then, they had shared many adventures—and much danger and hardship. Preacher had no better friends than these two.

So when he'd heard talk that they were headed for Dutch Charley's, an isolated trading post in the Bitterroot Mountains northwest of the Yellowstone country, he had pointed his stallion's nose in that direction, too, figuring he would find them there and trail along with them for a while.

As it turned out, he'd run into Audie and Nighthawk before any of them ever reached the trading post. Dutch Charley's was still a couple of days away on the other side of Wailing Woman Pass. The three of them would make the rest of the journey together.

The problem was, Audie and Nighthawk had trouble dogging their trail.

"We ran into a bunch of ne'er-do-wells three days ago," Audie had explained to Preacher as they sat next to the faintly glowing remains of a campfire their first night together. "They did everything correctly. They hailed the camp before they came in. They spoke respectfully and politely and shared some of their provisions."

"Umm," Nighthawk had chimed in.

"But as my esteemed friend points out, one could almost smell the villainy on them. We both saw how they eyed not only the pelts we've taken but also our supplies and our pack horses. Their avariciousness was as plain as the proverbial nose on your face."

"Did they have any pack animals with 'em?" Preacher had asked.

"No. The only supplies they had were what they carried on their saddle mounts."

"Umm."

Audie had laughed. "Indeed. They had lean and hungry looks, as the Bard had Julius Caesar say of Cassius, only their expressions were born of actual deprivation rather than naked political ambition. I'm not sure which is more dangerous, the hunger for power or the hunger for food!"

"They didn't try nothin' that night, though?" Preacher wanted to know.

Audie shook his head and said, "No, perhaps because they realized that the presence of strangers had put us on the alert and they would have preferred to take us by surprise. But ever since, our instincts have told us that we were being followed. I trust my own instincts quite a bit, but Nighthawk's are infallible. Those men are out there, all right, just waiting for a good chance to kill us and steal all our belongings."

Preacher had taken a sip of strong black coffee from the tin cup in his hand.

"I don't doubt it a bit," he said. "How many varmints are there?"

"Six that we saw. I suppose it's possible others could have stayed back out of sight and not come into camp."

Preacher mulled that over for a moment and then shook his head. "More than likely not. They only had three-to-one odds. I can see why they'd be a mite leery of tanglin' with you two."

Audie laughed and said, "Surely, they wouldn't have counted me as a full opponent. But of course, Nighthawk is approximately the size of two men, so that would balance things out, would it not?"

"Don't sell yourself short—so to speak."

That brought another laugh from Audie.

"Folks out here in the high country know who you and Nighthawk are," Preacher went on. "Chances are, those fellas have heard tell of you and don't want to risk a fight out in the open. They'd rather find someplace they can ambush you. That'd tilt the odds a mite more in their favor."

"That does sound like a reasonable scenario," Audie agreed. "Do you have any thoughts on where such a suitable ambush site could be found?"

"We got to go through Wailin' Woman Pass to make it to Dutch Charley's," Preacher had said. "Either that or go the long way around, and that'd add fifty miles to the trip. Did you happen to mention that's where you fellas are headed?"

"No," said Audie, "but they could see for themselves that we have a load of pelts. Charley's is the closest place we can dispose of them, so it being our destination is a logical assumption to make."

"Knowin' that, they could ride around you and push hard to make it to the pass first. Then they could lay in wait there like the skulkin' varmints you took 'em to be."

"I can certainly see that happening," Audie said, nodding. "We'll just have to be ready for them."

So, for the past day and a half, the three friends had traveled with all their senses alert but had seen no sign of potential trouble. Now they had reached Wailing Woman Pass, so called because when the wind blew at just the right speed through its narrow confines, it created a moaning sound like a woman consumed with grief.

On the other side, the trail led down into a beautiful landscape of rugged mountains, lush meadows, towering evergreens, and fast-flowing streams. The trading post was located on one of those streams and they would reach it by nightfall—but only if they survived the trip through the pass.

Almost sheer stone walls rose seventy or eighty feet on either side of the opening through a saw-toothed ridge that ran for many miles roughly north and south. The pass was no more than twenty yards wide.

What made it intimidating was that instead of cutting straight through the barrier, as most passes did, it zigged and zagged so that travelers had to cover almost a mile in length to traverse a ridge half a mile wide. A man couldn't ride more than a hundred yards without having to go around a sharp bend, followed by another and another.

Preacher, Audie, and Nighthawk had dismounted to study the pass as much as they could before they started through it. After the brief conversation about the possibility of riding into a trap, the men swung up into their saddles again, Nighthawk giving Audie a hand as he usually did.

Preacher nudged the heels of his high-topped boots into Horse's sides and sent the rangy gray stallion walking forward. He called, "Dog, stay with me."

The big, shaggy cur, who looked as much like a wolf as he did a dog, had started to bound ahead of the riders. He stopped at Preacher's call, looked back over his shoulder, and whined softly. He was used to ranging far out in front of the mountain man, searching for trouble as well as rabbits or any other small critters he might scare up.

Dog wanted to do that now, but he obeyed the mountain man's command. He and Preacher and Horse had been trail partners for a long time. They made a formidable team, but Preacher was definitely the leader.

"I don't want you runnin' into a bunch of no-count robbers," Preacher said to Dog as he caught up to the big cur. "Chances are they wouldn't shoot you 'cause they wouldn't want to tip their hands, but we can't count on that. Don't worry: if there's any fightin' you'll be able to get in on it."

Dog paced alongside the big stallion, clearly holding himself in and not liking it.

Preacher led his own pack horse, then Audie came next, followed by Nighthawk who led the two pack horses he and his friend had brought with them. One of those animals was loaded with the beaver pelts they had taken, while the other carried their supplies.

"Times sure have changed," Preacher said without looking around, knowing his companions could hear him in the close confines of the pass. "I remember a day when you'd have both o' them pack animals loaded down with plews and have to split up the provisions on your saddle mounts. I ain't sayin' the streams are all trapped out, but the beaver sure ain't as plentiful as they once were."

"The demand is less, too," Audie pointed out. "Gentlemen don't wear beaver hats as much as they used to, nor do ladies sport fur mufflers and jackets. Given time, the beaver population will recover."

"I hope you're right."

"Umm," Nighthawk said as he brought up the rear.

"You're right, the beaver will be as plentiful in the mountains as the buffalo are on the plains," Audie replied to his friend's comment. "Nothing could ever destroy all of them."

Preacher grunted. "I wouldn't put nothin' beyond the ability of civilization to destroy it."

"But civilization is progress."

"So they say," Preacher responded, "but I ain't convinced."

"In truth, neither am I. That doubt is a major reason I'm out here in the mountains instead of inside the ivy-covered halls of learning. I wanted to see this land in all its glory and majesty while I still had the chance."

The conversation was interesting, as it always was when talking to Audie and Nighthawk. They were a couple of mighty smart hombres.

But the talking served another purpose, as well. Preacher wanted it to sound as if he and his companions were just ambling along through the pass, not paying any particular attention to their surroundings, so that the bushwhackers—if there were any waiting for them—would believe they were riding blindly into the trap.

The reality was that Preacher's keen eyes were moving constantly, searching the walls ahead of them on both sides for any telltale signs of lurking danger. His rifle was ready in his hands. He could cock it, raise it to his shoulder, and fire in less than a heartbeat.

All he needed was a target.

The rifle was a .54 caliber model 1841 Whitney Armory weapon with a percussion lock rather than a flintlock like the rifles Preacher had used for many years. It was more dependable, more resistant to the elements, and a beautiful piece of work with brass trim and gleaming wood.

It fired only one shot, however. Preacher had become a mite spoiled by the Paterson Colt revolvers he had been carrying ever since a troop of Texas Rangers had presented them to him a couple of years earlier. He liked them so well he had bought a second pair that he kept stowed in his belongings.

The Colts carried five rounds apiece. When a fella wound up fighting for his life as often as Preacher did, having ten shots at your disposal could make a heap of difference. It could mean life or death, in fact.

He was still yammering on about the blight of civilization when he heard something from around the next bend. It was just a soft thump, but that was enough to tell him something had fallen from one wall.

At the same time, a low growl sounded from deep in Dog's throat and the hair on his neck ruffled up.

"I heard it," Preacher told the big cur. "Might be nothin'. Might be somebody gettin' ready to start the ball. Only one way to find out."

He drew the rifle's hammer back and held it one-handed as he guided Horse around the next turn. Spotting movement from the corner of his eye, he turned his head and lifted it.

A short distance ahead, at the top of the left-hand wall, a man's head and shoulders rose from behind a rock and a rifle barrel thrust out.

Preacher had only an instant to react and a small target at which to aim. Even so, he didn't hesitate.

The rifle sprang to his shoulder and boomed as he squeezed the trigger.

CHAPTER 2

The ambusher on the rimrock never got a chance to fire his own weapon. His head jerked back, and his hat flew off as the ball from Preacher's rifle smashed through his brain. The rifle slipped from his suddenly nerveless fingers and fell to the floor of the pass as its former owner slumped forward over the rock he had used—unsuccessfully—for cover.

Behind Preacher, another rifle boomed. Either Audie or Nighthawk had fired this shot; he didn't look around to see which because he knew it didn't matter.

From the top of the stone wall to the right, a man screamed. Preacher saw the ambusher lurch upright and topple over the brink, turning over completely in midair before crashing lifelessly to the ground.

A swift rataplan of hoofbeats sounded from around the next bend. Preacher rammed the empty rifle back in its saddle scabbard and put the stallion's reins in his teeth. He reached down to his hips and drew both Paterson Colts as he leaned forward and prodded Horse into a run with his heels.

Four men on horseback swept around the bend and charged toward Preacher and his friends. The would-be robbers had posted a single rifleman on each rim, their job being to cut down two out of the three intended victims. Then the other four would attack from the front and wipe out the remaining man.

But it hadn't worked out that way. Preacher, Audie, and Nighthawk were still alive and kicking, and they were ready to take the fight straight to their attackers.

That was what Preacher did, guiding Horse with his knees as he thundered toward the four men. The guns in his hands roared and spouted flame and powdersmoke.

One of the attackers flung his hands in the air and pitched off his horse, shot clean through the body by Preacher.

Another jerked backward and dropped the gun he held, but he managed to stay mounted as his horse veered to the side. That didn't do him any good because Dog raced forward, launched himself into the air, and crashed into the wounded man, knocking him out of the saddle. The big cur landed nimbly on all four paws and sprang on top of the man, whose yells turned into a grotesque, bubbling scream as Dog's sharp teeth tore into his throat.

Nighthawk charged up alongside Preacher, eager to get into the fight. The giant warrior's arm drew back and flashed forward. The tomahawk he threw spun through the air so fast it was hard for the eye to follow.

The weapon seemed to reappear almost as if by magic as it struck one of the remaining men in the forehead. The tomahawk's keen edge cleaved into the man's skull and lodged there as blood welled around it. The dead man fell, but one foot hung in a stirrup and the madly charging horse dragged him on past Preacher, Nighthawk, and Audie.

That left just one attacker, and by now he must have realized what a terrible mistake he and his companions had made. He hauled back hard on his horse's reins and tried to turn the animal. The mount stumbled and lost its balance, going down in a welter of flailing legs. It rolled right over its former rider.

Preacher and his friends reined in and were out of their saddles quickly. Nighthawk trotted around the pass, checking to make sure the would-be robbers were dead. He didn't bother with the one Dog was still savaging, nor with the one whose horse had fallen. Preacher and Audie approached that man, their guns out and ready.

After rolling over the man, his mount had struggled to its feet and moved off several yards. The animal appeared not to have been injured in the fall.

The same couldn't be said of its rider. The man lay on his back, gasping and moaning. The white, jagged end of a broken bone stuck out of his right thigh, with blood heavily staining that leg of his woolen trousers. His left arm was twisted at an unnatural angle, either broken or with a dislocated shoulder. And blood leaked from both corners of his mouth to make crimson trails across his bearded jaws.

"This one of the varmints who paid a visit to your camp?" Preacher asked Audie.

"Yes, I recognize him," Audie replied. He shook his head and said to the injured man, "I sincerely wish you had decided to resist temptation, my friend."

"You g-go straight to . . . to hell, you sawed-off little bas—"

The man got that far in his insult before a spasm went through him. His head jerked back, and cords stood out in his neck. More blood welled from his mouth.

"I'm all . . . b-busted up inside," he said when he was able to talk again. He stared up at Preacher and Audie, his eyes wide with agony. "P-Please . . . f-finish me off."

"I don't know," Preacher said. "I've never cottoned to low-down thieves, and you was about to call my friend here a dirty name, not to mention bein' so rude as to bring up him bein' short. There's a heap of wolves in these mountains. Seems to me it'd be fittin' if we was to go off and let them deal with you—"

Audie brought up the old flintlock pistol he held and squeezed the trigger. The weapon's dull boom echoed back resoundingly from the walls of the pass. The injured man jerked once as the heavy lead ball smashed into his forehead and put him out of his misery.

Nighthawk had come up behind them. As the shot's echoes faded, he said, "Umm."

"I agree, there was no point in prolonging the torment this poor fellow was enduring," Audie said. "I know you weren't being intentionally cruel, Preacher. The frontier is a harsh taskmaster and strips away much of a man's gentler nature."

"I was fixin' to shoot him," Preacher said. "To tell the truth, I figured he might not see it comin' as much with me jabberin' at him that way."

"Ah, I understand now. You were just trying to be kind in your own rough fashion."

"Well, I might not go quite that far," the mountain man said. "Like I told the varmint, I never have cottoned to thieves."

They rounded up the robbers' horses and drove them on through the canyon. They would trade the animals and the gear once they got to Dutch Charley's.

They left the dead men where they had fallen. As Audie had said, the frontier was a harsh taskmaster, and scavengers had to eat, too.

Even though, during his long, adventuring years, Preacher had traveled the length and width and breadth of the West and seen just about everything there was to see, when the three friends emerged from Wailing Woman Pass, he was struck by the sheer beauty of the landscape spread out before them. The colors were breathtaking—the deep blue sky, the dazzling white clouds, the soothing, restful, green pine-clad slopes. Rugged gray peaks reposed in the distance like huge, slumbering behemoths. Wildflowers provided splotches of bright color in the valleys.

White foam frothed on the icy blue, swiftly flowing streams. There was no prettier place on God's Earth than the high country, to Preacher's way of thinking. He might roam here and there and probably would always be too fiddle-footed to do otherwise, but this was home, and here he would always return until the day came for him to cross the divide. When he did, he hoped it would be here.

Something of what he was feeling must have shown on his face, because Audie looked over at him and said softly, "It's the same with me, Preacher. There's nowhere else like it."

The encounter with the thieves slowed them down enough that the sun had gone behind the Bitterroots and twilight was beginning to settle down over the land by the time they came in sight of Dutch Charley's Trading Post. It was a sprawling log building that had started out fairly small and been added on to several times over the years as Charley's business increased. Behind it was a barn with an attached corral, and not far from the barn was a squat building that served as a blacksmith shop whenever Charley wanted to fire up the forge.

One of the numerous creeks that flowed through the region ran nearby. Charley, who also had an engineering bent, had constructed a water wheel on it. He didn't use it for anything at the moment, but he liked having it and insisted that if enough people ever moved into the area, he would build a sawmill to go with it, or possibly a grain mill. Or both.

Numerous lights burned around the trading post, casting inviting yellow glows in the gathering dusk. As the three men rode toward the place, Audie commented, "You know, this is almost starting to look like a settlement."

"You hush up with talk like that," Preacher chided him. "You remember, six or eight years ago I got mixed up with those folks who had the bright idea of startin' theirselves a town out here, up north a ways."

"I recall that it was fairly successful for a while."

"Yeah, but it didn't last. There was always one sort of ruckus or another breakin' out, and the British kept stirrin' up trouble. The settlers finally gave up, and that should've been the end of crazy notions like havin' towns out here." Preacher shook his head. "We just don't need 'em."

"You can't stop things from changing with a wish and a hope, my friend."

"I reckon not," the mountain man admitted. "But that don't have to mean I cotton to it."

"A never-ending conundrum."

Nighthawk nodded solemnly.

In the fading light, Preacher studied the corral. He didn't see any horses, although some could be inside the barn. However, the weather was pleasant, and it seemed more likely any horses would be outside this evening.

"Looks like ol' Charley don't have much business goin' on."

"It's early yet," Audie said. "Some other travelers could arrive."

Without saying anything, Nighthawk leveled an arm like the trunk of a young tree and pointed across the creek.

"You're right!" Audie said. "Two riders approaching from the west."

Preacher saw them emerging from some trees about a hundred yards on the other side of the stream. They were too far away to make out any details, but he could tell from the way the horses moved with plodding gaits that they were tired, as if they'd been on a hard trail for a long time. The animals picked their way deliberately across the meadow toward the creek, one of them out in front of the other instead of side by side.

Preacher noticed something else. The rider bringing up the rear turned his head several times to look behind them as if he were checking to make sure they weren't being followed.

Preacher shifted his gaze to the trees again and watched to see if anyone else rode out of them. He didn't see anybody.

The two strangers splashed across the creek, which was fairly shallow here with a rocky bed. It was easy to ford, which was a major reason Dutch Charley had decided to build his trading post at this location. They reached the buildings well ahead of Preacher and his companions, swinging around the trading post itself to head for the barn and the corral.

"No pack animal," Preacher commented. "They're travelin' light, I reckon."

"In a hurry, perhaps," Audie said.

Preacher glanced over at him. "You got the same impression I did, didn't you?"

"That someone might be pursuing them? As a matter of fact, I did."

"Which don't make it any of our business."

"None at all," Audie agreed without hesitation. "And it's entirely possible we're misreading the situation. Even if we're not, it might well be inappropriate for us to become involved."

"Well, we wouldn't want to do nothin' inappropriate."

Both white men grinned. Nighthawk let out a grunt that was as close as he ever got to laughter.

The two riders dismounted. The larger of the two opened the corral gate and led the horses into the enclosure. The other one, carrying a large, apparently unwieldy pack of some sort, walked toward the trading post in a slow, weary gait.

Preacher frowned in surprise. Even though the light was poor, he was close enough now to see that the person heading into the trading post wore a dress over buckskin leggings.

A woman, more than likely an Indian.

After closing the gate, the other pilgrim pulled blankets from the backs of the horses and began rubbing the animals down. He had leaned a long-barreled flintlock rifle against the fence.

Preacher saw him glance toward the weapon as he, Audie, and Nighthawk approached, but he didn't make a move to retrieve it, concentrating on tending to the horses instead. The fellow didn't want to provoke trouble if none was brewing.

Preacher could tell that the man was watching them pretty closely from the corner of his eye. He was an Indian, still tall and straight but obviously of advanced years. His hair was iron gray and worn in simple braids, and his face was seamed and weathered.

A Flathead, Preacher guessed. The man's buckskins were plain and free of ornamentation so he couldn't go by that, but the Flatheads were the most common tribe in this part of the country.

Preacher reined Horse to a stop outside the corral. Audie and Nighthawk did likewise with their mounts. The old Indian swatted his ponies on their rumps and sent them trotting toward the barn. Then he turned to the newcomers and said in English, "I'll get the gate for you."

"Much obliged, Grandfather," Preacher said.

"I am not your grandfather," the old man replied with a hint of sharpness. He lifted the rope loop that held the gate closed and swung it back so the three men could ride in.

"Sorry," Preacher said as he nudged the stallion into the corral. "I don't reckon I meant any offense."

The old man waved a gnarled hand. "It is nothing. I was too quick to speak. It has been a long day."

"You and your wife have come a long way?"

"I do not travel with my wife. She is my granddaughter." The old man smiled. "So, I actually am a grandfather. I should not be insulted by being called one."

Preacher, Audie, and Nighthawk dismounted after leading their pack horses and the horses they had claimed from the dead robbers inside the corral.

"Folks call me Preacher," the mountain man said. "This here is Audie, and that walkin' mountain over there is Nighthawk."

"I am Sahale. It means 'in a high place.'"

"Pleased to meet you. You folks are Flatheads, is that right?"

Sahale frowned. "We are Salish. Our ancestors never flattened their heads. The first white men who came to this land were confused by our sign language and believed that was what our people were saying." He raised his hands and pressed the palms against the sides of his head. "This is just the sign for our tribe. It has no other meaning."

"It's easy for folks to get things wrong without meanin' any harm. What's your granddaughter's name?"

"Chimalus. It means 'bluebird.'"

"Pretty name," Preacher said. "We'd best tend to these horses."

Sahale looked at the half-dozen saddled but riderless mounts and commented dryly, "You seem to have an abundance of them."

"It's a long story. Well, come to think of it, I guess it ain't all that long. The fellas who owned these horses figured on robbin' and killin' me and my friends." Preacher spat. "They don't need the horses no more."

Sahale had nothing to say to that. He picked up the rifle, ducked between two poles in the fence, and walked toward the trading post.

"Quite a dignified old man," Audie said quietly. "I wonder what he and his granddaughter are running from."

"We could ask him, but I ain't sure he'd tell us," Preacher said. "He seems a mite proud and stiff-necked."

They put that question out of their minds for the next few minutes as they unsaddled all the horses and rubbed down the ones they had been riding. The horses went over to a long water trough to drink. Nighthawk found bags of grain in a shed and poured some into a bin so the animals could eat. The two ponies ridden by Sahale and his granddaughter joined in, although not without some squabbling among the horses as they established a hierarchy.

By the time Preacher, Audie, and Nighthawk left the corral and walked toward the trading post, all the light had faded from the western sky except a shallow arch of gold just above the mountaintops. Preacher pulled the latch string on the back door and led the way inside after telling Dog to stay put.

Flames leaped and danced in the huge fireplace that took up most of a side wall. A pot-bellied, cast-iron stove stood at the far end of the big main room. Between the two sources of heat, it was pleasantly warm. A tangy blend of tobacco smoke from Dutch Charley's pipe mixed with the smells of roasting meat and baking bread and filled the air.

Shelves packed with assorted trade goods took up much of the space in the room. A bar ran along the back with tables in front of it. Dutch Charley himself stood behind the bar with his huge hands resting on the polished planks. He was a tall, broad man with a red face, a sweeping mustache, and a halo of wispy fair hair around his head. His last name was Hennenburger, Preacher recalled, but everybody in the mountains just called him Dutch Charley.

His wife was an Indian woman he had met on the way out here and brought with him. She stood at a stove behind the bar stirring something—probably stew—in a large iron pot.

The other two people in the room sat at a table on the far side of the room, well away from the light of the fireplace and the glow cast by lanterns hanging on chains from the roof beams. Sahale sat with his back against the wall and the rifle lying on the table close at hand. He wasn't hunting trouble, but trouble might be hunting him. Clearly, he intended to be ready for it if it found him.

His granddaughter sat with her back to the room. At the end of the table, in the narrow space on the puncheon floor between the table and the wall, lay the large pack she had carried into the building earlier. She kept glancing over at it, Preacher noted, almost as if she were afraid it was going to get up and run away under its own power.

That odd thought had just gone through his head when she half-turned on the bench to look at him. The compelling beauty of the dark-eyed gaze she cast upon him stopped him in his tracks.

CHAPTER 3

Indian women were just like any other kind, Preacher had found. Some were mighty pretty, and some weren't. This young woman was pretty, with smooth skin, dark eyes, and hair like a raven's wing, parted in the middle and woven into two thick braids that draped over her shoulders and hung down in front of the fringed buckskin dress she wore.

In a voice that crackled with irritation, she asked in English, "What do you want, white man?"

"Not a thing other than to say howdy, ma'am," Preacher replied. "Me and my friends met your grandpa outside. We figured we ought to come over and pay our respects."

"You have done so," she said. "You should leave us alone now."

The old man spoke to her in their native tongue. Preacher savvied enough of it to know he was telling her there was no reason to be rude. Indians valued civility and nearly always were polite unless they were provoked.

On the other hand, Preacher wasn't one to force his company on anybody who didn't want it. He lifted a hand to the wide brim of his brown felt hat and touched a finger to it as he nodded.

"If that's the way you feel, we'll bid you a good evenin', then," he said.

"And safe travels in the future," Audie added.

Nighthawk just gave them a grave nod.

The three men strode over to the bar where Dutch Charley greeted them with a big grin on his ruddy face.

"Preacher, Audie, Nighthawk! So good to see you again!" The trader's voice held only a trace of an accent from his upbringing in Germany. "It has been quite a while since you've been through this way."

Audie climbed up on one of the rough stools so he could see over the bar and said, "Your business has grown, Charley. You must be prospering."

"*Ja*, my business has grown and so has my wife."

The Indian woman at the stove turned to beam at them and revealed a rounded belly that proclaimed she was with child.

"Our heartiest congratulations, madam," Audie told her.

"You hopin' the young'un is a boy or a girl, Charley?" asked Preacher.

Charley shook his head. "I don't care, although it would be nice to have a son to carry on this business when I'm gone."

"Well, you got our best wishes no matter which way it turns out." Preacher slapped his hands on the bar. "Now, it's been a mighty long day, and we could all use some coffee and bowls o' whatever that delicious-smellin' concoction your missus is cooking up might be."

A few minutes later, they were enjoying strong black coffee from large, earthenware mugs and wooden bowls full of savory stew with chunks of elk meat swimming in the dark broth along with wild onions and carrots and potatoes from Dutch Charley's garden. They had chunks of freshly baked rye bread to sop up the juices.

Meanwhile, the old Flathead called Sahale stood up from the table and went over to the fireplace where a quarter of venison was roasting on an iron spit. He took a knife from a fringed and beaded sheath at his waist and carved off several chunks of sizzling, dripping meat, the heat of which didn't seem to bother him as he carried the venison back to the table where his granddaughter sat waiting. He sat down again and divided the food between them.

Preacher observed that from the corner of his eye and said quietly to Charley, "You know those two? Have they been here before?"

Charley leaned forward and said equally quietly, "I never laid eyes on them until they showed up a short time ago. But you know my policy—everyone is welcome as long as they don't cause trouble."

"How about if trouble follows 'em here? We saw 'em ridin' in. The old-timer kept checkin' their back trail like he expected to see somebody on it."

Charley's massive shoulders rose and fell. "It does not matter. I would not turn away anyone who seeks the hospitality of my place."

"Nor would we want you to do so," Audie said. "Consider this a simple word of warning."

Charley nodded, reached under the bar, and brought out a heavy bungstarter. He placed it on the bar and then retrieved a pair of flintlock pistols that he set down flanking the bungstarter. He reached under the bar a third time and produced a double-barreled shotgun with the stock and barrels sawed off so that it could be aimed and fired with one hand if a man's arm was strong enough to withstand the recoil—which Charley's undoubtedly was. Finally, he added a scabbarded cavalry saber to the collection.

"Yeah, I'd say you're ready for trouble, all right," Preacher said with a grin. "Armed for bear, sure enough."

Audie said, "Actually, I'm not sure any of those weapons would bring down a bear except perhaps for the shotgun if it was fired at short enough range. But I doubt if you have bears coming into the trading post very often, do you, Charley?"

"I mind my own business," Charley rumbled, "but I maintain the peace in here, too."

Preacher chuckled and went back to sopping up stew with

a big piece of rye bread. That was enjoyable and occupied his attention for the next little while.

As he was drinking the last of his coffee, Preacher turned slightly on the stool and glanced at the table where the two Indians were. The old man still sat almost bolt upright, which seemed to be his habitual posture, but the young woman had leaned forward across the table and rested her head on her crossed arms. She appeared to be asleep.

Wherever they had come from, whatever they had gone through, weariness had claimed the young woman named Chimalus.

Bluebird, Preacher reminded himself. The name meant Bluebird, and he decided that was what he was going to call her. It fit her.

Although, given her lack of friendliness, he figured it was possible he'd never have occasion to speak to her again. More than likely, it didn't matter what he decided to call her.

Audie pushed away his empty bowl, shook his head to the unspoken question from Charley's wife as to whether he wanted more, and said, "We have business to discuss."

"You have brought in pelts?" Charley asked.

"These two have," Preacher said as he poked a thumb toward Audie and Nighthawk. "They're the industrious ones. I've been just sort of roamin' around for a while, too lazy to work at trappin' or anything else."

"We left the packs in the barn," Audie said. "Would you like for Nighthawk to fetch them in?"

Charley waved a ham-like hand. "Tomorrow morning will be soon enough to negotiate," he said. "I will give you the best price I possibly can, Audie, you know that, but the market is not what it once was."

"Yes, we're all too aware of the downturn it's taken. We were just talking about that earlier."

"There's more to trade," Preacher said. "We brought in some

extra horses, too. They look like decent saddle mounts, and they got saddles to go with them."

Charley's bushy eyebrows rose. "Should I inquire as to how you came by these horses?"

"It was honest enough. Their owners decided to ambush us. Probably figured on robbin' us after they killed us. We disabused 'em of the notion."

Charley nodded and said solemnly, "I see. You have no need of the horses?"

"I don't," Preacher said. "Already got a fine pack animal."

Audie and Nighthawk shook their heads. Audie added, "There's some other gear to go along with the horses and saddles, a few guns and tools and what have you. We'll keep the ammunition and supplies."

"I'm certain we can make a deal. Where will you go from here? Back to trapping?"

"Ain't quite figured that out yet," said Preacher. "The good thing is, we don't have to be nowhere at no particular time." He smiled. "So if you want to draw a mug o' beer to help wash down that fine grub, I wouldn't say no."

"More coffee for me," Audie said.

Nighthawk didn't ask for anything else.

For the next half-hour or so, the men sat at the bar chatting pleasantly with Dutch Charley. The trader's wife had retreated to another part of the building.

When Preacher glanced over his shoulder, he saw that Sahale had finally given in to his tiredness, as well. He was still sitting up, but his shoulders rested against the log wall behind him and his head drooped forward. His eyes were closed.

His granddaughter still dozed over the table with her head resting on her arms. Preacher wondered how far they had come today to be so tired.

A moment later, with no warning, the young woman jerked out

of her slumber and bolted to her feet. She let out a wordless cry and twisted back and forth as if looking around for something. Her gaze must have landed on the pack at the end of the table. She stared at it for a second and then heaved a huge sigh of relief.

Following her startled outburst, her grandfather had leaped to his feet, too, instantly awake. He grabbed the rifle from the table and lifted it to swing the barrel back and forth as if searching for a target. He stood there with his shoulders slightly hunched and a look on his weathered face that was frightened and angry at the same time.

"My friends, my friends, it is all right," Charley said in his booming voice as he held out his hands toward them and patted the air calmingly. "Nothing is wrong." He smiled. "I think you must have had a bad dream, *fraulein.*"

Although she probably didn't understand the German word, Bluebird must have known the trader was talking to her. She gave a little shake of her head and said, "Not a bad dream. An *evil* dream about evil men." Her features had relaxed slightly, but now they began to tense again. "They are close by. I can sense them."

"We left them far behind, granddaughter—" Sahale began.

"They have found us." Bluebird groaned. "They are coming. We cannot escape them."

Preacher's first impulse was to go to her and assure her that she and her grandfather would be all right. He and Audie and Nighthawk were here, and they wouldn't allow anything to happen to the two Flatheads. Charley Hennenburger's massive presence just added to that security.

He hesitated because she had been a mite standoffish earlier and he didn't want to spook her even more.

Nighthawk started across the room toward them. That was better, Preacher thought. Even though he was Crow and they were Salish, at least he was another Indian. Bluebird would probably feel more comfortable with him reassuring her.

Nighthawk was only halfway across the room when the trading post's front door was flung open with such force that it crashed back against the wall. Men boiled through the opening, bristling with guns, and one of them yelled, "There they are! Get those damn redskins!"

CHAPTER 4

Preacher wheeled away from the bar as his hands dropped to the butts of the Colts at his hips. The big revolvers slid smoothly from their holsters. He would have warned the newcomers to stop right where they were, but before he could get the words out of his mouth, one of the men charging into the room whipped up a flintlock pistol and fired at Nighthawk at almost point-blank range.

Nighthawk's reactions were lightning-fast, especially for such a big man. As flame gouted from the gun muzzle, he twisted aside and flung his left arm out. The pistol ball stirred the fringe hanging down from the buckskin shirt's sleeve, but that was as close as it came to the Crow warrior's flesh.

An instant later, Nighthawk's hand closed around the gunman's wrist and twisted. The man screamed as bones cracked and grinded against each other. The gun dropped from his suddenly useless hand.

One of the other intruders yelled, "Don't shoot, you damn fools! You might hit them!"

So they didn't want to kill Sahale and Bluebird, but despite that, Preacher felt sure they didn't have any good intentions for the two Indians. He pouched both irons and stepped up to take on the attackers hand to hand. More than likely, he could have driven them off with the Colts, but that would mean missing out on what might be a good scrap.

Also, he was curious. He wanted to get his hands on one of the varmints and find out just why the two Salish were so important.

Still holding the wrist of the man who'd shot at him, Nighthawk bent and grabbed the man's left leg at the knee, as well. Seemingly effortlessly, he jerked the man off his feet and hoisted him above his head. Nighthawk was so tall the man brushed against one of the hanging lanterns. His homespun shirt ignited, and he screamed and flailed as the flames caught and spread.

Nighthawk threw him into the faces of the other men.

That bowled over several of them. They wound up in a writhing mess on the floor, just inside the doorway. Unfortunately, enough room was left for another six or eight men to leap past them and continue the invasion of Dutch Charley's. In the confusion, Preacher couldn't get an accurate count of the attackers—not that it was important. He was going to tangle with them no matter how many there were.

One of the men tried to dart past him toward the corner of the room where Sahale and Bluebird had now retreated so their backs were against the wall. Preacher grabbed the fellow by the arm, swung him around, and slammed a hard right into his face. The man reeled back a step but caught his balance before he went down. With an angry roar, he came at Preacher, fists swinging wildly.

The punches were uncontrolled and artless, but the mountain man couldn't block all of them. A blow got through and caught him on the jaw, jolting his head to the side.

That allowed his opponent to close in and hook a fist into Preacher's midsection. The man was almost as tall as Preacher and more heavily built. The punch packed plenty of power. The impact bent Preacher forward.

He went with that and dived at the other man, tackling him around the waist. Both of them crashed to the rough puncheons.

Preacher landed on top and rammed a knee at the man's groin. The man twisted aside, took the knee on his thigh, and grabbed Preacher's shoulders. Grappling with each other, they rolled over a couple of times before they fetched up against the sturdy legs of a table.

While they were rolling, Preacher caught glimpses of Nighthawk battling three or four of the intruders at once. The giant Crow was like a grizzly bear standing tall as wolves surrounded him. His massive fists lashed out like mauls and knocked men off their feet, but more instantly took their place.

Dutch Charley had charged from behind the bar and was swinging the bungstarter, lambasting some of the strangers with it. He had left the other weapons sitting on the bar, probably not wanting to risk using them at close quarters, especially that sawed-off shotgun. Using the bungstarter, he had knocked two men off their feet before another stepped up behind him and struck him in the back of the head with a vicious stroke from a rifle butt. That drove Charley to his knees.

Preacher didn't see any more than that because his hands were full with the man he was battling. Growling like an animal, the man pulled his head down between his shoulders and butted Preacher in the chest. It was a smashing blow that momentarily robbed Preacher of his breath. That allowed his burly opponent to get his hands around Preacher's neck. He pulled the mountain man up a few inches and then slammed his head back down on the floor.

This was getting mighty annoying. A red haze dropped in front of Preacher's eyes, as if he were looking at his surroundings through a gauzy crimson curtain. That was either rage welling up inside him, or else he was about to pass out.

Passing out wouldn't be good. If he did, the big varmint he was wrestling with likely would choke the life out of him. Preacher cupped his hands and clapped them against the man's ears as hard as he could.

That made the man howl in pain and loosen his grip. Preacher brought his hands in close and drove them upward. He caught the man under the chin and wrenched his head back. A sharp crack sounded. Preacher's opponent went limp and collapsed on top of him.

Muttering curses, Preacher grabbed the dead man's shoulders and shoved him aside. Preacher rolled the other way and came up on hands and knees.

As he did, a big gray shape flashed in front of his face. Dog had gotten into the trading post somehow and was eager to join in the fight. He sprang up, sank his teeth into a man's arm, and the big cur's weight dragged the startled hombre to the floor. He began to yell in terror as Dog went after him with slashing teeth.

Preacher spotted Audie scrambling away from the back door and realized that the little man had opened it to let Dog in. Audie scooped up the bungstarter Dutch Charley had dropped when he was knocked out. Audie whirled the bungstarter over his head and swung it in a roundhouse blow. He was just the right height for that blow to land between the legs of an intruder. The man screamed in agony and dropped to the floor, clutching himself and curling up in a tight ball.

Nighthawk had planted himself between the two Flatheads and the attackers. Several men were sprawled on the floor around the giant Crow, moaning and twitching. But others still had him surrounded and were pummeling him with fists, feet, and gun butts. The attacking force had been even larger than Preacher realized at first. Obviously, more men had poured into the trading post to continue the assault.

As formidable as Nighthawk was, he hadn't been able to stop all of them. A few had gotten past him and closed in on Sahale and Bluebird. As one lunged at the young woman, her grandfather lifted his rifle and fired. The ball struck the man and staggered him, but as he fell, two more took his place and tried to grab Bluebird.

She had pulled a knife from somewhere. She slashed at the

nearest man and cut him badly on the hand groping for her. He yelled and jerked back. With his other hand, he yanked a gun from the waistband of his trousers, pointed it at Bluebird, and pulled the trigger.

After the earlier shouted warning from one of the men not to shoot, the sudden explosion was shocking. But not as shocking as the stunned expression on Bluebird's face as the pistol ball's impact drove her back against the log wall. She hung there, mouth open and eyes wide with pain. Blood welled from the black-rimmed hole in her buckskin dress between her breasts. She pitched forward, landing next to the wrapped bundle she had placed on the floor. Even in collapsing, she flung out an arm so that it covered the bundle protectively.

Brutally gunning down the girl like that changed everything. Even before Bluebird hit the floor, Preacher's Colts were in his hands, roaring and bucking as he triggered them. The gun-thunder was deafening as flames spewed from the revolvers' muzzles. A cloud of powdersmoke billowed around the mountain man.

Preacher's aim was deadly, but not even his swift volley of lead was in time to stop an attacker who leaped at Sahale and plunged a big-bladed hunting knife into the old man's chest. Sahale gasped and sagged against the wall. He still had enough strength to grasp the rifle with both hands and slam the breech into the face of the man who had just stabbed him. The blow shattered bone and made the man stagger backward.

Sahale dropped the rifle, pawed futilely at the bone handle of the knife protruding from his chest, and slowly slid down the wall.

Preacher emptied the Colts. An intruder fell with each crashing report. The ones still on their feet fled frantically. A couple reached the doorway and dashed out into the night, but Nighthawk caught the other two before they could escape. Grabbing each by the neck from behind, he smashed their heads together with such force that they shattered like melons.

Nighthawk tossed the dead men aside like discarded rag dolls.

Preacher ran to the door but paused as he heard the swift rataplan of hoofbeats from two galloping horses. The men who had fled had reached their mounts and were lighting a shuck away from the trading post as fast as they could.

Preacher turned back to a scene of devastation. More than a dozen bodies lay scattered around the room amidst overturned tables and chairs. One man was badly burned, another had been torn to pieces by Dog. Preacher's Colts had accounted for numerous others, and Nighthawk had broken a few skulls and snapped a few necks with his bare hands.

"Nighthawk, see if any o' them varmints are still alive," Preacher said. "If they are, don't kill 'em just yet."

Audie was kneeling beside Dutch Charley. As he rose to his feet, he reported, "Charley's unconscious, but he doesn't appear to be hurt badly."

"Glad to hear that," Preacher muttered as he headed for the two Salish. Audie hurried to join him.

Sahale was dead. The old man's eyes were open but lifeless as he stared straight ahead. His arms had fallen loosely at his sides as he sat propped against the wall.

Preacher expected to find Bluebird dead, too, after she was shot at close range like that, but a sudden moan from her made both Preacher and Audie spring to her side. Carefully, with the gentlest touch he could muster, Audie took hold of her shoulders and turned her onto her back. He sat down so that her head rested in his lap.

Preacher hunkered on his heels next to the wounded young woman. The bloodstain on the front of her buckskin dress was large and still spreading. Preacher didn't try to expose the wound. He knew there was nothing he and Audie could do for her except try to make her as comfortable as possible. Her life was fleeting and she had only moments.

Preacher had seen way too much death not to know these things.

"Rest easy there," he told her, making his normally rough tone as soothing as he could. "Don't you worry about a thing, Bluebird."

Her dark eyes opened, the lids fluttering. It took a moment for her gaze to find Preacher and lock on to him. She looked up at him and asked in a husky whisper, "How . . . how do you know . . . my name?"

"Your grandfather told us," Preacher said. "It's a mighty pretty name, too. Suits you."

"My grandfather—" She tried to turn her head, and Preacher knew she was looking for Sahale.

"He's gone on to the spirit world ahead of you," he told her. "His pain is over."

"He will be . . . waiting for me . . . soon."

Her eyes closed. Preacher thought she had slipped away, but after only a moment, her eyes opened again and once more she peered up at him with a strangely intent light shining in them.

"My pack . . . ?" She groped for it with a shaking hand.

"It's all right," Preacher assured her. "Nothin' happened to it durin' that ruckus. Whatever you got wrapped up in it oughta be just fine."

She touched the bundle and let out a long exhalation of relief, a sigh that turned into a grimace of pain and a sharply caught breath.

"Please . . . you will take care of . . . You must promise me . . . You will care for . . ."

Preacher wasn't going to make her journey into the realm of the spirits any more troubled than it had to be. He said quietly, "I give you my word, Bluebird, I'll take care o' whatever you got there. You don't have to worry about it even a little bit."

"And I promise, as well," Audie said. "Whatever needs to be done, my friend and I will help Preacher see to it."

Bluebird's head jerked up and down slightly in a nod. "Th-thank you . . ."

She sighed again, this time releasing the life to which she had clung until she had obtained the promise from Preacher and Audie.

A low, gravelly voiced chant came from Nighthawk as he stood over them. He was singing a death song for Bluebird and Sahale. It might not have been the song they would have sung had they been able to do it, but it would suffice as they traveled to the next world.

Audie eased Bluebird's head from his lap. Preacher straightened to his feet and turned to the trader. "You all right, Charley?" he asked.

By now, Dutch Charley had come to. His wife had helped him up and both of them sat at one of the tables. She clasped one of his hands in both of hers. With his other hand, he rubbed his head where he had been struck and winced.

"*Ja*, I will be fine," he said. "Thank God we Germans have hard, thick heads."

"Yeah, I ain't gonna argue about that. You said you hadn't ever seen those two Flatheads before. How about the bunch that busted in here? Any of them look familiar to you?"

Charley frowned in thought and opened his mouth to answer, but before he could say anything, Audie called, "Preacher!"

The surprise and urgency in his friend's voice made the mountain man swing around quickly. He saw that Audie had moved over to the blanket-wrapped bundle that had been so precious to Bluebird for some reason. He had pulled back one of the blankets slightly and was staring at what he had revealed.

The thin, wailing cry of a baby filled the powdersmoke-tinged air inside the trading post.

"What the hell!" Preacher burst out. A few long strides carried him across the room to the corner. Nighthawk joined him, and with a scrape of chairs, Dutch Charley and his wife got up from the table and followed.

The five of them gathered around the bundle lying on the floor and stared down at it as a second cry joined the first.

Two blond-haired, blue-eyed infants, possibly twins by the look of them, lay there swaddled in the blankets, their little red faces scrunched up as they cried and waved their tiny fists in the air.

CHAPTER 5

For a long moment, the infants' wails were the only sound in the room. Then Preacher said in a stunned voice, "Well, I'll be hornswoggled. Those are babies in there!"

"A quite unexpected eventuation," Audie agreed dryly. "And not to be too blatantly obvious in my observation, I don't believe this unfortunate young woman gave birth to them, although she certainly demonstrated a large degree of maternal devotion toward them."

"You mean she took care of 'em like she was their ma?"

"She fought to the death to protect them, and even mortally wounded, she clung fast to life until she had secured our pledge to care for them."

"Yeah, I reckon nobody could've done more for 'em," Preacher said. "But what I want to know is, where in blazes did they come from?"

"And why are they so important that those hardened, violent men were willing to kill to retrieve them?"

Preacher looked at his friend and asked, "You think these little'uns are what those varmints were after?"

"It seems to be the only logical conclusion."

Preacher frowned in thought, tugged at his earlobe, and then rasped a thumbnail along his beard-stubbled jawline as his brain turned over everything that had happened.

"When that fella yelled out not to shoot, he was worried about them tykes gettin' hit, not about Bluebird and her grandpa," he reasoned. "They didn't care about the two Indians, just the babes." Audie tickled first one infant and then the other under their chins, calming them and making their crying ease off before it died away entirely. The infants began to coo happily instead.

"You have a natural touch with them, my friend," Dutch Charley said. "I hope when my child is born, I'll be able to do such a good job of soothing it."

Charley's wife stepped forward and wordlessly held out her hands. Audie lifted one of the babies and gave it to her. The woman cradled the infant in her arms and rocked it back and forth.

Audie got to his feet, reached down, and picked up the second baby. He wrapped it in one of the blankets and gave the other blanket to Charley's wife.

Preacher looked at Nighthawk and asked, "Any of those varmints still alive?"

The Crow warrior shook his head.

"So we can't ask them about it," Preacher said. "We're back to what we were talkin' about before Audie found these young'uns. You recognize any of this gang, Charley?"

Audie and Charley's wife carried the babies over to the bar while Charley studied the faces of the dead men scattered around the room. Preacher and Nighthawk trailed him and waited for his verdict.

Finally, Charley sighed and said, "I feel certain that I have seen some of them before, but I cannot tell you their names or how long it has been since I saw them. I know only that they look familiar. But you know how many men pass through these parts and stop at my trading post, Preacher. The fact I have seen them before means nothing." The trader's brawny shoulders rose and fell. "I will continue to think about it. Something may come to me."

Preacher nodded and said, "Thanks, Charley. Don't reckon you've seen those babies before, have you?"

"They are the first infants who have ever been inside these walls. I thought my own child would be first, but fate has decided otherwise, *nein?*"

Preacher turned to the bar where Audie now sat on a stool with a baby in his arms. Charley's wife stood beside him holding the other infant.

"The little rascals have anything on 'em that might tell us who they are?" Preacher asked.

"We're not that fortunate," Audie replied, "but there is something interesting about them, Preacher. Look at these necklaces they're wearing."

Preacher came closer and squinted at the object lying in Audie's palm. It was a small stone attached to a rawhide thong looped around the neck of one of the babies.

"Each child is wearing one of these," Audie continued. "They were hidden by the blankets at first, which is why I didn't notice them until I picked the babies up. These stones are star garnets, Preacher."

The stone was circular, slightly flattened, and a rich dark purple in color. A lighter-colored striation ran around the stone's outer edge, and similar markings crisscrossed both faces, dividing it into twelve roughly equal segments. Preacher could tell that the markings were natural.

"I don't recollect ever seein' any rocks that look like this," he said.

"They're quite uncommon. As far as I know, they can be found in only two locations. There are deposits of them in India—"

"Dang it, that's all the way on the other side of the world, ain't it?"

"Indeed," Audie said, "and the only other place star garnets are found is in the valley of Emerald Creek."

Preacher frowned in recognition of the name. "That's what folks call a stream about a hundred and twenty miles northwest o' here, ain't it?"

"That's right."

"I did some trappin' there nine or ten years ago." Preacher glanced at the bodies of Bluebird and Sahale. "That's Flathead country up there, sure enough. You reckon that's where those two came from?"

"It seems to be a reasonable theory."

"Both of them and their horses looked wore out enough to have come that far," Preacher mused. "And if they'd been chased the whole way, it'd sure explain how tense and unfriendly they were." The mountain man nodded decisively. "They stole them babies from up there. Stole 'em from some white couple."

"Umm," Nighthawk said.

Audie said, "I agree, they didn't strike me as the sort who would abduct infants. Not without a very good reason."

"No offense, but Indians have stolen a whole heap o' white children over the years," Preacher pointed out.

"That's true. But it's impossible for us to know their motivation with the information we have now."

"And probably the only way we can find out why they done it is to find whoever them little ones belong to."

"We did promise Bluebird that we would take care of them," Audie said. "Since it seems clear that she and her grandfather were trying to get away from whoever was pursuing them, it's possible the young woman wouldn't think that we were fulfilling our pledge by returning the infants to wherever they came from."

"Well, blast it, Audie, what the hell else are we gonna do with 'em? We can't take 'em to raise our own selves!"

The babies began to cry again.

"A bit less vehemence, old friend," Audie said. "You've upset them."

Preacher grimaced. "Didn't mean to do that. You can settle 'em down again, can't you?"

"I'll try." Audie began rocking the infant he held back and forth as he spoke in low, soothing tones. Charley's wife did likewise. The babies grew quieter.

Keeping his voice down to a rumble, Preacher said, "The way I see it, we got to find out where they came from and who they belong to. That don't mean we have to just turn 'em back over to whoever their folks are, though."

Audie nodded slowly. "True enough. If we discover that they came from a bad situation, we'll have to figure out something else we can do. But we need more information in order to reach a wise decision."

Preacher chuckled and said, "Charley asked where we were gonna be goin' next. I reckon we know now."

Audie let the star garnet necklace dangle around the baby's neck again and tucked the blanket tighter around the infant.

"These little fellows are going to need names," he said. "Since we have no idea what their parents dubbed them, I suggest that we call them Romulus and Remus. According to mythology, they were orphaned and raised by wolves before eventually founding the city of Rome." Audie smiled. "We don't know whether their parents are still alive, but the three of us are a bit wolflike, I suppose. And then there's Dog, who has been mistaken for a wolf on many occasions."

"I reckon that'll work—" Preacher began.

Charley's wife spoke up, interrupting him. She had been poking around in the blanket in which the infant she held was swaddled. She smiled as she said something in her native tongue. Preacher understood some of it, and Nighthawk appeared to be even more fluent. He said, "Umm," to Audie.

"What's that? Are you certain?" Audie threw his head back and laughed. "In that case, Romulus and Remus aren't appropriate names at all. They were brothers, and what we have here are a boy and a girl! Brother and sister, beyond a doubt."

"Huh," Preacher said. "I reckon it's hard to tell at this age without takin' a closer look. What are we gonna call 'em, then?"

Audie gave that some thought for a moment and then said, "I propose that we dub them Apollo and Artemis, after Zeus's twin children. That will allow us to continue the mythological connection."

"Fine by me," Preacher said. "Apollo's the boy, right?"

"Correct."

"All right, we'll take 'em home and see if we can figure out why Bluebird and her grandpa were runnin' away with them."

"And if it turns out they had a good reason for taking the children?" Audie asked.

"Then we'll have to do some more figurin'," Preacher said.

Earlier, they had left the six dead ambushers where they had fallen in Wailing Woman Pass. Now, with twice as many corpses to deal with, they couldn't be quite so callous. Dutch Charley had a trading post to run, after all, and just throwing the carcasses in a gully as Preacher might have preferred would create an unpleasant odor and attract all sorts of scavengers.

Charley's wife prepared the bodies of Bluebird and Sahale for burial by wrapping them in blankets. Nighthawk placed them in a storeroom for the night. They would be laid to rest in the morning, as the Salish people were one of the tribes where the dead were interred in the earth rather than placed on scaffolds or in trees.

Preacher and Nighthawk dragged the other corpses behind the barn. If wolves carried some of them off during the night, that was fine. The ones that remained would go in a mass grave once Bluebird and Sahale had been tended to properly.

It was grim work but had to be done. All in all, that was a lot of killing for one day, Preacher reflected before he dozed off that night, but sometimes a man was forced into it.

He didn't lose a minute's sleep over any of the varmints he'd sent across the divide. They had murdered the two Indians and had it coming, as far as he was concerned.

He woke up the next morning to the sound of infants crying, something he hadn't experienced very many times in his life. He found Audie sitting at the bar trying to get the babies to suck on rags soaked with sugar water.

"Hilda said that when she cleaned Bluebird's body, she could tell the girl hadn't been nursing the babies, so it seems they've been weaned. I think they're just being contrary by refusing to cooperate with me."

"Hilda?" Preacher repeated.

"That's what Charley calls her. It's not actually her name, of course."

Preacher shook his head. "You know, it never occurred to me that I didn't know her name. She's always just been Charley's wife. Hilda, eh? Well, it kinda suits her."

"I agree."

"She's going to have a baby. You reckon she could nurse these two?"

"Unfortunately, no. Her milk hasn't come in yet. But we need to be able to feed them ourselves, anyway—we can't very well take Hilda along with us when we start out for Emerald Creek."

"You're right about that."

"Ah, here we go!" Audie said as the baby in his arms began to suck on the rag. "Apollo is feeding. I'm sure I can convince Artemis to, as well. It's not the best possible arrangement, of course, but at least we can give them some sustenance this way and keep them alive until we find out what we need to do next."

"This may come as a surprise to you," Preacher said, "but I don't know hardly nothin' about takin' care o' babies. I had little brothers and sisters . . . or maybe it was cousins . . . Been so long ago, I don't rightly remember for sure. But I never had much to do with tendin' to 'em when they was real little."

"I suppose you do know how to change a diaper, though, don't you?"

Preacher's eyes widened. "Good grief, Audie, are you serious?"

"Completely," the little man said.

Preacher sighed. "Well, I reckon I can manage if I have to."

"We promised to take care of these children. We're in this together, Preacher."

"You're right, I know. I won't let you down, nor Bluebird, neither."

"Good. I've already had this discussion with Nighthawk, and he's agreed to do his part."

"Umm," Preacher said under his breath.

By the middle of the day, the bleak chore of dealing with all the bodies had been taken care of. Bluebird and her grandfather were laid to rest atop a small hill about a hundred yards from the trading post with a beautiful view of the creek.

The men who had followed them intending to kill them and steal the babies were tossed into the large, shallow hole Preacher and Nighthawk had dug in a clearing back in the trees. It was better than they deserved, Preacher thought, as he and Nighthawk covered the grave, but at least it got rid of them.

With that done, Audie and Dutch Charley negotiated the trade involving the load of pelts and the extra horses and gear. They sealed the deal with a handshake.

The horses ridden by this latest batch of dead men had been nowhere to be found this morning. Preacher supposed they had followed the mounts of the two men who had gotten away.

The escape of those two nagged at his thoughts as he and his companions got ready to travel. While he was saddling Horse, he commented to Audie, "You know, there's a mighty good chance those fellas will head right back where they came from and tell whoever sent 'em about what happened here."

"Oh, I'd say that's entirely likely."

"Which means the varmints may be on the lookout for us."

"Of course. But they might also believe we'll continue heading east as Bluebird and Sahale were doing."

"And that means they could come after us."

Audie nodded. "Yes, it's possible we'll encounter them on our way to Emerald Creek."

With a puzzled frown, Preacher asked, "Why's it called Emerald Creek if you can find them star garnets there?"

Audie laughed and shook his head. "I have no idea," he said. "I suppose more than one variety of precious stone may be found in the area. Perhaps we'll discover that, too, when we get there."

Charley's wife, Hilda, had the two babies inside the trading post. Audie went to fetch them while Preacher and Nighthawk led the saddle horses and pack animals out of the barn. They had kept one of the extra mounts and rigged board-and-blanket slings on both sides of the saddle, similar to how Indian women sometimes carried their children, so the infants could ride securely in them part of the time.

Dog sat off to the side watching the preparations warily. The big cur didn't seem to know what to make of the babies, but he acted like he didn't want to get too close to them.

Audie came out onto the porch carrying one of the babies. Hilda followed with the other. Dutch Charley was the last one out the door, and he caught Preacher's eye as he emerged.

Preacher walked over to join him. Quietly, Charley said, "I've been racking my brain, trying to remember anything I could about those men who looked familiar, and something finally came back to me."

"You know who they were?"

Charley shook his head. "Their names, no. But I recalled that they were traveling with a whole group of ruffians led by a man named Mack Ozark."

"Mack Ozark?" Preacher repeated. "Mighty odd name. Who is he?"

"If the things I have heard are true," Charley said, "he is a bad man. A very bad man."

CHAPTER 6

"These are only rumors I've heard, you understand," Charley went on. "It's said that Mack Ozark is an outlaw, and a particularly vicious one, at that, for all his cunning. The one time I saw him, he caused no trouble, but simply looking at him made a shiver go through me. You know what I mean? Something about his eyes . . . It was like looking in a man's eyes and expecting to see a soul, but nothing was there except the cold, primitive essence of the serpent in the garden."

"That sounds like somethin' one of Audie's old poetry fellas might say."

"Poets have written about evil many times. Mack Ozark is an evil man." Charley made a face and went on, "I'm told he began his career of villainy in the mountains of Arkansas, from which he took his name."

"Yeah, Mack Ozark don't sound like the sort of name a fella would be born with," Preacher said.

"He killed his first man when he was twelve years old and assaulted his first woman not many years after that. He set houses afire and burned entire families alive. When a local constable arrested him, Ozark freed himself, took the lawman prisoner, and peeled off every inch of the man's skin with a dull knife while the poor man was still alive!"

"That sorta sounds like it might just be a story . . . but to be honest, I've run into a few fellas who were mean enough to do such a thing."

Charley nodded. "Such monsters are rare, but they exist. When Ozark was forced to flee the mountains, he fell in with a gang of thieves while he was still a young man. They made a practice of attacking wagon trains full of immigrants crossing the plains. The gang killed all the men and sold the women and children as slaves to Indians or to Mexicans who came up from the south. Ozark fit right in among them."

"Did you know all this when he stopped here at the tradin' post?" Preacher asked.

Charley shook his head. "No, these are things I've heard from others since then. When he and his friends were here, all I knew was that he made me nervous and I wished he would leave."

"I never knew you to be scared of anything, Charley, so that tells me just how bad this varmint must be." Preacher scratched at his jaw. "What's he look like?"

"Tall. Almost as tall as you. Very swarthy. His hair is dark and thick, and he has a mustache that hangs down on both sides of his mouth. No beard, or at least none then. Gray eyes. The color of ice when it's thick on a stream or a lake, and every bit as cold."

Preacher nodded slowly. "I reckon I'll know him if I see him."

"By the time you see him, it may be too late."

"We'll have to take that chance." Something else occurred to the mountain man. "You said he had some friends with him, includin' some o' them sons who killed Bluebird and her grandpa. How many were there, do you recall?"

"That day, only half a dozen. But since then, I have heard that he commands a large gang, perhaps as many as thirty or forty men."

"The same bunch he ran with over on the plains?"

Charley shook his head again. "Some of them, possibly, but I have no way of knowing."

"That gang was already robbin' wagon trains when Ozark threw in with 'em. Maybe he wound up bossin' it."

"That could be the case. But what really puzzles me is the connection between a man such as that and two innocent babes. What could that possibly be?"

Before Preacher could answer, Audie called from where the horses waited. "We're ready to go, Preacher."

"Be right there," Preacher told him. He turned back to Dutch Charley and said, "Maybe we'll find out once we get where we're goin'."

"Don't let those children fall into Ozark's hands, Preacher," the trader urged. "After seeing him, I truly believe that man to be capable of almost anything."

A few minutes later, Preacher, Audie, and Nighthawk rode out. Preacher was in the lead, with Dog bounding ahead as usual, followed by Audie who led the horse with the two makeshift cradle boards and their precious cargo. Nighthawk brought up the rear, trailing all three pack animals behind him.

As Preacher rode, he couldn't get the things Charley had told him out of his head. If somebody like Mack Ozark was holed up in the country toward which they rode, maybe it would be the smart thing to turn around and go the other way. The safest thing for those two young'uns, too.

But as he and his friends had discussed the previous day before they rode into Wailing Woman Pass, they never cottoned much to running away from trouble. Better to face things head-on and fight for what was right.

Maybe ol' Mack Ozark really was a ring-tailed roarer, just like Dutch Charley said. But Preacher had been known to do some pretty good bellerin' his own self . . .

The valley where Emerald Creek flowed was approximately 120 miles northwest of Dutch Charley's Trading Post. It would take

Preacher and his companions a little less than a week to reach it, assuming they didn't run into any significant delays along the way.

Those star garnet necklaces Audie had found on the infants were solid proof they had been in that valley. Preacher couldn't bring himself to believe they had come all the way from India on the other side of the world.

The first day passed uneventfully. Apollo and Artemis slept most of the time, rocked into slumber by the steady rhythm of the horse carrying their cradleboards. That evening, Audie got them to suck on rags soaked with sugar water. He also boiled and mashed up some carrots from Charley's garden that he had brought along. The babies were less fond of those but ate some anyway.

"How old do you reckon them little varmints are?" Preacher asked as they all sat by the fire that night.

"They're at least six months," Audie replied. "Possibly eight or nine. This isn't the first solid food they've had. Bluebird wasn't nursing them, so she had to be feeding them something else. We're lucky they've been weaned. It would have complicated matters considerably if they hadn't been."

"How soon are they gonna start walkin'?"

"Oh, not for another month or so, I'd say."

"Good. Then we don't have to worry about chasin' 'em down if they start runnin' off."

Audie laughed. "We may not have to worry about them running off, but at this age it's entirely possible they may be crawling. So we'll still need to keep an eye on them to make sure they don't get into any trouble."

Preacher rolled his eyes and shook his head, unsure why fate had chosen to saddle him with being responsible for a pair of infants. Whoever had come up with that notion was probably having a good laugh about it.

The next day, they pushed on and made good time across

mostly rolling terrain. Snow-capped mountains were visible in the far distance, well beyond their destination, but in this region, the wooded hills weren't too rugged. Broad valleys between them provided relatively easy routes. Occasionally the travelers were forced to detour around deep ravines cut by fast-flowing streams, and here and there, large rocky knobs dotted the landscape.

It was pretty country, sure enough, but Preacher didn't allow himself to be lulled into a sense of nonchalance. All his senses remained on high alert. His keen eyes scanned the countryside around them, searching for any signs of potential trouble.

Dog ranged well ahead of them, often out of sight, and Preacher was confident that the big cur would let him know right away if he encountered anything he thought was suspicious.

Game trails cut through this country as well as traditional travel routes used by the Indian tribes who lived here. Preacher and his companions were following one such well-trod path that ran between a rocky knob to their right and a low, saw-toothed ridge to their left. The opening between the two geographic features was perhaps seventy yards wide.

One of the babies picked that moment to start squalling. Naturally, the second infant, ensconced on the blanket-wrapped cradleboard on the horse's other side, sympathized and began howling its lungs out, too. Preacher reined in and hipped around in the saddle to look meaningfully at Audie.

"I think they're getting tired of me," Audie said. "Why don't you see if you can quiet them down for a change?"

Preacher's shaggy eyebrows went up. "Me?"

"You're as much their caretaker as I am, you know."

Preacher muttered a few choice words under his breath as he swung down from the saddle. Audie was right, of course, but that didn't make Preacher any fonder of the idea of dealing with two crying infants.

"Which one's which?" he asked as he approached the horse carrying the babies.

"Apollo on the left, Artemis on the right. Apollo is the one who started crying this time."

"I'll see if I can settle him down first."

Carefully, Preacher loosened the blankets enough to lift Apollo out of the snug nest. Audie had cut up one of the spare blankets to form diapers and stuffed moss in them to serve as an absorbent so the cloth could be used again. Preacher checked the diaper tied around the infant's hips and found that it didn't need to be changed.

"What's wrong, you dadgum little varmint?" he asked as he cradled the blond-haired youngster against his chest and bounced him up and down a little. Tears still ran down the scrunched-up face as Apollo continued to cry.

Preacher tickled the baby's belly and under his chin. He ruffled Apollo's hair. None of that did any good.

Sitting nearby on horseback, Nighthawk wore his usual solemn, almost expressionless mask, but Preacher saw amusement lurking in the giant Crow warrior's eyes. Nighthawk raised a hand, pointed, and said, "Umm."

"I agree, it's worth a try," Audie said. "Why don't you blow on his belly, Preacher?"

"You mean the young'un's belly?"

"Well, I certainly don't mean Nighthawk's!"

That brought a faint grunt of laughter from the towering Crow.

Preacher made a face again, then lowered his head, placed his lips against Apollo's belly, and blew. He fluttered his lips to make a sputtering noise. Apollo kept crying, and Preacher blew harder.

Nighthawk actually laughed out loud this time, which was almost unheard of, and Audie howled with hilarity. Preacher jerked his head up and glared at them.

"Why don't you two dadblasted jackanapes just hush up that dang mule-brayin'?" Preacher burst out. "Why, I oughta—"

He continued ranting at his friends, indulging in one of his rare but extremely colorful outpourings of profanity. Audie and Nighthawk just laughed louder and harder. Nighthawk pounded his saddle horn.

Audie wiped at his eyes as he raised his voice to interrupt Preacher's stream of invective. "Look, Preacher," he said. "Apollo has stopped crying."

Preacher fell silent and frowned as he looked down at the infant in his arms. Apollo was staring up at him with keen interest. The baby cooed and gurgled.

"I think he enjoys your inventive vocabulary," Audie added.

"Umm," Nighthawk said.

"You're right, that won't work with Artemis. He can't speak to a lady like that!"

Preacher shook his head, growled deep in his throat, and said, "You two jaybirds just keep it up. It'll be your turn before you know it, and then we'll see how you do at placatin' these little varmints."

"I've already been doing that, remember?" Audie pointed out.

"Yeah, yeah," Preacher muttered. "You reckon ever' time these rascals start cryin', I'm gonna have to cuss a blue streak at 'em to hush 'em up?"

"Well, I suppose if it works . . ." Audie replied with a grin on his face. "And it seems to be catching. Once Apollo stopped crying, Artemis did, too. You're fortunate."

"Yeah, mighty lucky," Preacher said. He held Apollo under both arms and swung the now-happy baby back toward the cradleboard. "Let's get you squared away again, you leather-lunged little heathen."

But before he could lower Apollo into the sling-like arrangement of blankets, something whipped viciously past his head, missing only narrowly. Preacher recognized the telltale hum instantly and didn't need to hear the crack of a rifle a split-second later to know that some low-down bushwhacker had just missed a shot at him.

Apollo chose that moment to kick and squirm, and him jerking around like that, combined with Preacher's surprise over almost having his brains blown out, made the mountain man lose his grip on the baby. Apollo slipped right out of his hands like a flopping fish.

Luckily, Preacher's reflexes were almost supernaturally swift. His left hand shot down and snagged the back of the diaper before Apollo hit the ground. The knots Audie had tied held.

Another rifle barked somewhere not far off. Preacher didn't know where the ball went, but he wasn't hit and he didn't hear this one. He wrapped his left arm around the infant and pressed Apollo against his chest as he whirled away from the horse.

Nighthawk had already leaped out of the saddle and one fast stride of his long legs brought him up on the other side of the mount that had been carrying the babies. He plucked Artemis from the blankets and held her against his chest as Preacher was doing with Apollo. Hunching his massive shoulders in an attempt to do a more effective job of shielding the youngster, he turned and loped toward the mound of rocks to the right of the trail.

Preacher saw a spurt of powdersmoke from the saw-toothed ridge, followed an eyeblink later by a handful of dirt kicking in the air as the ball struck the ground near him. He tightened his grip on Apollo as his right hand dropped to the Colt on that side and palmed it from the holster.

Swinging the revolver from left to right, he thumbed off three rounds as quickly as he could. The revolver boomed in his hand, and he hoped it wasn't hurting Apollo's ears too much. He didn't figure he would hit any of the ambushers, but he wanted to give them something to think about, maybe even make them duck for cover for a few seconds.

With that done, he whirled and dashed after Nighthawk, heading for the nearest sanctuary—which happened to be that rocky knob.

Preacher hoped there weren't any bushwhacking skunks hidden up there, too.

CHAPTER 7

Nobody shot at Preacher and Nighthawk from the rocks as they dashed toward the knob with the babies. Behind them, Audie yelled at the pack horses and spooked them out of the line of fire. He reached over to grab Preacher's rifle and drag it from the scabbard lashed to Horse's saddle, then kicked his mount into a run after his friends.

With his long legs, Nighthawk made it to the knob first. Several boulders were scattered at its base. Moving with great care and gentleness, especially for his size, the warrior ducked behind one of them and leaned down to place Artemis on the ground. The big slab of rock would protect the baby, although there might still be some danger from ricochets.

Preacher wasn't far behind him. He eased Apollo down next to Artemis.

A rifle ball whined off the boulder and passed close by Preacher's ear. He crouched lower and again fired the Colt toward the ridge. The range was too far for the handgun to be effective, although a lucky shot was always possible.

Nighthawk ran around the rocks and held out his arms as Audie galloped up. Audie barely slowed his mount before he left the saddle in a dive, bringing his rifle and Preacher's with him. He dropped the weapons as he sailed through the air for an instant before Nighthawk caught him. They had carried out this maneuver in many fights over the years when Audie needed to dismount in a hurry. Nighthawk used Audie's momentum to help him turn and swing his diminutive friend to the ground.

Preacher was out in the open, too, as the men hidden on the ridge continued firing. A rifle ball stirred the fringe on his buckskin shirt's left sleeve. He scooped both rifles from the ground and tossed Audie's toward Nighthawk. The warrior caught it. The weapon looked a little like a child's toy in his massive paw. He passed it on to Audie as both of them ran behind the boulders again.

Preacher hunted cover behind another of the big rocks. He stayed low while he checked his rifle. It was loaded but didn't have a percussion cap on the lock. He carried a pouch containing shot and caps attached to his belt behind the holster for the right-hand Colt, as well as a small, brass-plated powder flask. A patch box on the rifle's stock held cloth patches in which to wrap the lead balls before they were shoved down the muzzle with the rifle's ramrod.

With those supplies, Preacher could get off several more rounds, but the capacity certainly wasn't endless. He would need to make every shot count.

He eared back the hammer and thumbed a percussion cap onto the nipple. After taking his hat off and setting it aside, he edged his head up for a quick look at the ridge where the ambushers were holed up.

Their rifles had fallen silent. Now that Preacher, Audie, and Nighthawk had taken cover, the would-be killers no longer had any easy targets. They weren't very good marksmen in the first place, Preacher mused; otherwise, they wouldn't have missed all the shots they had taken so far.

On the other hand, he recalled that the two infants were important to these men and they didn't want the little ones hurt. Preacher didn't doubt for a second those were more of Mack

Ozark's men over there, so they might be taking extra care not to hit the babies.

He said as much to Audie, calling over to the former professor, "That's got to be more of Ozark's bunch takin' potshots at us."

"It's certainly the most reasonable explanation," Audie agreed. "If this fellow Ozark has as many followers as Dutch Charley said, he could have split them up into smaller search parties. The two men who escaped from the trading post could have run into some of the others and joined forces with them to orchestrate this ambush."

Preacher looked along the trail. Horse and the other animals had trotted a couple of hundred yards before stopping to graze. They were well out of the line of fire, although Horse would come galloping back without hesitation if Preacher whistled for him. Preacher wasn't going to do that unless it was absolutely necessary; he wouldn't place the stallion in harm's way without cause.

He wondered briefly where Dog was. He was a little surprised the big cur hadn't warned them about the ambush. He hoped nothing had happened to the shaggy varmint.

Worrying about that could wait until later. For now, he watched the ridge with keen interest. He was ready to snap the rifle to his shoulder and fire if he spotted a suitable target. Both sides, though, seemed to have settled into a waiting game.

The tense silence stretched out for long minutes. Preacher wasn't prone to nerves. He could wait, silent and unmoving, for hours when it was necessary to force an enemy into making the first move. That ability had saved his life numerous times in the past.

Most men couldn't do that. They would get antsy after a while and do something even when it wasn't in their best interest. Preacher wasn't surprised when a shout came from the ridge on the other side of the trail.

"Hey, you boys over there in the rocks! You hear me?"

It was a harsh, male voice. Preacher didn't recall ever hearing it before. He glanced over at Audie, who shook his head. Preacher took that as agreement that he shouldn't respond yet. Better to let their enemies stew a little more.

"I know you can hear me, damn it!" the man yelled after a minute or so. "Listen, we don't want to kill you!"

Preacher grinned. After everything that had happened, nobody in their right mind would believe that claim.

"All we want is those babies! You give 'em to us, and we'll let you ride away. I give you my word on that, boys. Turn 'em over to us, safe and sound, and I swear nothin' will happen to you."

Preacher waited a moment longer just to draw things out and then called back, "How do we know we can believe you?"

"Because I give you my word!" the spokesman answered without hesitation.

"That ain't nowhere near good enough! How about this? You let my friends get the horses and ride on out of gunshot range, and then you can have these younkers. But until my friends are safe, I'll be waitin' right here to cut these babies' throats if you try to double-cross us!"

Even though Audie had to know Preacher was bluffing, a horrified expression appeared on his face.

The gunman on the ridge sounded equally horrified. "You'd murder innocent children? What kind of a man are you?"

"The kind who ain't all that eager to trust somebody who's been shootin' at him!"

The man on the ridge didn't respond immediately. Preacher figured he was talking things over with the rest of the ambushers.

After a few minutes, the man shouted, "All of you can ride away and leave the babies there in those rocks. We won't shoot at you. What do you think about that?"

"I think you're still askin' me to believe you! I ain't loco enough to do that, mister!"

Frustration was obvious in the man's voice as he responded, "Why the hell do you even care about those young'uns? They ain't yours! You just threatened to kill 'em, so you can't have any strong feelin's for 'em!"

"Maybe they're worth money!"

In truth, Preacher and his companions had no idea why Mack Ozark's men wanted so badly to reclaim the babies. It made sense that there had to be some good reason, though—and money was the reason men did many things.

The suggestion drew a response. "Wait, you're thinkin' about sellin' those infants? To who?"

"Maybe to whoever meets our price."

"What's your price?"

"You tell us what they're worth to you, and we'll tell you if it's enough!"

Once again, silence settled down. Preacher wasn't going to sell Apollo and Artemis, of course. He was both stalling for time and trying to tease out some possibly useful information from their enemies.

But the faint sound of a rock shifting somewhere above and behind warned him that other people could try to stall for time, too. His instincts took over as he dived to his right, rolled over, and came up propped on his left elbow as he looked up the knob's slope.

A shot blasted above him as Preacher caught a glimpse of a man pulling himself over the rocks. The pistol ball splattered against the boulder he'd been using to shield himself from the killers on the other side of the trail. Preacher's right hand jerked up with a Paterson Colt gripped in it. The heavy revolver boomed and gouted powdersmoke.

The man who had climbed over the knob to attack them from behind had gotten to his feet. He fired a second shot just as Preacher squeezed off his first. The attacker's shot went wild and landed in the trail between the knob and the ridge.

The mountain man's aim was more accurate, even though firing uphill like that was tricky. The bullet struck the man's left foot and knocked that leg out from under him. He went down hard, letting out a startled yell as he toppled over, and then he came rolling down the steep slope straight at Preacher.

The fall was pure happenstance, but it was bad luck for Preacher. He snapped another shot at the falling man but missed. Then, as Preacher tried to get to his feet, the out-of-control hombre smashed right into him.

The impact drove Preacher against the rock at his back. Pain lanced through him, centered around his ribs. He knew he wasn't badly hurt—yet—but the ambusher was doing his best to change that. He grabbed the wrist of Preacher's gun hand with his left hand and forced it aside; with his right, he hammered punishing blows at the mountain man's face and torso.

Preacher brought his knee up and sank it into the attacker's groin. The man howled in pain and bent forward. The grip on Preacher's wrist slipped, allowing him to jerk free. He slammed the heavy revolver into the side of the man's head and heard bone crunch as the blow smashed the skull. The man fell to the ground at Preacher's feet and jerked and twitched uncontrollably as he died.

He hadn't been alone in the attack from behind. Two more men fired down at Audie and Nighthawk from the top of the rocky mound. The Crow warrior and the diminutive former professor flung themselves in opposite directions as bullets whistled and whined around them.

Nighthawk rolled, came up on his knees, and drew his arm back. It flashed forward and the tomahawk he threw turned over and over in the air as it flew toward the gunmen. The throw was perfect. The tomahawk's keen edge struck one of the men on the right cheek and cut deeply into his face, blinding him on that side and making him shriek as he stumbled and fell.

Audie's short-barreled rifle cracked and the other attacker lurched back as the ball struck him in the left shoulder. He managed to hang on to his gun, though, and continued firing.

The heavy booms from the weapon told Preacher the man had a Paterson Colt, too.

Preacher aimed through the cloud of powdersmoke around the man and fired. He couldn't tell at first if the shot found its target, but then the man sagged forward and began rolling down the hill. The loose-limbed tumble was ample evidence that he was dead. The man who had been downed by Nighthawk's tomahawk was still screaming, but the sound stopped abruptly with a gurgle proclaiming that death had claimed him, too.

No more attackers came over the top of the rocky mound, but a fresh volley of shots crashed from the ridge on the other side of the trail. Preacher and his friends were forced to dive for cover again. As he twisted around, Preacher spotted four men charging toward the boulders, attacking from that side under cover of the resumed gunfire.

Preacher had set his rifle aside, but he didn't need it for close work like this. This was the sort of fight the Patersons were made for. He filled both hands, came up in a crouch behind the rock where he had taken cover, and yelled out his rage as he began firing. The Colts boomed and bucked in his hands, left, right, left, right, as he laid down a deadly storm of lead that scythed through the men charging toward him.

They were devastated by the mountain man's firepower. Two men staggered and fell immediately, cut down by Preacher's lethal onslaught. Another bent double, clutched his bullet-torn belly, and began stumbling around in circles. The fourth man threw on the brakes, but any thought he might have had about retreating vanished as Nighthawk hurdled over a stone slab and caught the man's shoulder in his left hand.

At the same time, the knife in Nighthawk's right hand buried itself in the man's body in an upward-angling thrust. Once, twice, and again a third time, the blade ripped into the attacker, turning the man's midsection into a bloody mess. Nighthawk tossed the dying man aside and began running across the trail toward the ridge.

Preacher saw a man rise up over there to take aim at the charging warrior with a rifle. The mountain man snatched up his own rifle and fired first, a snap shot guided solely by instinct.

But it was deadly accurate and the would-be killer disappeared as the ball from Preacher's rifle struck him and knocked him backward. A heartbeat later, Nighthawk reached the base of the ridge and started climbing.

Audie had reloaded his rifle and fired another shot at the crest to cover Nighthawk's ascent. No one else stuck a head up, and Nighthawk reached the top in a matter of moments. He scrambled over and stood up as he looked around. Then he turned toward Preacher and Audie and spread his arms wide.

"They're gone," Audie said. "Either we killed them all, or the ones who were left fled."

Preacher stepped over to the boulder where Apollo and Artemis had been placed for safety. He knelt beside the infants, who were making restless noises but not really crying.

After a moment, he looked up at Audie and announced, "The young'uns are fine, just annoyed by all the racket. None o' those ricochets came close to 'em."

"Thank heavens for that," Audie said as he came over to join Preacher. "Nighthawk is coming back."

Nighthawk slid down the ridge and trotted back over to the mound where he and his companions had taken cover. With a mixture of sign language and grunts, he communicated that he had heard more than one horse swiftly departing the area.

"Several of them got away," Audie said, "which means that they'll probably join forces with the rest of Ozark's men."

"And we'll have to deal with 'em again," Preacher said with a grim look on his rugged face.

"Yes, I'd say that's highly likely. But we've fended off one attack and the children are fine, so we have to be thankful for that."

Nighthawk pointed. Preacher looked up the trail and saw Dog trotting toward them. The big cur came up to him and nuzzled his leg.

"You missed the whole fight, you shaggy varmint," he said. "Didn't you hear all that shootin' goin' on?"

Dog just looked up at him. Preacher laughed and shook his head.

"I'm glad you're all right, old son," he said as he scratched Dog's ears. "I was a mite worried that somethin' had happened to you. Next time we're headin' into an ambush, I expect you to let us know about it."

Dog turned and ran off again.

Audie laughed and said, "Sometimes he seems to have such an unusual connection with you that I almost forget he isn't human, Preacher. Don't be too hard on him."

"That ain't likely," Preacher said. "He's saved my hide too many times for that." He smiled as Dog stopped, looked back at the humans, and wagged his shaggy tail. "And I reckon there's a good chance he probably will again."

CHAPTER 8

The next two days passed uneventfully as the mountain man and his companions continued heading northwest. They were more than halfway to their destination, Preacher estimated.

As they sat beside their small campfire that night, he said, "I'm a mite surprised we ain't run into more of Ozark's men. Maybe ol' Mack his own self."

"Based on our previous encounters with them, they know we're heading in the same direction they came from," Audie pointed out. "That conclusion is based, of course, on the assumption that Ozark is making his headquarters somewhere in the vicinity of Emerald Creek. If that's the case, he could have decided that the most efficient course of action is simply to wait for us to come to them."

"That makes a heap o' sense, all right," Preacher said. "And they're liable to have a warm welcome waitin' for us when we get there, too."

"Indeed."

Knowing that they might not run into any more ambushes didn't make Preacher any less alert. He was still watchful as they traveled on through the beautiful, thickly wooded hills the next day.

Audie had Apollo and Artemis eating potatoes, carrots, and beans he had brought from Dutch Charley's garden. He cooked the vegetables thoroughly until they were soft and easily mashed to a consistency the youngsters could handle. He worried that they weren't getting enough healthy food, but there was only so much he could do in that respect.

The three men took turns standing guard at night, plus Dog and Horse were close by and would let Preacher know immediately if they sensed anything threatening. He was asleep that night while Nighthawk had the sentry duty, but Dog nosing his arm woke him. Instantly, he was fully awake and alert. As he lifted his head to look around, Horse suddenly let out a startled whinny. The stallion was disturbed, too.

Something was wrong, no doubt about that. Preacher pushed himself up on an elbow. The fire had burned down to embers and gave off only a faint glow, but that was enough for him to spot Nighthawk on the other side of the clearing where they had made camp.

The Crow warrior was on his feet, facing toward the trees, his tomahawk gripped in his hand as he stood there tensely, obviously aware of a threat. Preacher didn't say anything because he didn't want to distract Nighthawk or warn whoever might be lurking out there in the darkness.

A heartbeat later, there was no longer any question about what was wrong. A towering shape loomed out of the shadows and loosed a terrible roar.

The single most terrifying creature in the mountains—a grizzly bear—had come out of the night to attack the camp.

A huge paw with deadly claws jutting from it swiped at Nighthawk with blinding speed. But Nighthawk's reflexes were incredibly swift, as well. He ducked under the grizzly's attack and struck with the tomahawk, aiming the blow at the beast's belly as it stood up on its hind legs. Then Nighthawk dived to the side as the bear continued lumbering forward.

Snapping and snarling ferociously, Dog darted toward the bear and drew its attention away from Nighthawk. The grizzly made a swipe at the big cur, too, but Dog was too fast and avoided it.

At the same time, Audie scrambled out of his bedroll and scooped both infants from the ground. He scurried away to put some distance between himself and the unwanted visitor to the camp.

Preacher surged to his feet and drew both Colts. The .36 caliber balls in the revolvers wouldn't do much damage to a grizzly bear; not enough, at least, to put such a monster down unless the ball went through an eye and penetrated the creature's brain.

Preacher was ready to shoot all ten rounds in the guns at the bear's head, hoping for just such a lucky shot, when he had to hold his fire. Nighthawk had rolled and surged up on his feet again, leaping in to strike at the grizzly's head with his tomahawk.

More than once, Preacher had engaged a grizzly bear in close combat, armed only with a hunting knife. He had lived through those encounters and the bears had died, but he had suffered a lot of punishment in the battles. Most men who had to fight a grizzly were doomed to a painful, bloody death.

Nighthawk was taller than Preacher, although the bear still towered over him. His shoulders were broad and powerful, his body covered with layered slabs of muscle. The bear outweighed him anyway, was stronger and just as fast, if not faster. Nighthawk had the tomahawk, and Preacher saw that the Crow had drawn a knife with his left hand and was wielding it, too. But the bear had claws and teeth.

No matter who won, it was going to be a hell of a fight between those two.

Preacher stood watching the epic combat. Dog backed off, as well, the hair on his neck still ruffled in instinctive anger and hatred toward the predator as a low growl sounded in his throat.

Nighthawk thrust with the knife, hacked with the tomahawk, and whirled away from the bear's slashing claws as much as he could. A dark bloodstain began to show on the left shoulder of his buckskin shirt where the claws had ripped through it and gouged trenches in Nighthawk's flesh, although fortunately they hadn't penetrated very far.

The bear was bleeding, too, from wounds that Nighthawk's weapons had opened, but Preacher could tell the injuries were superficial. The grizzly had such a thick layer of fat and muscle over its entire body that it was hard for a blade to reach anything vital.

As the bear tried to wrap both front paws around Nighthawk and catch him in a crushing grip, the warrior ducked quickly and dived between the animal's rear legs. Once he was behind the bear, he twisted lithely and chopped at the grizzly's legs, trying to hamstring it.

The bear bellowed in pain and dropped to all fours. It whirled around with speed and agility that would have done a bucking bronco proud. Nighthawk tried to get out of the way, but the creature's shoulder caught him. It was an inadvertent blow but powerful enough to knock Nighthawk to the ground and make him roll over a couple of times.

The bear lunged after him, but once again Dog leaped into the fray. He bounded onto the bear's shoulder and sank his teeth in. The bear roared again and twisted away from Nighthawk to paw awkwardly at Dog. The big cur released his jaws and dropped away before the grizzly's claws could reach him.

That gave Nighthawk time to recover his wits and spring back to his feet. The bear was facing away from him now because Dog had distracted it. Nighthawk jumped onto its back, wrapped his legs around the thick body, and looped his left arm around the bear's neck under those immensely powerful jaws. He began slamming the tomahawk into the back of the bear's head, again and again.

A grizzly's skull was so thick that sometimes a rifle ball would just glance off and fail to deliver a fatal wound. A pistol round was even less likely to be effective.

But not even a grizzly's skull could stand up to repeated impacts from a tomahawk, especially one wielded by a warrior as strong as Nighthawk. Preacher had once heard Audie refer to the Crow as a copper-hued Hercules, and even though the mountain man didn't know all that much about mythology, he figured that was a pretty accurate description.

The bear began to stagger as Nighthawk continued hitting it in the head. Preacher could almost feel sorry for the critter, but it had picked this fight, not the humans.

Finally, the bear collapsed. Nighthawk hit it again a couple of times, burying the tomahawk in its brain just to make sure the massive creature was actually dead. He wrenched the tomahawk free, pushed himself to his feet, and staggered a little as he tried to step away from the carcass. The fight had taken a lot out of him.

"I know that varmint got you at least once, Nighthawk," Preacher said. "Are you all right?"

"Umm," Nighthawk said with a nod.

Preacher pouched his irons and then hunkered next to the fire to stir up the embers. He added wood to them, and within a few moments flames began dancing again and throwing a feeble glow across the campsite. It was bright enough for Preacher to get a better look at the bloodstain on the shoulder of Nighthawk's shirt. He agreed that it didn't appear too bad, although those gashes from the bear's claws would need to be cleaned so they didn't fester.

Dog went over and licked Nighthawk's hand. The Crow's usual impassive expression didn't change, but he rubbed Dog's head and scratched the cur's ears. Dog's swift and daring actions may well have saved the big warrior's life.

Preacher realized that Audie hadn't returned to camp with the babies. He would have expected Audie to reappear and check on his old friend before now. He turned and called into the woods, "You can come back and bring the young'uns, Audie. Ol' Ephraim's dead and won't be botherin' nobody else."

Many of the mountain men referred to grizzly bears as "Old

Ephraim." Preacher didn't know where the nickname came from, but he'd heard it ever since he had come west to the mountains more than thirty years earlier during the Shining Times. Audie would be aware of that, too, and know what Preacher was talking about.

Yet there was no response to Preacher's call. His eyes narrowed as he listened intently. The night was quiet, all the birds and small animals having fled because of the roaring from the bear. None of them wanted anything to do with a grizzly. A hush hung over the landscape. If Apollo and Artemis had been crying, Preacher would have heard them.

"Where in blazes did Audie get off to with them little sprouts?" he said to Nighthawk.

The warrior just shook his head, clearly as puzzled as Preacher was.

"Dog, find Audie," Preacher ordered. "Find Apollo and Artemis."

Dog took off into the woods. Preacher said to Nighthawk, "We'll take a look around, too. I'll head this way"—he gestured— "and you see if you can find any sign of 'em over yonder."

Nighthawk nodded and disappeared into the trees, moving opposite to the direction Dog had taken. Preacher went yet another way.

From time to time, he called Audie's name. Worry was growing inside him. Audie was mighty good at taking care of himself, but his small stature meant that he would often be at a disadvantage. That was just a physical fact.

Not only that, but Audie had also had the two infants with him when he hurried away from the campsite. His goal had been to get them as far out of danger as possible, which Preacher certainly agreed with. But that meant that if he had run into any problems, he would have been saddled with taking care of the babies as well as dealing with whatever peril he had encountered.

Preacher had seen which way Audie went when he left the camp, but he could have changed course and be just about anywhere out here in the night.

"Audie, dadgum it, where are you?" Preacher said out loud.

He didn't get an answer, but a moment later he heard something else that sent a pang of alarm through him.

"Preacher!" Nighthawk called in a voice that rumbled like thousands of tons of rock sliding down a mountainside.

Preacher turned and hurried through the woods, being careful despite his haste that he didn't run into any tree trunks along the way. He made his way to where Nighthawk waited in less than a minute.

The huge warrior was on one knee. He had Audie propped against the upraised knee. The little man groaned and shook his head slowly.

"Audie, are you all right?" Preacher asked.

"I . . . I will be. Someone . . . hit me in the head and knocked me unconscious."

Preacher felt a cold ball of fear in his belly. It was a very unaccustomed sensation for him, and he never would have experienced such a reaction on his own behalf.

Right now, though, he was afraid for someone else. Two someones, in fact.

"Where are the babies?" he asked.

Audie tried to sit up straighter, but Nighthawk's big hand on his shoulder held him back.

"They're around here somewhere," Audie said. "They have to be!"

"You sit here and take it easy," Preacher told him. "I'll fetch a torch from the fire and have a look around."

Despite his calm tone, uneasiness continued welling up inside him. He whistled for Dog as he hurried back to the campsite some thirty yards away. The big cur reached the clearing at the same time Preacher did.

"Find the babies, Dog," the mountain man commanded. "Find Apollo and Artemis."

He pointed in the direction where he had left Audie and Nighthawk to indicate where Dog should begin his search. As soon as Dog bounded off into the trees to pick up the trail, Preacher plucked a burning branch from the fire and quickly returned to the spot himself.

A circle of light spread from the makeshift torch as Preacher held it above his head. The flickering glare revealed the trickle of blood that had flowed down the side of Audie's face from a cut on his head. He also had a swollen lump just below his hairline. Somebody had walloped him a good one.

"I tell you, they should be right here," Audie insisted. A frantic note crept into his normally strong, confident voice. Preacher knew he was talking about Apollo and Artemis.

Preacher walked back and forth, examining the surrounding area in the light from the torch. He saw no sign of the infants.

As soon as he'd realized that Audie had been knocked out, he'd had a pretty good idea what happened. He was sure Audie did, too. Audie just hated to admit it.

But that reluctance wasn't going to change anything. Audie sighed and said, "Somebody took them. Whoever struck me absconded with the babies. When he saw that I was unconscious, he took them, the unspeakable reprobate!"

"Could be he even figured you were dead," Preacher pointed out. "Reckon you were lucky he didn't cut your throat just to make sure, while he was at it."

"Lucky," Audie repeated with a hollow note in his voice now. "Yes, I suppose so."

"You didn't even catch a glimpse of who it was?"

Audie shook his head and then winced. The movement must have sent fresh bursts of pain through his battered skull.

"No, I heard just the briefest rustle in the brush, and then it was as if someone dropped a mountain on my head. I didn't know anything after that until I regained consciousness. I moaned a bit, and then Nighthawk was here helping me to sit up."

"Let's get back to the campfire," Preacher said.

"But the infants—"

"I put Dog on their trail. He'll find 'em if anybody can. We need to take a better look at that head o' yours, and Nighthawk's got some little scratches that need patchin' up, from that tangle he had with the grizz."

"Good heavens, that's right! What happened to the bear? Were you able to chase it off?"

"Before it was over, that ol' bear must've wished he hadn't come bargin' into our camp like that. Nighthawk killed it. Stove its head in with his tomahawk."

"That's incredible! A herculean feat, to be sure."

"I was just thinkin' the same thing a while ago."

Nighthawk rose to his feet, bringing Audie with him. Preacher knew Audie didn't cotton to being toted like that, but there wasn't much he could do about it. The Crow warrior carried Audie back to camp and set him down carefully near the fire.

Preacher tossed the burning branch back onto the flames and knelt beside Audie.

"Lemme take a look at that head."

Audie jerked his hand in a curt gesture. "I'm fine," he said. "See to Nighthawk's injuries."

"Umm," the Crow said.

"You two can argue later about how the other one's hurt worse," Preacher told them. "Quit your fussin', Audie, and let me take a look."

The former professor's injury was a simple one. From the looks of it, Preacher figured somebody had struck him with a gun butt. That had opened up a cut, raised a lump on Audie's head, and knocked him cold. Preacher probed around the goose egg, but although it was painful, judging by the faces Audie made, Preacher didn't think the skull was busted.

He told Audie as much, then added, "Good thing you got a nice, hard head."

Nighthawk grunted in amusement.

"You never can tell, though," Preacher went on. "I've knowed of fellas who got walloped like that, seemed to be all right, and then up an' dropped dead a few days later without no warnin'. Try not to do that."

"I'll certainly endeavor not to drop dead," Audie said.

Preacher had Nighthawk take off his buckskin shirt and then examined the deep claw marks left on the Crow's shoulder by the bear attack. The wounds were already scabbing over, but Preacher fetched a bottle of whiskey from his saddlebags and soaked a cloth with the fiery stuff anyway. He cleaned off the partially dried blood and then poured whiskey directly on the wounds.

"Burns like blazes, don't it?" Preacher said, even though Nighthawk acted as if he didn't feel a thing.

"There's no point in trying to get a response from him," Audie said as Nighthawk pulled his bloodstained shirt back on. "Nighthawk is, perhaps, the most perfect example of stoicism I've ever encountered. His visage might as well be carved from solid granite."

"The Great Stone Face, eh?" Preacher nodded. "Pretty good description of him."

The next moment, some rustling in the brush made him turn sharply. Dog pushed through the branches into the open, came to a stop, and gazed intensely at the three men for a moment.

Then, with an emphatic bark, the big cur turned and ran back to the edge of the woods, where he stopped again and looked over his shoulder at them.

"He's found 'em," Preacher said. "He knows where Apollo and Artemis are."

CHAPTER 9

They traveled on foot because they could do so without making as much noise as they would if they were mounted. Also, since they were moving through thick woods, it was easier on foot than on horseback.

Audie rode on Nighthawk's shoulders so as not to slow them down as they followed Dog. Preacher had suggested that Audie remain at the campsite since he'd been knocked out and probably needed to rest, but the little man wasn't having any of it.

"What I don't understand," Audie said as they followed Dog, "is what the connection could be between that bear and Mack Ozark."

"Ain't no connection, more than likely," Preacher said. "The bear wasn't workin' for Ozark, if that's what you're thinkin'. That ol' grizz just happened on us and decided he was mad at us. Mad enough to come stompin' into our camp bent on raisin' hell. Who knows how a bear thinks?"

"The attack was just an unfortunate coincidence, is that what you're saying?"

"Seems to be the most likely explanation. Figure it this way. Some o' Ozark's men have been keepin' an eye on us, probably sendin' word back to Ozark his own self, wherever he's holed up, lettin' him know that we're still headed in his direction. But then, they heard that bear a-bellerin' and headed toward the camp to take a look, but then who do they run smack-dab into? You and the very young'uns the varmints are tryin' to get their hands on. So one of 'em wallops you, and they grab the kids and take off for the tall and uncut."

"How many, do you think?"

"Might have been just one hombre. More likely two or three, I'd say. But probably not the whole bunch or they would've tried to kill us—assumin' the blamed bear didn't. I've got a hunch Ozark's gathered up most of his gang to wait for us, like you were sayin' earlier."

"Yes, I did say that, didn't I?" Audie mused. "And I should have already grasped the scenario you just laid out, Preacher. In hindsight, it seems blindingly obvious."

"Nothin's obvious when you been walloped on the head. After somethin' like that happens, thinkin' through anything takes a heap more work for a spell. I ought to know. I've had this ol' noggin o' mine dented more times than I like to think about."

Preacher was in the lead with Nighthawk and Audie close behind him. They kept their voices pitched low as they talked, although they weren't really worried about getting close enough to their quarry to be overhead. Dog would warn them before that could happen.

Preacher was using his instincts and his keen senses to follow the big cur as it led them on the trail of the stolen babies. They had left the horses back at the campsite, about a mile behind them.

Dog doubled back and nudged Preacher's leg. That told the mountain man they were getting close to their destination. He put out a hand to stop Nighthawk. In a voice barely above a whisper, he said, "You fellas stay here. I'll scout ahead a mite."

With Dog still leading the way, Preacher moved through the trees as noiselessly as a phantom. His ability to travel through a forest without making a sound was uncanny. There was a very good reason why, among his mortal enemies the Blackfeet, he was known as the Ghost Killer. He had sent many of their warriors across the divide without them having any idea he was even in the vicinity.

A few minutes later, Dog stopped next to Preacher's leg and whined softly. Preacher sniffed the air and dropped to a knee beside the big cur.

"Yeah, I smell it, too," he whispered. "Woodsmoke. Somebody's got 'em a campfire up yonder. They must be mighty confident nobody's gonna find 'em. If I'd stolen somethin' important like those young'uns, I reckon I would've made a cold camp tonight, just to be on the safe side." He leaned closer to Dog. "Let's go, old son. Slow an' easy now."

They crept forward, and it wasn't long before Preacher caught sight of a faint, inconstant glow through the brush. That was the campfire he had smelled. He went to hands and knees and crawled ahead slowly, moving the brush aside a bit at a time to avoid making any racket.

As he drew closer to the fire, he stretched out on his belly. Dog was close beside him, scooting along as carefully as Preacher. Hearing low-pitched male voices ahead of them, Preacher stopped and parted some branches to create a gap through which he could peer.

Fifty yards away, a ridge jutted up from the landscape, rising to a protruding eminence that bulged out and overhung some flat ground forming a cave-like area under the rock. A small campfire burned in a ring of rocks underneath that overhang. The smoke drifted out into the darkness. Two horses were picketed off to the side, away from the camp. One man sat cross-legged beside the fire while another paced restlessly back and forth nearby.

On the other side of the fire lay two small, motionless bundles. Preacher recognized the blankets in which Apollo and Artemis had been wrapped the last time he saw them.

He would have felt better if the babies had been squalling or even moving around a little. The way they were lying there so quietly worried him.

Of course, it was possible they were just sleeping, he told himself. Right from the start, Mack Ozark's men had acted as if they didn't want any harm to come to the infants, although they hadn't cared at all who else they hurt or killed.

Preacher couldn't make out the words as the men talked. The one on his feet seemed upset about something. He waved his arms as he paced. Maybe he believed this was a foolish errand Mack Ozark had sent them on. Recovering the babies had cost quite a few men their lives. Maybe this hombre didn't believe they were worth it.

Or maybe something else entirely was bothering him. Preacher might ask him later—assuming he didn't kill the baby-stealing son of a buck first.

It wouldn't take him long to go back to where he'd left Audie and Nighthawk and tell them what he'd found. But as he studied the situation, he decided that might not be necessary. A plan formed in his mind. He whispered to Dog for a few minutes, instructing the big cur on what he needed to do. Most folks would think he was crazy, trusting a dog to understand him like that, but Preacher knew from experience that this dog could grasp more things than anybody else would believe.

"Stay," he concluded, and was confident that Dog would wait right here until Preacher was ready for him to carry out the other commands he'd been given.

Preacher backed off a ways and then got to his feet. He moved to his left, staying low and being as quiet and careful as he had been approaching the camp. When he had gone a quarter of a mile or so, he angled back toward the ridge. In the thick shadows of night, he was well out of sight of his quarry when he reached it. He could still see the campfire's faint glow in the distance, but the two men couldn't see him.

He scrambled up the slope with ease, using rocks and the roots of the brush that grew there for footholds and handholds. He was cautious in his ascent, making sure not to dislodge anything that would fall and make a noise.

When he reached the top, he catfooted toward the large, bulging rock that hung out over the camp.

Within minutes, he had crawled out onto that rock and could see the trees and thick underbrush where Dog waited. He couldn't see the camp itself, but the flickering light from the fire spilled out onto the open ground in front of it.

The two men below him were quiet. If they had been arguing about something earlier, they had settled the dispute or at least given up on it for the night. Preacher could tell by the quality of the firelight that the flames were dying down. The two men must have turned in for the night.

Preacher cupped his hands around his mouth and made a quiet, hooting sound. If the two men even noticed it, they would take it for a night-hunting owl.

Dog knew better, though. That was the signal for the big cur to put Preacher's plan into action.

Dog pushed through the brush and stalked into the open. He stopped at the edge of the light from the fire and let out a loud, menacing growl.

The two horses reacted immediately, throwing up their heads and trumpeting frightened neighs. That finished the job of waking the two men. One of them yelled, "What the hell!"

The other man cursed and said, "It's a damn wolf! Shoot it!"

"Take it easy," the first man responded. "That old mountain man and his friends may be looking for us. I don't want a gunshot to lead them right to us if I can help it."

"But the wolf—"

"I'll scare it off."

So far, the men were reacting just the way Preacher hoped they would. He moved closer to the rock's edge. Out there at the boundary of the light, Dog continued growling and snarling, acting like he was going to attack at any second.

"Do something!" the first man urged. "If we let a wild animal drag those babies off, Mack will kill us."

There was confirmation the two varmints were working for Mack Ozark, Preacher thought. Not that he had doubted it for a second.

"Keep your blasted shirt on," the second man said, raising his voice to be heard over the commotion Dog was creating. "I don't care if it is a wolf, it's bound to be scared of fire."

The man strode out from under the overhang, brandishing a burning branch he had taken from the fire. He waved it toward Dog and yelled, "Get out of here, damn you! Go away!"

Dog stood his ground, his hackles rising even more. The man drew back his arm as if he intended to throw the branch at the big cur.

Preacher leaped off the rock.

He only fell about twelve feet before his feet slammed into the man's back, but that was far enough to give him considerable momentum. The unexpected weight and impact drove the man forward and knocked him to the ground. The torch flew out of his hand and sailed toward where Dog had put on his threatening show.

The big cur was no longer there, however. He was already dashing forward, headed for the cave under the rock.

Preacher landed on his feet and nimbly kept his balance. The man he had just jumped on was sprawled in front of him. Preacher sprang forward, planted a knee in the middle of the man's back to pin him to the ground, and drew his right-hand Colt. He pressed the muzzle to the back of the man's head.

The man had started trying to move as he regained his senses after being knocked to the ground, but he went absolutely still when he felt the gun barrel prodding him.

"That's mighty smart," Preacher told him. "Stay still like that and maybe I won't blow your brains out. Maybe."

He glanced over his shoulder as terrified screams rang out. Dog had knocked the other man onto his back and was ripping at him with razor-sharp fangs. The man flailed madly but couldn't get away from the animal. Gradually, his struggles weakened as he lost more blood through the gaping wounds Dog's teeth had opened in his throat. He stopped screaming and then lay still. Dog savaged him for a few more seconds before backing off and continuing to snarl as blood dripped from his muzzle.

"You hear that?" Preacher said to the other man. "You give me any trouble and I'll turn you over to that wolf of mine. He'll rip you to pieces just like he did your partner."

Dog wasn't a wolf, of course, but the prisoner didn't have to know that. He said, "Please, mister, whatever you want, I—I'll go along with it. Don't let that beast anywhere near me!"

Preacher took the gun away from the man's head, rose to his feet, and backed off a few steps. He kept the Colt trained on the man as he said, "All right, get up. Don't try anything."

The man climbed shakily to his feet. He didn't appear to be carrying a pistol, but he had a sheathed knife at his waist. Preacher reached in from behind with his left hand and drew the blade from its sheath. He tossed the weapon aside, well out of reach.

Then he moved around where the man could see him and motioned with the revolver.

"Go on back to the fire. You damn well better hope those little ones are all right, or else you're sure gonna pay for whatever happened to 'em."

"They're fine," the man said. "Clark and me took good care of them, I swear it. Our boss wants the little varmints back safe and sound."

"That'd be Mack Ozark, eh?"

A look of surprise crossed the man's beard-stubbled face. "You know Ozark?"

"I ain't never crossed trails with him, but I sure as blazes know who he is."

A sigh of resignation came from the prisoner as he said, "Then you know why you might as well go ahead and shoot me, mister. When Mack finds out we had those babies and then lost them, he'll kill me. He's liable to take his time about it and make me suffer, too."

"Don't sound like a very good fella to work for."

"Not in some ways. But he always comes up with good ideas for us to make money. Once you're part of the bunch, though, there's no way out except dying. So men are willing to do whatever it takes to keep him happy."

As they moved under the overhang, the prisoner stopped to stare down at the gruesome carcass of his former comrade. Dog growled at him and made him shy away.

"Poor Clark," he muttered. "He never had a chance."

"No, but you do," Preacher said. "Why does Mack Ozark want them babies so bad?"

The prisoner laughed, but the sound held no genuine humor. He seemed to have gotten over his momentary fear of Dog and was now more concerned about the threat of Mack Ozark's wrath.

"Do you think I'd tell you, even if I knew? Crossing Ozark is the best way to wind up dead." The man shook his head. "But as it happens, I don't know, and that's the God's honest truth. When he found out they were gone, he sent out search parties to look for them, and then once he got word that the old Indian and the girl were dead and some other fellas had the babies, he just about went crazy. He never told us what's so important about them, though, just that we'd better find them and bring them back to him just like they were when they disappeared, even wrapped in the same blankets and everything."

"Who do they belong to? Are they Ozark's kids?"

"I've told you all I'm going to tell you, mister." The prisoner scowled. "What business is it of yours, anyway? Why are they so important to you? Judging by what I've heard from the fellas who made it back from Dutch Charley's, you never even saw those babies until the fight at the trading post."

"I gave that Flathead gal my word I'd take care of 'em," Preacher said. "Seems to me the best way to do that is to take 'em back to their ma. Tell me who that is and where to find her, and maybe you'll come through this whole mess alive."

"I'm not saying anything else, mister. Hell, you can even sic that wolf of yours on me. I'd rather that than have Mack Ozark mad at me."

"You're a damn fool," Preacher snapped. "But if that's what you want—"

He was about to order Dog to threaten the prisoner, but before the words could come from his mouth, the big cur whirled around and growled as he peered out at the night. Preacher knew instantly from Dog's reaction that some other danger was lurking out there in the shadows, so he wasn't surprised when he saw orange muzzle flame rip the darkness apart.

CHAPTER 10

The crack of a rifle sounded at the same time. A split-second later, Preacher sensed as much as heard the wind-rip of a rifle ball past his head as he darted aside and threw himself forward onto his belly.

By the time he landed on the hard-packed ground, he had drawn the second Colt. With irons in both hands, he opened fire on the spot where he had seen the muzzle flash.

The guns hammered out a crashing melody as Preacher thumbed off shot after shot. Tongues of flame a foot long licked from their muzzles as they bucked in his strong hands.

When the hammers fell on empty chambers, he rolled to one side and kicked out at the fire, scattering the burning chunks of wood so the flames wouldn't light up the cave-like area. He made sure to kick the fire away from the two blanket-wrapped bundles lying nearby.

While he was doing that, Preacher caught a glimpse of the prisoner he had been questioning. The man lay on his back with his arms flung out to the sides. He wasn't moving. Preacher remembered the rifle ball that had missed him so closely and wondered if it had flown on to strike the prisoner.

He could check on that later, assuming he survived this fight.

For the moment, the fella didn't appear to be any threat, so Preacher wasn't going to worry about him.

Preacher holstered the Colts and crawled quickly over to the infants. He scooped them up and moved closer to the rock wall at the back of the camp where the shadows were thicker. Apollo and Artemis began to squirm and fuss. Those cries were welcome sounds. They proved to Preacher that both babies were still alive and evidently unharmed.

He settled them on the ground and stayed on his knees beside them as he began reloading the Patersons. He carried spare, already-loaded cylinders so he could swap them out quickly when he needed to. He felt a little better when he had ten rounds ready to fire again.

So far, only the one shot had come from outside the cave. Preacher glanced at the prisoner again. The man still hadn't moved. Preacher was convinced the stray shot had struck him and either killed him or badly injured him.

A grimace crossed the mountain man's face. He probably could have found out more from the man if he'd had the chance to keep questioning him. Now that opportunity might well be lost.

Apollo and Artemis stopped crying quite so frantically, although they still made fretting noises. Preacher tried to shush them, but it didn't do any good. He hoped they wouldn't cover up any sounds an enemy might make trying to sneak up on him.

He didn't see any sign of Dog and knew the big cur must have taken off in an attempt to find whoever had fired that shot at them. Dog was smart enough to know there was an enemy out there in the shadows, and he would do his best to deal with that threat.

A few moments later, a familiar voice called, "Preacher! Where are you?"

That was Audie. If he and Nighthawk were out there, the unknown rifleman must have fled. Preacher was cautious, anyway, as he moved closer to the open and replied, "Over here at the base of the ridge under this big rock."

Audie and Nighthawk both had keen enough vision to locate the place he was talking about. Most of the flames had died out since Preacher had scattered the campfire, but a few of the embers still glowed enough to cast a faint light. That light revealed Audie and Nighthawk as they approached the cave. Dog trotted up with them.

"I heard Apollo and Artemis crying," Audie said. "Are they all right?"

"I ain't had a chance to check them over yet," Preacher said, "but they sound like they're fine. Leather-lunged, just like always."

"Nighthawk, gather up that wood and build the fire up again." Audie knelt next to the infants and added over his shoulder, "Preacher, I thought you were going to come back and get us once you'd scouted the situation. Then the next thing we know, we hear those Colts of yours thundering as if all hell were breaking loose."

"When Dog led me up here, I realized I stood a good chance o' dealin' with those two varmints my own self," Preacher explained. "Darned near did, too, but there must've been a third one I didn't know about, or else he came up lookin' for them just like I was. He took a potshot at me, so I figure he must've been one of Ozark's men, too."

"There didn't seem to be anyone around when Nighthawk and I arrived."

"He lit a shuck after he saw he'd missed me and I started throwin' a heap of lead right back at him."

"That makes sense." Audie had unwrapped one of the babies by now and held the infant up to have a better look. "Apollo doesn't seem to be hurt, thank goodness."

Apollo must have recognized Audie. He was making cooing

noises now, sounding much happier than he had been only moments earlier.

Audie wrapped up the little boy again. Nighthawk had the fire blazing by now, and by its light Audie checked on Artemis, too. "She's all right," he reported with obvious relief in his voice. "Once again, fortune has smiled on us. The question is, how long will it continue to do so?"

Preacher went over to have a look at the man he'd been interrogating. He had a dark-rimmed hole in his forehead where the rifle ball had struck him and was as dead as he could be. Luck had ended his life just as surely as it had preserved those of Apollo and Artemis.

"I tried to find out from this fella why Ozark wants those young'uns so bad," Preacher said. "He swore up one way and down the other that he didn't know, only that Ozark ordered his men to find the kids and bring 'em back safe and sound. I asked him who their ma is, but he wouldn't tell me that and I didn't get around to forcin' it out of him before the shootin' started."

"So actually, we don't know any more than we did before," Audie said.

Preacher grunted. "Well, we know this here Mack Ozark is one mighty bad hombre. That fella saw what Dog did to his partner and that spooked him pretty bad at first, but when I threatened to let Dog loose on him unless he talked, he still didn't want to cooperate. Said he was more scared of what Ozark would do to him if he ever found out."

"And that's the man who wants to get his hands on these children," Audie said with a shake of his head. "We can't allow that to happen, Preacher."

"We won't," the mountain man said. "You can bet a hat on that. But what if their ma is dead, or worse, is willin' to turn the little ones over to Ozark?"

"No mother would ever do something like that!"

"I reckon you have a heap more faith in human nature than I do."

Audie frowned. "Think about it, though. Perhaps she sent the children away with Bluebird and her grandfather because she wanted to get them away from Ozark."

"If that's what happened, then we're takin' 'em right back to where their ma didn't want them to be."

Audie sighed with a nod. "It's a conundrum, all right, but there's one thing we can be sure of."

"Yeah," Preacher said. "The answers are waitin' up there somewhere ahead of us."

Preacher was confident now that he and his companions were being watched as they continued riding northwest toward Emerald Creek the next day. Mack Ozark's men were out there keeping an eye on them, but they probably wouldn't do anything unless Preacher and the others turned back.

Why would they come out in the open when Preacher, Audie, and Nighthawk were taking those babies right where Mack Ozark wanted them to go?

A showdown with Ozark was inevitable—and the odds would be against them, Preacher knew. They would fight that battle when it came, though, taking it head-on just as they had faced every other danger they had encountered in the past.

Because of the way the situation had developed, no one else tried to stop them on their journey, just as Preacher expected. Six days after leaving Dutch Charley's, Preacher, Audie, and Nighthawk reined in at the top of a hill and looked across the beautiful landscape in front of them.

Snow-capped peaks rose in the distance, but closer lay an inviting terrain of wooded hills and broad valleys carpeted with lush grass and colorful wildflowers. Thick stands of evergreens looked like dark cloaks draped over shoulders formed by the hills.

Audie pointed at a line of vegetation snaking its way through one of the valleys.

"That's Emerald Creek," he said. "I remember it from the last time we came through this area."

Nighthawk grunted and nodded in agreement.

"Is there a particular place along the creek those star garnets come from?" Preacher asked. "Or can you find them just anywhere in these parts?"

"Honestly, I don't know," Audie replied with a shake of his head. "All I'm sure of is that I've heard people say they found such stones along Emerald Creek."

Preacher thought it over and then said, "We'll follow the creek north and see what we come to, unless you fellas have some good reason for goin' the other way."

"When you don't know where your true destination lies, one way is as good as the other, isn't it? Philosophically speaking, I mean."

"I reckon." Preacher nudged Horse into motion. "Let's go."

They reached the creek in late afternoon and decided to go ahead and make camp for the night. While Preacher was tending to the horses and Nighthawk gathered wood to build a fire, Audie took Apollo and Artemis out of their cradleboards and found a good place on the bank for the babies to lie. Both infants seemed to be in a good mood, gurgling, waving their arms, and kicking their feet, but of course that could change in the blink of an eye, and they could start wailing furiously in discontent.

Preacher could see them from the corner of his eye as he un-saddled Audie's horse. For a moment, he didn't fully comprehend what he was witnessing as Apollo rolled over, pushed himself up on hands and knees, rocked back and forth for a few seconds, and then began crawling toward the creek. Audie had turned away and hadn't noticed what the little boy was doing.

"Audie!" Preacher exclaimed. He pointed. "Grab that kid!"

Audie jerked around, his eyes widening as he spotted Apollo approaching the stream. The infant was moving faster than it seemed like he ought to be able to. Audie yelped in alarm and scrambled after him.

"Wait just a blasted minute, lad!" Audie bent down and grabbed Apollo's diaper just before the baby toppled off the bank's edge into the water. He picked up the baby and held him securely. "What in the world do you think you're doing? How long have you been able to crawl like that?"

Preacher and Nighthawk joined Audie. "The way he was scurryin' along, it sure didn't look like that was the first time he'd been up crawlin' around," Preacher commented.

"It certainly didn't. And yet, every time I've left them somewhere, they've been right there when I came back. It's not like I've left them unattended, either. Anytime I haven't been very close by, one of you fellows has been watching them." Audie laughed, shook his head, and tickled Apollo under the chin. "But you were definitely a speedy little devil just then. I'm going to have to keep an even closer eye on you from now on."

"Let's just hope he ain't already taught his sister how to do that," Preacher said.

"I've seen no signs of Artemis crawling yet—but I didn't expect Apollo to go trotting off like that, either!"

With that potential catastrophe narrowly averted, the men continued setting up camp. As he went about the chores, Preacher sensed that he was being watched. It was a common feeling these past few days. Would Mack Ozark's men launch another attack? Or would they wait to see what Preacher and his companions were going to do?

As usual, they had to remain alert and be ready for trouble at any moment. A guard would be posted all night, as always.

It was Preacher's turn to take the first shift. After Audie had fed the children their supper, changed their diapers, and gotten them settled down to sleep, he and Nighthawk stretched out on either side of the babies and rolled up in their blankets. Like most frontiersmen, they possessed the ability to fall deeply and completely asleep almost as soon as their eyes closed, whenever they got the chance.

Preacher moved a short distance away from the dwindling campfire, sat down to prop his back against a tree trunk, and made sure not to look into the flames even though they were dying down. He kept his attention focused on the shadows surrounding the camp. That would keep his night vision as keen as possible.

Dog lay down on the ground beside him, head resting on his paws in front of him.

An hour or more had passed before Preacher heard something that made him sit up straighter. The night was so quiet he had been able to hear birds flitting around in the trees and small animals rustling in the brush, but this was different. It was a heavier sound, the rasp of a misplaced foot, followed by what might have been a sharp intake of breath as whoever was skulking around out there realized he might have made a misstep.

Preacher didn't make a sound, and as Dog stirred, he rested his hand on the big cur's head to keep him quiet. He knew the shadows were so thick around them that they couldn't be seen. He stayed where he was and waited, thinking his lack of a response might draw the stranger in farther. If this was one of Mack Ozark's men stalking them—and Preacher couldn't think of who else it could be—he might get another chance to interrogate a prisoner and find out more about Ozark's connection with those babies.

From where Preacher sat, he could see the blanket-wrapped shapes between the slumbering Audie and Nighthawk. Audie had stacked a barricade of small stones around Apollo and Artemis so that if either of them tried to crawl off, they would knock the stones over and make a noise. That would bring Audie and Nighthawk awake instantly.

More time dragged by, and then Preacher felt the rumble as a growl began to build in Dog's throat. He pressed down harder on the big cur's head and breathed, "Shhh."

Dog didn't make any noise, but Preacher could feel how tense his muscles were. Dog was ready to spring into action. More than ready—he was eager to do battle.

A shadowy figure appeared, moving from the trees into the open area along the bank where the group had made camp. It stole closer. Preacher couldn't make out any details except that the intruder wasn't overly tall and was rather thick-bodied.

The mountain man leaned down and whispered, "Stay," in Dog's ear. Then he came to his feet, uncoiling to his full height without any sound. The intruder was only a few steps away from Audie and Nighthawk now.

Preacher dived forward, tackling the man and knocking him to the ground.

The intruder yelled in surprise and alarm as he fell. Preacher landed on top of him and grabbed his hair to jerk his head back. If he'd had a knife in his other hand, he would be in perfect position to cut the intruder's throat. But that wasn't what Preacher wanted right now, so he looped his left arm around the man's throat instead and locked it into place. His knee dug painfully into the intruder's back as Preacher put pressure on him and bent him backward.

The man made gurgling sounds and writhed in Preacher's grasp, but he was no match for the mountain man's strength. Hearing the commotion, Audie and Nighthawk were awake instantly and came out of their blankets clutching weapons, ready to fight. Audie brandished a brace of flintlock pistols while the Crow warrior was armed with his tomahawk and knife.

"It's all right, boys," Preacher said. "I got this one, and it seems like he's the only one skulkin' around."

"One of Ozark's men, no doubt," Audie said as he came over to the spot where Preacher knelt on the intruder.

That made the prisoner grunt harder as he tried to force words past the iron grip of Preacher's arm across his throat. He struggled even more but had no chance of breaking loose.

Audie kept his pistols ready and scanned the trees in case of more menace lurking there. Nighthawk was equally alert.

"Dog, hunt," Preacher told the big cur. If anybody else was around, Dog would find them in a hurry. With that done, Preacher turned his attention to the man he had captured. He said, "I'm gonna let up a mite so you can talk, mister, but don't try to yell for help or pull any other tricks. You won't like what happens if you do."

Preacher eased his grip and took his knee out of the prisoner's back. The man lifted his head and gasped for breath, gulping down air he hadn't been able to get while Preacher was holding him.

When he had recovered somewhat, he struggled to say, "I . . . I don't work . . . for Mack Ozark!"

The words were in English. Preacher had already decided, based on the long hair slick with bear grease and worn in braids, as well as the buckskin clothing he had felt, that the prisoner was an Indian. That didn't mean the fella wasn't one of Ozark's men.

But the voice sounded young, and that seemed strange to Preacher. Every one of Ozark's men he had laid eyes on so far had been in his twenties or older.

This one didn't sound like much more than a kid.

"Stir up the fire and get us some light," Preacher said. Nighthawk moved quickly to do that. Preacher maintained his grip on the prisoner as the flames began to take hold and dance again, but he wasn't holding on as tightly now.

When the fire was big enough to cast a circle of light around it, Preacher let go completely and stepped back. His hands dropped to the butts of the Colts in case he needed them, but he saw quickly that that wouldn't be necessary.

The prisoner rolled over onto his back and lay there with his chest rising and falling rapidly as he tried to catch his breath and recover from being tackled. The flickering glare of the firelight washed over his round face and revealed that he was indeed young—no more than fourteen or fifteen, Preacher judged.

The stranger might still be a threat despite his youth. "Who are you," Preacher demanded, "and why in blazes were you sneakin' around our camp?"

The young man pushed himself up on an elbow and then struggled to sit up all the way, grunting with effort as he did so. His buckskin shirt was tight across his ample belly.

"I . . . I heard there were strange white men coming this way," he said when he had caught his breath.

"Umm," Nighthawk said sharply.

"Strange white men and a Crow warrior," the youth corrected himself hastily. "And that you have two babies with you." A stricken look came over his face. "That's not true, is it? You didn't bring them back here? Tell me you didn't bring them back here!"

"Tell us who you are and what your connection is to all of this, and then perhaps we'll share some of our information with you," Audie said.

"My name is—" He pronounced a name in the Flathead tongue that Preacher couldn't translate despite his familiarity with the language.

Nighthawk understood it, though. He rumbled, "Little Bear," and then let out a grunt to show that he was amused.

"Yes, that's right, Little Bear," the prisoner agreed. He didn't sound as if he cared for the name all that much.

"All right, Little Bear," Preacher said. "You still claim you don't work for Mack Ozark?"

"Of course I don't work for him! I don't have anything more to do with the man than I have to." He stared defiantly at the men for a moment, but then his gaze dropped, and he went on in a subdued tone, "Jonathan was my friend. Annie is my friend.

I would never betray them by throwing in with a . . . a monster like Mack Ozark!"

"I reckon maybe we're in agreement about what sort of fella this Mack Ozark is," Preacher said. "But who are Jonathan and Annie?"

Little Bear frowned. "You truly don't know who they are?"

"Never heard of 'em."

Little Bear raised a hand and pointed at Apollo and Artemis, who still slept securely in their blankets.

"Jonathan and Annie Collins are the parents of Edward and Elizabeth there," he told Preacher, Audie, and Nighthawk. "Or rather, I should say they were the parents of those little ones."

CHAPTER 11

A grim silence filled the air around the campfire for a moment after the young Indian's statement.

Then Preacher said, "You mean they're dead? The babies' folks are dead? They're orphans?"

Little Bear shook his head. "You're making me all confused. Jonathan is dead, but Annie is still very much alive. At least, she was a few days ago, the last time I saw her."

Audie said, "The children's names are actually Edward and Elizabeth? We've been calling them Apollo and Artemis."

"After the figures from mythology?"

"That's right."

"Who the hell are you?" Preacher asked. "From your hair and the way you're dressed, you look like a Flathead, but you talk like a white man."

"I am Salish," Little Bear responded with a note of pride in his voice. "But Annie taught me how to speak English and let me read her books. Jonathan always made sure she had plenty of books. She loves to read, and . . . and I do, too."

"I don't think this young man means us any harm, Preacher," Audie said.

"I don't," Little Bear said. "I just wanted to find out if what I heard about the twins is true." He shook his head. "Now I know it is, but I wish it wasn't. You shouldn't have brought them back here."

Preacher thought for a moment and then nodded. "You can move on up by the fire," he told Little Bear. "I reckon we've got some talkin' to do, and we might as well be comfortable while we do it."

The young Indian got to his feet, came closer to the fire, and sat down cross-legged beside it. Preacher and Nighthawk sat down flanking him while Audie said, "I'd better check on Apollo and Artemis, although they seem to be sleeping soundly." He shook his head. "Calling them Edward and Elizabeth is going to take some getting used to."

Little Bear said, "It sounds strange to me when you call them Apollo and Artemis—although I have to admit, the names do seem to fit them pretty well."

"First of all," Preacher said, getting down to business, "what's your connection with Mack Ozark?"

"I don't have any connection with him. Well, not really. My people trade with him sometimes. Our village isn't far from his compound. We provide Ozark and his men with fresh meat in return for some of the goods they have."

Little Bear scowled as he continued, "Some of our young women have gone to the compound and been forced to stay there. They shamed themselves by going in the first place, but they believed the promises of the white men."

"Ozark's got hisself a whole compound, does he?" Preacher said.

"Yes. Cabins for the men, a stable and corral for their horses, a blacksmith shop, a smokehouse, and some storage buildings. There's even an actual house where Ozark lives. There are more than a dozen buildings in all, with a stockade wall around them to make the place easier to defend—although no one would dare attack it."

"Where do you suppose Ozark gets the goods your people trade for?"

Little Bear's scowl deepened. "I know he and his men steal them and probably kill many of the people they rob. The men often talk freely around me. Some of them know I understand their tongue, but they see an Indian and they forget to be cautious. I've heard them talk about attacking wagon trains and robbing trading posts and ambushing caravans of freight wagons farther south along the Santa Fe Trail. They'll ride hundreds of miles to carry out their evil plans, if they believe they'll make enough money to make it worthwhile."

"They sound like a pretty bad bunch," Preacher said. "That matches up with the stories we've heard about 'em. But where do this fella Jonathan Collins and his wife come into the deal?"

"Jonathan Collins was the leader of the gang before Mack Ozark."

That flat statement made Preacher, Audie, and Nighthawk glance at each other in surprise.

Audie said to Little Bear, "You mean the father of those two children was an outlaw?"

"Yes, he was. There's no getting around that fact. I'd like to think he wasn't as ruthless and vicious as Ozark, but I don't really know that. He led the gang for several years. He was in charge when Ozark joined them down in Kansas."

Preacher said, "I reckon Ozark must've worked his way up to takin' over the gang."

Little Bear nodded. "That's what happened. Jonathan trusted Ozark with more and more responsibility as time went on. That was a mistake. I suppose Jonathan never thought that Ozark would turn on him and overthrow him as the leader. But once Ozark had gained enough support from the other men, that's exactly what he did." The young Indian sighed. "Jonathan never expected that betrayal."

"Ozark killed him, I suppose," Audie said.

Little Bear shook his head and said, "No, even worse. He made him a prisoner. Tortured him. Humiliated him. We all thought he would kill Jonathan, but by the end, the few friends he had left wished that Ozark would just go ahead and put him out of his misery."

Several moments of grim silence went by. Preacher tugged at his earlobe and scraped a thumbnail along his jawline as he pondered everything the young Flathead had just told them. Finally, he asked, "Did the gang have this compound before Ozark took over?"

"That's right."

"And Collins had his wife there? This lady called Annie who's the young'uns' ma?"

"Yes. Several other members of the gang are married, too, and have their wives with them. Jonathan and Annie lived in the house where Ozark lives now. After Jonathan . . . died . . . Ozark took over the house and moved Annie into a cabin that's a half-mile or so from the others, outside the compound. I suppose even a man like Ozark doesn't always want to be reminded of the terrible things he's done."

Audie said, "To be brutally honest, I'm surprised he didn't claim the poor woman for his own as part of the spoils of his victory over Collins."

"I know that's what Annie thought would happen. Was afraid it would happen. She told my sister that she would end her own life before she would give herself to Ozark. The only reason she hadn't already done so was because of the children. She had to stay alive to care for Edward and Elizabeth."

"Are you sure they're not really Ozark's kids?" Preacher asked. "They ain't even a year old yet."

"No, Jonathan was their father. After . . . after Ozark betrayed him, while Jonathan was a prisoner, Ozark allowed him to spend time now and then with Annie. I suspect that was just another way of torturing him, allowing them to be together and then forcing them to be apart again."

"This fella Ozark sounds more and more like he needs killin'," Preacher said. "But what was that you said about your sister?"

"She's Annie's best friend. Her name is Chimalus." Little Bear smiled. "It means 'bluebird.'"

Preacher stiffened. In the back of his mind, he supposed he had been waiting for just such a revelation. It made sense in light of everything Little Bear had told them so far. He and Audie and Nighthawk had learned a great deal from talking to the young man—but none of it was good.

Little Bear's thoughts must have started proceeding along the same lines. He leaned forward with a look of concern on his face and went on, "Wait a minute. Bluebird and our grandfather left with the babies a couple of weeks ago. Annie had been begging her for a long time to take them and flee, but Bluebird believed she would miss them too much once they were gone. Finally, she gave in, and they took Edward and Elizabeth one night. But if you have the babies now . . ."

He came to his feet, clearly growing agitated.

"Where are my sister and grandfather? What's happened to them? Are they all right?"

Audie stood up and went over to him. "I'm truly sorry to have to tell you this, Little Bear," he said, making his voice as comforting as he could. "Both of them were killed at a trading post about a week's ride southeast of here. That's where we met them briefly, and unfortunately one of Ozark's search parties caught up with them there."

Little Bear raised his hands, clenched them into fists, and pressed them against his temples. He squeezed his eyes closed as if he wanted to shut out everything around him. But he couldn't shut out the grief that welled up in his heart and soul. It escaped in a harsh, inarticulate wail of sorrow.

"I knew it, I knew it," he moaned. "I knew it wasn't a good idea for them to take the children. For some reason, Ozark wants them back."

"Sit down, son," Preacher told him. "I know it hurts like blazes. For what it's worth, the two of 'em died defendin' those kids. They were laid to rest proper-like, and most of the varmints responsible for what happened to 'em are dead. And the young'uns your sister was so worried about protectin' are right here, safe and sound."

"But you brought them *back*!" Little Bear looked around at the three men as his face flushed darker with anger. "How long will they stay safe if Mack Ozark gets his hands on them?"

"We don't know that," Audie said. "Honestly, we didn't know anything except that, before she passed, your sister asked us to look after the infants. We hoped that by bringing them back where they came from, that was what we were doing. We wanted to locate their parents so the family could be reunited."

Preacher added, "We didn't have no way of knowin' their pa was dead. And we still don't know why they're so important to Ozark if they don't belong to him. But he gave his men orders not to let them little ones get hurt. That's one thing we got on our side."

Little Bear sank to the ground again and hung his head.

"I suppose you're right," he said, "but you can't trust Ozark, not for a second. When he wants something, he'll do anything to get it."

"How far are we from this compound of his?"

Little Bear looked up. "It's about four miles west of here, on another little stream that flows into Emerald Creek."

"How did you know where to find us?" Audie asked.

"I didn't. I just heard men talking about how you were heading in this direction and had the twins with you. I've been waiting out here, scouting the area, for a couple of days. I was hoping I could find you first and warn you not to go on."

The young man's voice took on a new tone of urgency as he continued, "You should turn around and go back the way you came from. Put as much distance as you can between yourselves—and those babies—and Mack Ozark. If you really want to protect them and honor my sister's last wishes, that's what you'll do."

"Run away, you mean." Preacher's words held a harsh note. "That ain't somethin' we're particularly good at."

"You mean you're too proud to do it. You'd rather risk the lives of those innocent children."

"That's not it," Audie said. "Ozark has already demonstrated ample evidence of his willingness to send men after Apollo and Artemis—I mean, Edward and Elizabeth. If we turn and flee now, he'll just come after us. If there has to be a confrontation, it's possible it might be better at a time and place of our choosing, rather than Ozark's."

"But if you could stay ahead of them and reach the cities back east—St. Louis, for example—the children would be safer there."

"Bein' what some folks call civilized and bein' safer ain't always the same thing," Preacher pointed out. "We still ain't sure what's behind all this, and until we know, it's better that we don't cut and run." He rubbed his chin and frowned in thought. "You're right about one thing, though, Little Bear. We can't just go waltzin' in there and demand to know what this Ozark varmint is up to. We're gonna need to do some investigatin' first."

"What are you thinking, Preacher?" Audie asked.

"You and Nighthawk take the little ones and find a good place to hole up with them for a spell. Little Bear and me will go on to Ozark's place and I'll see if I can talk to this Annie Collins. She's their ma, and if she wants us to take the young'uns back east, I reckon that's what we ought to do."

The mountain man paused and then went on, "But if she wants to get away from Ozark and come with us, we'll sure do our best to see that she gets the chance."

Little Bear sounded excited now as he said, "You'd do that? You'd help Annie escape?"

Preacher nodded. "If that's what she wants."

"After everything you've told us, I can't imagine that she'd want to stay there," Audie said. "I suppose she felt like she couldn't leave, even to save the children, while her husband was still alive."

"That's right," Little Bear said. "As long as Jonathan was alive, she wouldn't desert him, and then after he was . . . gone . . . Ozark kept a guard on her and wouldn't let her leave."

Preacher said, "That's twice now you've sounded a mite funny about this Collins fella dyin'. Is there something else you need to tell us about that, Little Bear?"

"Not really. Nothing that makes an actual difference. It's just that . . . Well, Ozark didn't kill Jonathan, and he didn't die from the torture. He did away with himself. He tore up some bedding and made a rope out of it and . . . hanged himself."

"I'm sorry," Audie murmured. "He may have been an outlaw, but I can tell you were fond of him."

"He always treated me nice. He was almost like an older brother or an uncle to me. He didn't deserve what happened to him."

Preacher wasn't so sure about that; the gang had already been known for raiding wagon trains when Mack Ozark threw in with them, so it was pretty likely that Jonathan Collins had been a murderer as well as a thief.

But he didn't see how pointing that out to Little Bear would serve any purpose. The young man probably realized the truth already, anyway, whether or not he wanted to admit it even to himself.

Little Bear got to his feet and nodded. "I'll take you there," he told Preacher. "You know it'll be dangerous, though. If they catch you, they'll probably kill you. And you'd be lucky, at that. Ozark might decide to make an example of you."

"I've followed some perilous trails now and then, son," Preacher said dryly. "I reckon I'm willin' to run the risk."

"What about you, though?" Audie said to Little Bear. "If Ozark believes you're helping one of his enemies, you'll be in danger, too."

"I'll do it to help Annie and the twins, and . . . and to pay back some of what I owe Jonathan."

"It's settled, then," Preacher said. "Ozark's liable to have spies lurkin' around these parts—"

"I'm sure he does," Little Bear put in.

"So you and Nighthawk be as careful as you can while you're hidin' out, Audie. Take the little ones and go tonight. Find a place where nobody's liable to come across you, and one where you can put up a fight if they do."

Audie nodded. "I understand. You be careful, too, Preacher, and look out for our young friend here."

Preacher hoped Little Bear really was their friend. The youth seemed sincere enough in everything he had told them. His statements about Jonathan Collins had smacked of hero worship. That feeling might be misguided, but if it were true, it was likely that Little Bear genuinely wanted to help.

For now, that was how they would have to proceed.

Audie gathered up the children. They didn't care for being roused from sleep and complained about it, but not with any great enthusiasm. He bundled them into their cradleboards while Nighthawk handled the other chores of breaking camp.

"How will you know where to find us when you get back?" Audie asked Preacher.

"I'll be able to pick up your trail. Just because Ozark's men won't be able to track you, that don't mean I can't."

Audie laughed. "That's true. If a better tracker than you ever crossed the Mississippi, I don't know who it might be, Preacher. You may be in a hurry, though, especially if you have Mrs. Collins with you and Ozark and his men in pursuit."

"If that's how it turns out, don't let me lead Ozark right to you," Preacher warned. "You see any signs of trouble like that, you and Nighthawk take off for the tall and uncut and take them babes with you."

Audie nodded. "The safety of the twins comes first."

"Damn right."

Little Bear was still sitting by the fire when Dog came out of the woods and sat down to stare at him with a suspicious, unfriendly look.

"Is . . . is that a wolf?" the young Indian asked nervously.

"Well, he might be part wolf," Preacher said, "but he's mostly dog, and that's what I call him. Dog, come over here."

The big cur stood up and stalked toward Preacher and Little Bear, who looked like he wanted to run.

"Dog, this here is Little Bear," the mountain man said. "He's a friend. You understand that? Friend."

"Does he know what you're saying?" Little Bear asked.

"Oh, he knows, all right. He won't bother you now."

"He still looks like he wants to eat me."

"Naw, he's just sort of naturally intimidatin'. You'll be safe enough around him now—unless you try double-crossin' us."

"I would never do that, I swear. All I want is to help Annie and her babies."

Preacher nodded. "All right, then. Come on and show me how to find that compound where Mack Ozark and his gang are holed up."

CHAPTER 12

A udie and Nighthawk took all the pack horses with them. Preacher led Horse, and Dog padded alongside them as they walked through the night with Little Bear.

Dog still made Little Bear nervous. Some folks were scared of dogs in general, Preacher knew, and this particular dog was an unusually fierce specimen.

Perhaps to distract himself from his general uneasiness at the situation in which he found himself, Little Bear said, "Tell me what happened at that trading post you mentioned. Dutch Charley's, isn't that what you said it's called? I think I may have heard of it."

"You don't really want to hear about that, kid," Preacher said. "Like we told you, your sister and grandfather gave their lives tryin' to protect those young'uns. You can't get no better ending than that."

"Yes, you can," Little Bear said bitterly. "You can do what you set out to do and still survive."

"Yeah, but sometimes that just ain't in the hand life deals you." To get the youngster's mind off his loss, Preacher said, "Tell me about Annie Collins."

"She's beautiful," Little Bear said without hesitation. "She has curly hair as yellow as wildflowers in spring, and the bluest eyes you ever saw, and she's smart—smart enough to teach me how to speak and read English, and to read all those books she has in her cabin."

It sounded to Preacher as if the young man was sweet on Annie Collins himself, which wasn't surprising. Any young fella Little Bear's age who spent enough time around a good-looking older woman was going to have feelings for her, especially if she was kind to him. He remembered a gal named Jenny . . .

He pushed those thoughts aside. That chapter of his life had ended badly, and there was no point in dwelling on it.

"How did she wind up married to an outlaw?"

"Jonathan wasn't always an outlaw. He was a schoolmaster back in Illinois. That was where he and Annie met and got married. Then something happened . . . I don't really know what it was, they never talked about it . . . and he had to leave. She went with him. They headed west."

Little Bear sighed and continued, "I suppose Jonathan fell in with bad company. That's usually the way it happens, isn't it? He told me once that he tried to convince Annie to leave him. He told her he was no good and she deserved better. But she wouldn't listen to him. And so they stayed together."

"And wound up out here on the frontier," Preacher mused. "Fate has a way of leadin' people on trails they never thought they'd be takin'. And speakin' of trails, we ought to be gettin' close to that outlaw compound by now."

"It's not much farther," Little Bear agreed. "You might want to tie your horse here, and leave the dog, too."

"Dog comes with us," Preacher said, "but we can leave Horse here."

"You named them Dog and Horse?"

"You have any better suggestions?"

"Well, no, I suppose I don't. Those are very practical names."

This was far from the first time someone had questioned Preacher's names for his trail partners. It never bothered him to explain, and no one had ever come up with anything better to call them.

Preacher tied Horse's reins around the trunk of a small tree. He, Dog, and Little Bear moved on through the woods. A few minutes later, Preacher caught a whiff of woodsmoke from a chimney or cooking fire. He could have followed the smell to the outlaws' compound, but he didn't say anything and allowed Little Bear to complete the job of leading him there.

They reached the edge of the trees and stopped while still in thick shadows to look out across several yards of open ground to the small stream Little Bear had mentioned earlier. It was about ten feet wide and probably not very deep. Preacher could hear the bubbling whisper of water flowing swiftly over a rocky bed.

On the far side of the creek, the ground rose twenty feet in a fairly steep slope to a wide, level bench that backed up to more wooded hills. From where they were, Preacher could see the stockade fence around the compound's buildings but not the buildings themselves.

"That's it?" he asked Little Bear.

"Yes. You can see the gates."

Preacher did, as well as the watchtower that rose on one side of the gates.

"Where's Mrs. Collins's cabin?"

Little Bear pointed along the creek to the west. "Half a mile that way. It's around a little bend, so you can't see it from here, but you can't miss it when you go along the creek. It's an old trapper's cabin that was there before the compound was built. Annie had to fix it up when she moved in."

"If she's livin' there by herself, why don't she just leave?"

"Ozark keeps a guard watching the place. She might be able to slip away if she tried, but I'm not sure she cares enough anymore to do that. Once Jonathan was dead and she'd sent the children away . . . well, I don't think she believes she has anything left to live for."

"How old are you?" Preacher asked.

The question seemed to surprise Little Bear. "I've known fifteen winters," he said. "Why do you ask?"

"You seem to think about things more than most younkers your age do."

A soft laugh came from the rotund youth. "You mean I don't spend all my time thinking about hunting and fighting and becoming a warrior so I can impress the young women? I've never been good at those other things, Preacher. I try, but I'm never going to be a fierce warrior. I'm just not cut out for it."

"You never know. Most folks would look at Audie and figure he should've stayed back east. They'd say he didn't have no business bein' out here on the frontier and should still be teachin' at that college."

"Is that what he used to do?"

"Yep. He was a professor for a long time. But somethin' inside kept tuggin' on him, tellin' him he ought to go west and see what there is to see out here. Finally, he did, and he fit right in better'n anybody ever would've dreamed. Better than even he expected to, I imagine. Then he met Nighthawk and the two o' them became good friends, and they've made one hell of a team ever since. They're the best pards I've got out here, that's for sure, except for Dog and Horse."

"But how can Audie be a frontiersman? There have to be a lot of things he can't do."

"He's smart enough to figure out ways around 'most any problem. And his heart, well, his heart's as big as anybody else's. As big as Nighthawk's, I'd say." Preacher poked a finger against Little Bear's chest. "What's in there is mighty important, too, you know. Livin' ain't all about how strong you are or how fast you can run or how good you are at shootin' a bow and arrow."

"But sometimes those things will save your life," Little Bear insisted.

"That's true. And sometimes it takes fast thinkin' to save your life. Do what you can do, son, and try to get better at the things you ain't so good at, and in the end, if you're lucky, it'll balance out."

"That's good advice, Preacher. I'll remember it."

"You do that. Right now, though, take me to the cabin where Mrs. Collins lives."

They stayed in the trees as they moved to the west. According to Little Bear, Mack Ozark kept a guard posted in the watchtower all the time. Preacher didn't want to risk them being spotted out in the open.

They followed the creek around the bend. The bank on the other side wasn't as tall, so Preacher was able to see the cabin sitting about fifty yards back from the stream. No lights were burning inside it. More than likely, Annie Collins had turned in for the night hours earlier.

A short distance to the right of the cabin was a crude shed of some sort. It was dark, too.

"Where does that guard usually stay?" Preacher asked in a whisper.

Little Bear said, "I've seen one sitting on a stool by the door, but no one's there tonight. There's that shed over there where Annie keeps a milk cow. The guard could be in there."

"Any chance he's sleepin'?"

Little Bear hesitated for a moment before answering. "It's possible, but I don't think it's very likely. The men are all too afraid of what Ozark might do if they failed on a job he gave them."

"All right. You stay here. I'm gonna have a look around and see if I can figure out where the varmint is. If I can, I'll get him out of the way so we can talk to Mrs. Collins without bein' disturbed."

Preacher heard Little Bear swallow hard. Then the young Indian asked, "Do you mean you're going to kill him?"

"Are there any of this bunch with clean enough hands that they don't have it comin'?"

Little Bear thought about that again and said, "No, to be honest, I don't think there are."

"Whatever happens, then, don't go losin' any sleep over it," Preacher advised him.

Little Bear sighed and nodded.

"Dog, stay here with Little Bear," the mountain man went on. "He won't let nothin' happen to you."

"Are you talking to me or him?" Little Bear asked.

"Well, I was sayin' Dog won't let nothin' happen to you. If any trouble breaks out, you won't have to tell him anything. He'll know what to do. You just lie low and wait for the ruckus to be over. And if it goes really bad and I don't come back, you rattle your hocks back to the spot where we left Audie and Nighthawk. You can find it, can't you?"

"I'm pretty sure I can."

Preacher nodded. "Then you head for there, and one of those fellas will find you. You can bet a hat on that. You throw in with them and do everything they tell you to do. You'll be all right."

"That's not going to happen, though, is it? I mean, I've heard of you, Preacher. Everyone knows you can take care of yourself."

"That's what I figure on doin'. But there ain't no guarantees in this life, old son." Preacher squeezed the young man's shoulder for a second. "Thanks for the help you've given us so far. We're obliged to you."

With that, he slipped away into the shadows. To Little Bear, it must have seemed like he was there one second and gone the next, vanished into thin air.

The Ghost Killer was prowling the night once more.

Preacher crossed the creek about two hundred yards upstream where trees grew down close to the water on both sides and cast dappled shadows on the surface. That would make him more difficult to see just in case anybody happened to be looking in his direction.

His guess about the creek's depth proved to be correct. It

wasn't more than a foot deep, and he waded across it easily, the sound of his footsteps lost in the chuckling of the stream's flow.

Once he was on the same side as the cabin, he circled around so he could approach the log structure from the rear. It was as dark and quiet back here as it was in the front.

He saw the shed Little Bear had mentioned. It was made from rough-hewn planks, and a plank fence enclosed a small pen in front of it. The shed had a roof and three sides but was open on the side that faced the cabin. Preacher made out a dark bulk in the shadows under the roof and figured that was the milk cow Little Bear had mentioned.

As Preacher stood there silent and motionless, watching the shed, he spotted a tiny orange glow. Someone whose eyes weren't as keen might have missed it entirely, but he recognized it as the luminance from the bowl of a pipe as the man smoking it inhaled on it.

The guard was in there, all right, sharing the shed with the cow.

That meant Preacher was going to have trouble getting to him. The fence around the pen had a gate in it, but Preacher couldn't very well just walk up and open it. He needed to lure the guard out into the open somehow.

While he was pondering that, fate took a hand. The man stepped out from under the shed roof, stretched, and went to the gate. It was possible he took a turn around the cabin every hour or so to make sure everything was all right. He might be about to do that now.

Preacher smiled in the darkness. With the overwhelming odds he and his friends were facing, he would take any bit of good luck he could get.

The guard unlatched the gate and stepped through to swing it closed behind him. The aromatic smoke from his pipe drifted to Preacher. As the man went around the front of the cabin, Preacher dashed noiselessly to the other end of the building. He drew his knife and waited.

More than likely, the guard never fully understood what happened in the brief time he had left. As he stepped around the corner, Preacher's left hand slapped the pipe out of his mouth and then clamped around his jaws to prevent him from crying out. At the same time, the mountain man's right hand drove the knife into the man's chest. The blade scraped on a rib but penetrated all the way to the heart. Preacher felt the spasm go through the man as he died.

He left the knife in place and lowered the corpse to the ground before removing the blade. He wiped it on the man's shirt and then sheathed it.

Stepping to the door of the cabin, he lifted the latch and pulled the door open a few inches. He had his right hand on the butt of the Colt on that hip, although since Annie Collins was supposed to be alone there, he didn't expect to need it.

He heard the distinctive, metallic double clicks of a shotgun being cocked. That ominous warning from the darkness made him pause right where he was.

"If you step in here, I'll put both loads of buckshot right through you, and you know it," a woman's voice said. "What are you thinking? You know better than to try to come in here."

"I reckon I know now, ma'am," Preacher said, "but I didn't before."

Silence greeted his words. That moment stretched out, and then the woman said, "You're not Hoskins. Who are you?"

"Hoskins was the fella who was standin' guard?"

"That's right. You know him."

"Matter of fact, I don't. Didn't, I should say. The fella's crossed the divide."

A faint gasp came from the woman. Preacher couldn't see her, couldn't make out a thing in the stygian darkness inside the cabin.

"He's dead?"

"Yes, ma'am. I'm sorry if you find that disturbin'."

"I don't," the woman responded. "Floyd Hoskins was a despicable man. I've heard him talk about some of the things he's done. It was sickening."

"That makes me feel a mite better about killin' him, although to tell you the truth, I wasn't all that worried about it to start with."

"Who are you?" she asked again.

"A friend. Folks call me Preacher. And you'd be Mrs. Annie Collins, I reckon."

"I am. How in the world do you know that?"

"Another friend o' yours told me. Young Flathead fella name of Little Bear."

"Oh!" This time she really did sound worried. "Is he all right?"

"He was fine as frog hair the last time I saw him. That was a few minutes ago when I left him on the other side of the creek. He's the one who brought me here."

"What do you want with me?"

"Just to talk to you, ma'am."

"Talk to me? What about? I don't know you."

"No, ma'am," Preacher agreed. "You never heard of me until just now, more than likely. But for the past week or so, I've been helpin' to take care of a couple of little rascals my pards and me have been callin' Apollo and Artemis." He paused. "You know them as Edward and Elizabeth."

CHAPTER 13

This time the gasp of shock from Annie Collins was louder.

"Oh, my heavens!" she said. "My children! Are . . . are they all right?"

"Yes, ma'am," Preacher assured her. "Two of my friends are lookin' after 'em, and you couldn't have a better pair of guardians than Audie and Nighthawk doin' that."

He heard Annie lower the hammers on the shotgun she claimed to be holding. Preacher didn't doubt that she actually was—and that she would have used the weapon if the guard called Hoskins had intruded in here where he wasn't welcome.

"Come in," she told Preacher. "I—I don't understand any of this, but if you know something about my children, I want to hear it. They're not supposed to be anywhere near here!"

"No, ma'am, I understand that now. We'll get it all straightened out."

Preacher pulled the door open wider and slipped into the cabin. He closed the door behind him. A moment later, he heard the distinctive sound of a lucifer match being scraped to life. Flame burst from the match's tip with a glare and a whiff of sulfur. The light from it illuminated Annie's face and cast shadows over it at the same time.

She held the flame to the wick of a candle sitting on a rough-hewn table. The candle caught and the flickering glow from it spread in a circle through most of the one-room cabin.

The furnishings were sparse and primitive: the table, a couple of chairs, a bunk with a corn shuck mattress and a thin blanket against one wall.

The only thing that really stood out in the place was a stack of books several feet high in one corner. Little Bear had said that Annie liked to read. The numerous, well-worn leather-bound volumes were proof of that.

Preacher wondered fleetingly how many of them had been looted from wagon trains raided by Jonathan Collins's gang of killers and thieves.

Annie straightened from the candle. She was as pretty as Little Bear had described her. Preacher figured she was in her late twenties, probably not thirty yet, although strain had put a few lines around her mouth and eyes. Despite that, Preacher thought she was quite attractive.

"All right, tell me what this is about," she said. "Why do you have my children? They're supposed to be with a friend of mine. She promised to keep them safe."

Preacher nodded. "You're talkin' about Bluebird."

"You've met her?"

"Her and her grandfather both, but not for long, I'm sorry to say. My friends and I ran into 'em at a place called Dutch Charley's, a tradin' post southeast of here."

Speaking simply and directly, he explained to Annie Collins what had happened. The woman put her hand to her mouth in grief and horror when Preacher described how Bluebird and Sahale had been killed battling Mack Ozark's men. She sank into one of the chairs as her strength had deserted her.

"Before she passed on, Bluebird asked me and my friends to promise to take care o' what she had in the pack," Preacher went on. "We wanted to make it as easy for her as we could, so we swore we would. We didn't have no idea what we'd find once we unwrapped them blankets, though."

"Babies," Annie said in a hollow voice. "My babies."

"Yes'm. And I want to tell you, they're as fine a pair of youngsters as I ever laid eyes on. They don't give no trouble—well, not much, anyway. I reckon all young'uns need some takin' care of. But these two are mighty good little varmints."

"You're sure they're safe?"

"Sure as I can be. Audie and Nighthawk—them friends I mentioned—they're plumb attached to those kids. They'd do anything to protect 'em."

"Including die—like Bluebird and her grandfather did?"

"Yes, ma'am, I reckon they would," Preacher said. "So would I. You see, our word means a powerful lot to us, and we gave it to Bluebird before she died. Ain't no way we're ever backin' down from that."

"I appreciate that, Mr. Preacher. I really do."

"Just 'Preacher,'" he told her. "You can forget that 'mister' business."

Curiosity got the better of her other emotions for a moment. She asked, "Are you actually a minister? I have to say, you don't look like any I've ever met."

He shook his head. "No, ma'am. I'm a fur trapper by trade, I suppose you'd say, but mostly I just seem to amble around and get in trouble. If you want to hear about how come I'm called Preacher, just ask Audie sometime. He pure-dee loves to spin that yarn. I've had about enough of it, my own self."

Annie didn't say anything else for a moment, then she murmured, "Poor Bluebird. I knew I was asking her to run a terrible risk when she agreed to take the children and leave, but I hoped she and her grandfather would be able to get away safely. They were going to another Salish village where they had relatives. They would have been among friends there. The villagers would have hidden them. That monster Ozark never would have found them."

She drew in a ragged breath. "That was my hope, anyway," she continued. "I thought surely that whatever he's after, eventually he would give up looking for them."

"Hold on a minute," Preacher said. If he and Annie were going to get out of here, they probably ought to be moving, but he wanted to find out as much as he could about the danger they would be facing. "You don't know why Ozark wants those young'uns back?"

Annie shook her head. "No, he just showed up one day and said he wanted Edward and Elizabeth to come live in his house with him. I refused, of course."

"Couldn't he have just taken them?"

"He could have, of course. But no matter how horrible he may be, Mack Ozark is no fool. He knew it wouldn't sit well with some of the men in the gang if he ripped a woman's babies away from her. Some of the men are married, and their wives certainly wouldn't stand for that. Ozark rules with an iron fist, but at the same time, he wants to keep peace within the group."

That made sense, Preacher supposed. Not having met Mack Ozark, he couldn't pretend to know how the man thought. But as long as Annie was a virtual prisoner here, Ozark had the upper hand. He could afford to take his time about getting what he wanted.

Sooner or later, though, his patience was bound to wear out. Knowing that was probably what drove Annie to take the risk of sending the children away with Bluebird and Sahale.

Annie sighed and said, "It would have been better if you had taken the children and gone on east. I—I probably never would have seen them again, but I was willing to accept that as long as they were safe."

"You keep sayin' things like that," Preacher said with a frown, "like you figure Ozark's gonna do somethin' terrible to those kids.

He ordered his search parties to make sure they were safe. It ain't like he's gonna roast 'em and eat 'em or somethin'. He's an outlaw, not some witch from one o' them old German fairy tales."

Audie had told him about fairy tales and the gruesome things that went on in them. Preacher had never read such stuff and didn't intend to.

What he had just said caused another thought to pop into his mind. "Ozark is an outlaw," he repeated. "Somehow, those babies are worth money to him."

Annie just stared at him for a second and said, "I don't see how. They're just . . . babies."

"I don't know," Preacher admitted, "but from everything I've heard about Ozark, he's more interested in loot than anything else. Maybe we can figure it out."

Annie pressed her hands against the table and came to her feet with a determined expression on her face.

"No," she said with an emphatic shake of her head. "I don't care. It doesn't matter why he wants them. He can't have them. You go back to your friends, Preacher, and then the three of you take my children and get as far away from here as fast as you can."

Her voice softened a little as she added, "If you want to do something else for me, take Little Bear with you. He's a kind, sweet boy, and very intelligent. He deserves better than to grow up in a village where everyone is under the thumb of a man like Mack Ozark."

"I haven't known the young fella for very long, but he does seem like a good one," Preacher agreed. "I don't know whether he wants to leave these parts, though." The mountain man paused. "But I'll bet he would, if you came with us."

Annie looked shocked, as if the idea had never even occurred to her. She confirmed that by saying, "Ozark would never let me leave."

"I wasn't plannin' on askin' his permission."

"Escape . . ." Annie sat back in the chair and seemingly

struggled to grasp the concept. "I knew I could never leave as long as Jonathan was alive . . . You know about Jonathan and what happened to him?"

Preacher nodded and said, "Little Bear told me. I'm mighty sorry for your loss, ma'am."

"I started losing Jonathan long ago," she said. "But that didn't mean I could bring myself to desert him. And then, once he was . . . gone . . . I knew I couldn't take the children and run. I wasn't capable of surviving on my own with them. Ozark would just come after us and bring us back. It seemed to me they would have a better chance with Bluebird and her grandfather. They at least knew how to live in this wilderness."

"I reckon you could have gone with them," Preacher suggested.

Annie shook her head. "I would have just slowed them down. Speed was the most important thing. By staying here, I managed to keep it a secret for several days that Bluebird and Sahale had fled with the children. That gave them a chance to forge a lead. But sadly, not enough of one."

"You won't slow me and my friends down, I can promise you that. And if Ozark comes after us, well, I'll just send Audie and Nighthawk on ahead with you and the young'uns and Little Bear while I stay behind to slow down Ozark and his bunch."

"You'd be throwing your life away if you did that."

He grinned. "Maybe not. I've taken on plenty of bad hombres in the past, includin' whole bands of Blackfoot warriors. I'm used to bein' outnumbered. And I'm still here, alive and kickin'."

"Yes, I suppose you are." Annie stared down at the table in the candlelight for a moment and then lifted her head. "Do you really believe we could get away?"

"I reckon we've got a good chance. And a good chance is all I've ever asked outta life."

She took a deep breath. "We'll do it. Now that I know my babies are so close by, I have to be with them again. Take me to them, Preacher, and then let's get away from here as fast as we can."

"Sounds like a mighty fine idea to me. You want to pack a few things to take with you?"

She shook her head again. "There's nothing here that means enough to me to wait. I can't carry my books—they're too heavy and they would slow us down—and nothing else here is important to me." She took a shawl from a peg on the wall and wrapped it around her shoulders, then picked up the shotgun from the table. "I'm ready to go."

"Let's light a shuck, then."

Preacher leaned over and blew out the candle. Annie was already heading for the door. She opened it and stepped outside—then stopped short.

"Preacher," she said, her voice taut with strain again.

Preacher moved up behind her and looked past her, and in the silvery light from the stars that washed over the landscape, he saw what had stopped her cold.

More than a dozen men stood there between them and the creek, most of them holding rifles. One of the group, a big, broad-shouldered man whose face Preacher couldn't make out in the darkness, stepped forward. In harsh, gravelly tones, he said, "Going somewhere, Annie darlin'?"

Preacher knew without being told that he was about to meet the infamous Mack Ozark.

CHAPTER 14

Annie started to raise the shotgun, but Preacher quickly stepped up beside her and caught hold of the twin barrels before the weapon could come level.

Mack Ozark seemed to be a complicated hombre and clearly didn't want Annie dead, or he would have made sure of that before now.

But if she menaced him and his men with a shotgun, he would probably give the order to shoot both her and Preacher full of holes. It was hard not to respond when somebody threatened you with a weapon like that.

"Don't go to shootin' just yet," Preacher told her as he pressed the barrels down toward the ground. "Let's see what he wants first."

"Listen to the man, Annie," Ozark said. "There's no need for you to get hurt."

He turned his head to look at Preacher. "You, on the other hand, mister . . . Where's my man Hoskins?"

Preacher gestured with a thumb toward the shadows at the side of the cabin.

"No point in lyin' about it. You'll find him anyway once you take a look," the mountain man said. "He's over there around the corner."

"Dead?"

Preacher shrugged. "Seemed like the thing to do at the time.

I didn't figure he'd let me talk to the lady, no matter how polite I was when I asked him."

Several of the men shifted their feet and muttered angrily. Floyd Hoskins, despicable though he was, according to Annie, must have had friends among the gang. They would want to settle the score with Preacher for the man's death.

Ozark shook his head and said, "That's too bad. I might have been able to let you live if you'd cooperated, but I can't very well do that after you've killed one of my men. How would that look?"

Preacher nodded toward Annie. "The lady's done nothin' wrong. You don't have no reason to hurt her."

"You don't know what reason I have to do anything," Ozark snapped, dropping his amiable tone—which Preacher hadn't believed for a second.

Preacher ignored that and said to Annie, "Ma'am, you go on back inside now. I'll deal with these fellas."

"I won't do it," she said stubbornly. "I'm tired of living under that awful man's thumb. I'm going to stay right here beside you no matter what he does."

She raised the shotgun a few inches to emphasize her determination.

Preacher grimaced in the darkness. Annie didn't understand. If she would just retreat into the cabin, he could slap leather and open fire on Ozark and his men with his Colts.

He was confident he was fast enough on the draw to ventilate Ozark before any of the outlaws could stop him, even though they already had their rifles pointed in his direction.

They would blast him to hell a split-second later, of course, but if he could kill the leader of the gang, sacrificing his life might be worth it. Preacher knew that with Ozark dead, Audie and Nighthawk would stand a better chance against the rest of the outlaws.

And his friends *would* avenge his death. Preacher had no doubt about that.

They would do what they could to help Annie Collins and

protect her babies, as well. But Preacher couldn't put any of that possibility in motion as long as Annie was standing right here beside him. If he opened fire on the gang, they would shoot back and kill her, too.

Problem was, he couldn't very well explain all that to Annie with Ozark standing right there, backed up by a dozen ruthless killers.

"Tell me one thing, Ozark," Preacher said, stalling for time. "How'd you know there was anything wrong here? I was careful not to make any racket."

"You mean while you were killing Hoskins?" Ozark laughed, a harsh, unpleasant sound. "One of his friends walked down from the compound to visit with him. He knew that Floyd always posted himself in the shed except when he was taking a walk around the place, so when he didn't find him there and he didn't show up after a while, my man knew something was wrong. He didn't look around, he just hurried back to the compound to let me know Hoskins was missing."

Ozark spread his hands and went on, "And so here we are, ready to put things right." His voice hardened. "Annie, go back in the cabin."

"No," she said. "I won't do it. Don't you understand, I'd rather be dead than have things go on the way they are. Especially if you're dead first. You—"

Preacher heard the hysterical note in her voice, saw the shotgun's twin barrels start to rise even more. She was going to force all hell to break loose.

He couldn't afford that. His hand shot out, closed again around the shotgun's barrels, and wrenched them upward this time as she jerked the triggers.

Both barrels boomed. The double report was deafeningly loud as it pounded against Preacher's ears like giant fists.

The buckshot flew harmlessly into the air, though, and Ozark must have realized that because he shouted, "Hold your fire, hold your fire! Get that man! Don't hurt Annie!"

Several men tossed aside their rifles and swarmed forward. Preacher could have drawn his guns and cut them down with the Colts, but if he started shooting, Ozark's men would disregard their leader's order and return the fire. Annie would be hit.

He still had hold of the shotgun, so he wrenched it out of her hands and gave her a shove that made her cry out as she stumbled toward the cabin's open door.

He whirled back toward the men attacking him. The shotgun was empty, but it made an effective club when he swung it at the closest outlaw.

The shotgun's stock crashed against the man's jaw and knocked him off his feet. He fell in front of two of the other men and they tripped over him to sprawl forward.

Preacher darted to his left and rammed the shotgun's butt into the belly of another man. The blow doubled the outlaw over and put him in position for Preacher's knee to come up and slam into his face.

The mountain man ran out of time to carry the fight to his enemies. The lone attacker who was still on his feet launched himself in a diving tackle that caught Preacher around the waist and dragged him to the ground.

Preacher struck a backhanded blow with the shotgun that knocked his assailant away from him, but the two who had tripped over their comrade had scrambled back to their feet and now closed in from both sides.

Preacher couldn't avoid the kicks they aimed at him. Boot toes hammered his ribs and rocked him back and forth. They kicked the empty shotgun out of his hands.

He ignored the pain—years of desperate fights had taught him how to do that—and rolled onto his side to grab the leg of one man. A sharp heave upended that hombre and sent him crashing to the ground on his back.

A kick from the other man landed in the small of Preacher's back. The agony from that one was hard to set aside. He would be passing blood for days, he thought—assuming he lived longer than just tonight.

The Good Lord had left out any surrender when He made Preacher, though. The mountain man shoved himself onto hands and knees and surged upright. The man who had just kicked him in the back lunged at him, swinging a mallet-like fist.

Preacher twisted aside. The blow landed on his left shoulder and sent needles of hurt down his arm, but his right arm was fine, and he used it to smash a fist into the middle of his attacker's face. The feel of cartilage crunching as the man's nose flattened was satisfying to Preacher's soul.

The next instant, strong arms closed around him from behind, pinning his arms to his sides.

"I got him!" a man yelled in his ear. The varmint's breath was laden with fumes of whiskey, onions, and rotted teeth and almost made Preacher gag. "Whale the tar outta him, boys!"

Two more attackers loomed in front of Preacher, obviously intent on doing just that. As the first one got too close, Preacher jerked a leg up and kicked him in the belly. The man flew backward.

The second one was smart enough to come in at an angle. He clubbed a punch that landed on Preacher's jaw and slewed his head to the side.

A third man crowded in from a different direction and hooked a fist to Preacher's belly. These outlaws, without exception, were big, powerful men, and Preacher had already taken quite a beating from them. He tried to hold in a groan, but it slipped out despite his best efforts.

Another punch landed on his right cheek. He didn't know where that one came from, only that it jerked his head back the other way. Then somebody hit him again.

And again.

Consciousness was rapidly slipping away from him now. He knew that; he could sense the black tides washing in all around him. He tried to fight off the darkness and summoned all his strength in a last-ditch attempt to break free from the bear hug of the man behind him.

He couldn't do it, and as fists slammed into his face and body again and again, landing like sledgehammers, the last of his awareness faded away.

Oblivion claimed him.

Preacher had been knocked out often enough in his life that regaining consciousness was a familiar sensation to him.

He knew exactly what was going on as the black nothingness surrounding him began to recede and dim light seeped in to take its place.

Gradually, the light grew stronger. It had a reddish quality, and it was inconsistent, brighter, and then dim again before once again blossoming.

Eventually, he felt heat against his face, too, and realized that he was facing a fire.

He became aware of other things, as well. His arms were above his head, pulled high and held in place somehow. He was standing up with his feet on the ground, but enough of his weight hung on his arms that his shoulders ached in their sockets.

Something tight was looped around his wrists. A rope? Had to be.

As that thought formed in his mind, he realized that he was strung up somewhere. The heat felt the same on his face as it did on his chest.

That was because his chest was bare. He'd been stripped to the waist.

His eyes were still closed. He hadn't opened them or made a sound because he didn't want anyone who might be around to know that he was conscious again.

Sometimes it came in handy if folks believed you were still out cold. They might say or do things they wouldn't if they knew you were aware of what was going on. He hung there for several minutes, limp and unmoving. Somewhere not far away, footsteps came closer and then receded. Preacher could tell by the way they sounded, hard boot heels clicking on boards, that whoever made them was walking around on a wooden floor, not dirt.

They were inside a building. Probably in Mack Ozark's compound.

Preacher's eyes were closed. He opened them to mere slits, just enough to be able to tell that he was facing a fireplace with a thick, heavy mantel above it. A good-sized blaze burned on the hearth. The flames were responsible for the light and heat he experienced.

Heavy footsteps approached him again. A man stopped in front of him and muttered, "I'm tired of this."

A heartbeat later, an open-handed blow exploded against Preacher's face, knocking his head to the side. He tried to brace himself for the backhand he knew would follow, but it came too quickly. This time the man's knuckles struck Preacher's face with a stinging impact.

Preacher opened his eyes. He didn't see any point in standing there letting somebody wallop him.

He wasn't surprised to see Mack Ozark standing in front of him. That put Ozark's back to the massive stone fireplace and threw his face into shadow, but the firelight reflected back enough to give Preacher his best look so far at the outlaw leader.

Ozark matched the description Dutch Charley had given Preacher. The hawklike nose, the dark, deep-set eyes, the drooping mustache were all there. He was an ugly man—nobody would ever argue that he wasn't—but at the same time, his features had a compelling power to them.

Ozark grinned as he said, "I was hoping you'd keep on pretending to be unconscious for a while longer. That way I could have hit you a few more times trying to wake you up."

"I don't reckon there's anything stoppin' you from wallopin' me again," Preacher said. His voice sounded rusty and strange in his ears. "You probably enjoy beatin' up on helpless fellas."

"You make me sound like a cruel man. Some sort of inhuman monster."

"That's what everybody says about you. I figure there must be somethin' to it. You know what they say about there always bein' fire anywhere there's smoke."

Ozark shook his head and backed off a step.

"I don't enjoy being cruel," he insisted. "I just don't let anything stand in the way of me getting what I go after. Anybody who does that is weak. Ever since I realized the world is out there for the taking if you're strong enough, I've never again allowed myself to be weak."

Ozark sounded as if he had some education, Preacher thought. Not at the same level as Audie, by any means, but more polished than Preacher would have expected a notorious outlaw's education to be.

Of course, the sort of life the man had led before he turned bad didn't matter. Only the evil he had done since then was important.

Ozark moved to Preacher's right, going out of sight. He came back a moment later carrying a tin cup.

"Have a drink," he offered as he held the cup to Preacher's lips.

The mountain man smelled whiskey. It wouldn't serve any purpose for Ozark to poison him. He opened his mouth and swallowed some of the cup's contents.

It was plain whiskey, all right. The fiery stuff stung his lips, which were battered and cut from the fight earlier.

But it burned his gullet going down and kindled a fire in his belly. Preacher drew strength from that, so he didn't mind the pain. He welcomed it, in fact, because it helped clear his head.

"Better?" Ozark asked as he took the cup away from Preacher's mouth.

"Why do you care? You don't give a damn whether I live or die."

"That's not true. You'll die soon enough, no doubt about that, but it's important to me that before you do, you tell me what I want to know."

"What's that?"

"Where those two infants are."

Preacher laughed hollowly. "You really think I'd tell you that, after everything that's happened?"

"Why not? Those youngsters don't mean anything to you. They're not your children."

"They're not yours, either. You got no right to 'em."

"Never mind about that," Ozark said. "I'll make you a deal. Tell me where to find them and I'll make sure you die quick and as painlessly as possible, my friend. Otherwise, if you make me force the information out of you, I'll turn you over to my friends when I'm finished with you—and your death will be anything but quick and painless."

Ozark laughed again, an ugly sound devoid of any genuine humor, and added, "Hell, if you help me get my hands on those kids, I might even let you live."

Preacher didn't believe that for a second, not that he would have been tempted by the offer anyway.

Instead, he said, "Whatever you're gonna do, you might as well get on with it, because I ain't tellin' you anything, old son—except to go to hell."

Smiling, Ozark threw the whiskey that was left in the cup into Preacher's face, blinding him for a second. The boss outlaw dropped the empty cup, stepped in, and slammed a punch to Preacher's midsection.

There wasn't an ounce of fat on the mountain man's body to start with. Strung up and stretched out like that, he had no protection from the force of the blow. It rocked his guts and made a ball of sickness form in his stomach. His lips drew back from his teeth as he grimaced.

Ozark set his feet and struck again, hitting Preacher twice more, hooking in left and right fists. The blows jerked Preacher's body back and forth.

"I can do this all night, *old son*," he said mockingly, "and all day tomorrow, too, if that's how you want it."

Preacher gathered up as much spit as he could. It wasn't much, but it was enough to splatter on Ozark's face when the mountain man launched it from his lips.

Ozark snarled, wiped away the moisture, and hit Preacher again, in the face this time. He threw punch after punch, and after a while, Preacher knew he was still getting hit, but he didn't really feel it anymore.

Eventually, Ozark stopped and backed off. Preacher dangled there with his head hanging forward. Blood seeped from his mouth and dripped on the floor in front of his feet. He watched the crimson drops falling in what seemed to be slow motion, down and down and down until they exploded against the boards.

Ozark was breathing hard from his brutal efforts. The rasp of air in his throat slowed as agonizing moments crept by.

Finally, he said, "You're stubborn. I can almost admire that. But not quite. You're in my way, and I won't stand for that. Your life is over if I don't get what I want. And so is hers."

The implication of those words made Preacher drag his head up. He saw Ozark motion curtly to somebody else, and a moment later, one of the outlaws came into view with his arm clamped around Annie Collins's arm. Her face was pale and frightened as he dragged her forward.

Annie stumbled as Ozark took hold of her other arm and pulled her in front of him. With her back to him so that she faced Preacher, he yanked her against his broad chest and used his other hand to pull a knife from a sheath at his waist.

He pressed the blade's keen edge against Annie's throat and said to Preacher, "She refuses to tell me what I need to know, and I'm tired of fighting with her, just like I'm tired of dealing with you. Tell me how to find those children or I'll cut her throat. You have until the count of ten . . ."

CHAPTER 15

W hat Preacher did next surprised Ozark. He could see it in the man's eyes as he said, "Don't waste your breath countin'. Go ahead and do it. I never laid eyes on the gal until tonight. She don't mean nothin' to me."

Annie seemed surprised, too, by Preacher's apparently callous response. But then a look of gratitude appeared in her eyes as she realized what he was doing. She took it a step further than Preacher, however.

"Yes, go ahead and kill me," she urged Ozark. "I don't have anything to live for anymore."

Ozark glared at both of them in frustration. He took the knife away from Annie's throat and gave her a shove that sent her stumbling away from him. She might have fallen if the other outlaw hadn't moved quickly. He caught her arm and helped her keep her balance.

"Take her and lock her up again," Ozark ordered the man. "Make sure there's a guard on her at all times and nobody can get to her. Then come back here."

"Sure, boss."

Jerking roughly on Annie's arm, the man led her away, out of Preacher's sight.

But she called back to him, "Don't tell him anything, Preacher. I'm begging you!"

A door slammed somewhere behind him before the mountain man could reply.

He looked at Ozark and saw that the man's eyes had widened slightly, as if he were surprised again, and a moment later Preacher realized why.

"Preacher," Ozark repeated. "That's your name?"

"That's what folks call me. Ain't the name I was born with, of course, but I ain't used that one in so long I sort of disremember what it is."

That wasn't the least bit true. He knew perfectly well that his given name was Arthur. He had been known as Art when he first came west after leaving his family's farm in Ohio and fell in with the mountain men Clyde Barnes and Pierre Gameau.

Clyde and Pierre had saved his life and begun his education in all the things he needed to know in order to survive on the untamed frontier. Several years had passed before he picked up the name Preacher, although now it seemed to him as if he had been known by it forever.

"You've heard of me, have you?" he asked Ozark with a faint smile.

The outlaw's lips curled into a sneer under the thick, drooping mustache.

"Yeah, I've heard of you," Ozark replied. "The stories about you claim you're the deadliest fighting man west of the Mississippi. You're supposed to be Daniel Boone, Davy Crockett, Jim Bridger, and Mike Fink all rolled into one."

Preacher chuckled dryly. "Happens I've met all those fellas except ol' Dan'l, and I wouldn't make no far-fetched claims like that."

"Maybe not, but you still have quite a reputation. When my men brought word to me that three strangers were headed in this direction and had Jonathan Collins's children with them, it never occurred to me that one of them would turn out to be Preacher."

Ozark shook his head and went on, "I should have figured it out, though. I'd heard about how you were known to be friends with a dwarf and a giant Indian, like the ones reported to me. But I just thought you were some old mountain man who failed to realize that the Shining Times are over."

"You reckon the Shinin' Times are over?"

Another harsh laugh came from Ozark. "They're dead and gone. The future belongs to men like me. Men who know what they want and take it."

"You'll be doin' me a favor by killin' me, then. I don't want to live to see a future like that."

"Oh, you'll live for a while longer," Ozark told him. "You haven't given me what I want yet, so you won't die until you have."

Preacher figured they were in Ozark's house, the dwelling that had belonged originally to Jonathan and Annie Collins. His vision had cleared a little since Ozark stopped hitting him, and he had been able to take a look around the room.

It was comfortably furnished with a table and several chairs that had been made in an actual factory somewhere, not hacked out of tree trunks and nailed together. Preacher wasn't sure how Collins had gotten the furniture all the way out here, but he supposed if you had enough money, most things were possible.

Woven rugs of Indian design were scattered on the floor. One wall was studded with pegs on which hung rifles, pistols, powder horns, and several swords in scabbards.

The swords looked old, as if maybe they came from Revolutionary times. Preacher wondered if Jonathan Collins had acquired them, or if that was Ozark's idea.

A door opened behind him. Footsteps sounded. Ozark looked

past Preacher at whoever had just come in, probably the man he had sent to place Annie back in captivity.

"Go get three or four more men," Ozark ordered. "We're going to lock Preacher in the smokehouse."

"Preacher? That's Preacher?" The man swallowed audibly. "Maybe you better just go ahead and kill him, boss, while he's in bad shape and you've got the chance. I've heard stories about Preacher. He's supposed to be a mighty bad man to have for an enemy."

"So am I!" Ozark roared as his face darkened with anger. "Are you trying to tell me how to run this gang?"

"No, sir, no, sir, not at all," the man replied hastily and fearfully. "I didn't mean nothing by it, boss, I swear. I was just surprised to find out that this fella is Preacher, that's all."

Ozark jerked his head in a curt nod and snapped, "Go do what I told you."

"You bet, boss."

"Wait a minute," Ozark said as his subordinate started to turn away. "Did you do like I said with Annie?"

"I sure did. She's locked up in the storeroom in the warehouse, and Royce and Barker are right outside the door. She can't go anywhere even if she managed to get out somehow, which she won't."

Ozark waved a hand. "Go on."

Footsteps hurried out and the door slammed.

Preacher grinned, even though stretching his cracked and bloody lips like that was painful.

"Looks like I got your boys spooked," he said.

"Don't you worry about my men," Ozark said. "They'll do as they're told."

"I ain't worried about 'em. When the time comes, they'll die just like all the other varmints who thought they had the upper hand on me."

Ozark sneered again. "You're awfully sure of yourself, aren't you?"

"Don't see no reason not to be. I'm still here, and a whole heap o' fellas who've tried to kill me ain't."

Ozark grinned back at him. "I can say the same thing, you know." He slapped his chest. "I'm still here, damn you."

The boss outlaw turned and stalked away, out of Preacher's view. Preacher heard glass clink against glass and figured Ozark was pouring himself a drink.

A moment later, Preacher heard the sound again. Despite Ozark's bold words, he might be trying to fortify himself with a few shots of liquor.

This time, Ozark didn't offer Preacher a drink, but at least he didn't throw one in his face, either.

After a few minutes, several men trooped in.

"Cut him down and take him to the smokehouse," Ozark told them.

One of the men came up behind Preacher. The mountain man felt his arms move back and forth as the outlaw sawed on the rope holding him up. By this time, his hands were numb from the tightness of the rope around his wrists and the pressure it put on them.

The rope parted. Preacher collapsed. He had known that was possible and would have preferred to stay on his feet, but his muscles simply refused to cooperate. They had been put under too much of a strain.

The men left the rope around his wrists. A couple of them grasped his arms and lifted him. Two more stood back and aimed pistols at Preacher, ready to shoot him if he tried anything.

That wasn't going to happen, Preacher thought grimly. He was capable of a lot, but not even he could take on four hardened killers given the shape he was in at the moment. He managed to make his legs work awkwardly as his captors half-dragged, half-carried him toward the open door.

Preacher twisted his head around and looked up, satisfying his curiosity as he saw that the rope holding him up had been looped around a rafter. He'd wondered about that. It wasn't important, of course, but he'd wanted to know anyway.

The outlaws took him out into the night. The coolness of the air was refreshing. Preacher saw quite a few other members of the gang standing around watching as his captors led him to a small, sturdy-looking log building with a flat roof. He had seen many smokehouses and recognized this one for what it was.

It had been built for more than smoking meat, however. The brackets on either side of the open door and the thick beam leaning against the wall indicated that it was designed to do double duty as a prison.

The men steered Preacher to the doorway. The two holding his arms stopped, and a man behind him planted a foot on Preacher's rear end and shoved hard just as the other two let go. He flew forward through the opening.

His hands were tied in front of him, so he was able to get them down and break his fall with them, rather than landing face-first on the ground. As he sprawled there, the door slammed shut behind him. He heard the bar drop into the brackets, effectively sealing him in here.

The darkness was complete. The smokehouse wasn't airtight, but it had to be close to that in order to keep the smoke in while meat was being prepared. The tiny cracks here and there weren't big enough to let in any starlight.

Preacher lay there on his belly for long minutes, the breath rasping in and out of his throat. Eventually, he summoned all the vestiges of strength he could muster from his body and pushed up onto hands and knees.

He couldn't feel his hands, but he knew they were on the ground supporting him as he inched forward.

When his head bumped the wall, he let himself sag over to his side and struggled to sit up with his back propped against the logs. Again, he had to sit there for a while to recover some of his strength before he attempted to do anything else.

But eventually, he was able to lift his arms. He lowered his head and found the loops of rope around his wrists with his mouth. He began pulling at them with his teeth, trying to loosen them, and as he worked to free himself, he started figuring out how he was going to escape.

And what he was going to do to Mack Ozark when he did.

CHAPTER 16

In such thick, suffocating darkness, it was impossible to tell how much time was passing. When the sun came up in the morning, it would grow lighter in here, but until then, one moment was pretty much like the last.

Preacher worked on the rope for a while, but eventually, exhaustion and the punishment he had taken caught up with him. His head tipped back and rested against the log wall as he dozed off.

He fell into a sound sleep.

When his eyes opened again, he realized after a moment that a faint gray glow was stealing into the makeshift prison. He bit back a groan. That was the light of dawn seeping in through the cracks. He had slept away the night instead of freeing himself.

Before long, Mack Ozark would send men to fetch him and start trying again to force him to reveal the twins' whereabouts. Preacher knew he'd die before he cracked under that pressure, but he'd just as soon not have to endure more torture in the meantime.

He went back to work on the rope binding his wrists, stubbornly tugging and gnawing on it with his teeth. Finally, the strands began to part.

Somewhere outside, a volley of shots crashed with no warning.

Preacher's head jerked up at the unexpected sound. Audie and Nighthawk had to be responsible for that gunfire. Somehow, they knew he was a prisoner and were making an attempt to rescue him.

Preacher wasn't surprised. Ever since he'd been captured, the possibility that his friends might come to help him had been in the back of his mind. He had known that Little Bear was watching when he slipped up to the old trapper's cabin to look for Annie Collins. Seeing him and Annie taken prisoner by Ozark, Little Bear's first instinct would have been to go looking for Audie and Nighthawk so he could let them know what had happened.

Preacher might have hoped that they would abandon him to his fate and concentrate on keeping the infants safe instead, but at the same time, he knew Audie and Nighthawk would never turn their backs on a friend. They would try to find some way to rescue him and still protect Edward and Elizabeth.

He hoped his friends had found someplace safe to leave the babies. More than likely, they had left the young'uns in Little Bear's care. The young Flathead wouldn't be much help in a battle like this, but he could watch those babies and protect them to the best of his ability.

Preacher went back to work on his bonds with a new ferocity as he heard shouts from elsewhere in the compound. He could tell by the dimness of the light that dawn hadn't been approaching for long. It was still gray and shadowy outside.

Like the keen strategists they were, Audie and Nighthawk had picked the best time to launch their attack. Ozark's men would be groggy with sleep.

The rope had frayed quite a bit, and Preacher was about to try breaking it when he heard the bar rattle in the brackets on the other side of the door. Someone removed it, and a moment later, a towering, broad-shouldered figure jerked the door open and stood there filling up the doorway.

"Nighthawk!" Preacher exclaimed.

The giant Crow warrior ducked his head low to come through the door. One long stride brought him to Preacher's side. He bent over the mountain man, hooked his fingers in the frayed rope, and snapped it as if it were nothing more than a slender thread. Preacher shot to his feet. The sleep he had gotten, short though it had been, had restored some of his strength. His iron constitution didn't require as much time to recover as some.

"The babies safe?" he asked Nighthawk as he flexed his fingers.

"Umm!"

"Glad to hear it."

Blood began flowing back into Preacher's nerve-deadened fingers, bringing with it stabbing jolts of pain. He ignored the discomfort. He was just glad to have some feeling in his hands again.

Nighthawk pulled a tomahawk from behind the rawhide sash tied around his waist and pressed it into Preacher's hand. The mountain man nodded. It felt good to be armed again, although he would have liked to have his Colts.

"Let's get outta here," he said. "We need to get Annie Collins. She's supposed to be locked up in the warehouse, wherever that is."

Nighthawk nodded. He ducked to step back through the doorway and leveled an arm as soon as he was outside.

One of Ozark's men sprawled on the ground beside the door. His head was twisted at an odd angle on his shoulders.

Preacher knew that Nighthawk had gotten hold of the varmint standing guard outside the smokehouse and broken his neck with one good wrench of his hands. As Preacher followed, he saw that the big Crow was pointing toward a large, log structure on the other side of the blacksmith shop. That was probably where the gang stored the goods they looted from wagon trains and trading posts and used to trade with the Indians.

As Preacher followed, he saw that the big Crow was pointing

toward a large log structure on the other side of the blacksmith shop.

Suddenly men swarmed from the cabins and ran to the stockade wall. They bounded upstairs to the parapet that ran around the inside and began firing rifles over the wall, aiming toward the woods across the creek.

Preacher wasn't sure what they were shooting at, but he assumed Audie was responsible for some sort of distraction over there. After the first volley, more shots continued from that direction, but they were spaced out now.

More than likely, Audie and Nighthawk had placed rifles and pistols in various places, and Audie had rigged a line so he could fire all of them at once, making it seem like a much larger force was attacking the compound.

Then he could dash from one weapon to the next, reload, and fire again to maintain the illusion. It probably wouldn't take Ozark's men long to figure out what was going on, but outlaws generally weren't the brightest hombres, so Preacher and Nighthawk had a little time to work with.

Or so Preacher hoped, anyway.

The two friends dashed toward the warehouse, keeping to the shadows as much as possible. However, those shadows were thinning as the eastern sky grew lighter, so the guard posted at the warehouse door spotted them and opened his mouth to yell an alarm as he jerked his rifle to his shoulder.

Preacher acted so swiftly the guard never got the chance to warn any of his compatriots. The mountain man's arm flashed back and then forward while he was on the run. Despite that, the throw was perfect, and the tomahawk struck the outlaw in the forehead, cleaving through his skull and into his brain, killing him instantly.

The dead man's knees buckled, and his finger involuntarily jerked the trigger in its final spasm. The rifle blasted, but the barrel had already dropped so the ball dug harmlessly into the ground in front of him.

So much shooting was going on in the compound that one more report seemed to go unnoticed as the guard fell forward on his face.

The warehouse had large double doors so wagons could be driven inside and unloaded. They weren't locked but had a simple bar across them holding them closed. Nighthawk lifted it loose and tossed it aside, then grabbed one of the big doors and pulled it open.

Preacher bent just long enough to yank his tomahawk from the dead guard's head and rushed inside. The shadows were still thick in the building's interior, but he made out an area to one side that had been partitioned off and had a door leading into it.

From the depth of the shadows in that direction, muzzle flame bloomed like a crimson flower. Ozark had put a guard in the room where Annie Collins was locked up. The fella had rushed his shot, though, and the ball hummed past Preacher's ear.

Preacher dashed toward him. The man gave up trying to reload his rifle and used it instead to block the tomahawk Preacher swung at his head.

By thrusting the rifle upward with both hands, the guard left his midsection open. Preacher kicked him in the belly. The man gasped and took a step back. Preacher tried to close in, but he had to duck as the guard made a sideways swipe at his head with the rifle butt.

While he was bent over, Preacher slashed the tomahawk at the man's knee. Bone crunched under the blow. The man screamed and started to fall as Preacher straightened from his crouch. The mountain man struck upward at an angle, and the tomahawk caught the guard in the throat.

Blood spurted hotly over the back of Preacher's hand as the weapon opened a gaping wound in the guard's throat. Gurgling grotesquely, the man collapsed. Preacher stepped back to avoid as much of the crimson flood as he could.

The door into the smaller chamber had an actual lock on it instead of a simple latch or bar. Mack Ozark might be the only one with a key.

Nighthawk didn't bother with a key. He stepped over the guard Preacher had killed and rammed his shoulder against the door. With a crunching and splintering of wood, the frame gave way, and the door popped open.

"Come on, Mrs. Collins," Preacher said. He held out his left hand since it wasn't covered in blood. "We're gettin' out of here."

For a heartbeat, there was no response. Then Preacher saw a pale shape that resolved into Annie Collins's face as she stepped forward into the dim light.

"You're alive," she murmured.

"Yes'm."

"Ozark didn't kill you."

"Not yet, but I expect he'll get around to tryin' again mighty soon, especially if we don't light a shuck outta here."

She hesitated, but only for a second, before taking his hand. Nighthawk headed for the door and Preacher was right behind him, grasping Annie's hand to make sure she kept up.

A man appeared in the doorway just before Nighthawk reached the opening. He started to let out a yell, but Night-hawk grabbed him under the arms and jerked him off his feet. The giant Crow stepped outside and flung the man away from him.

Yelling and waving his arms and kicking his legs, the outlaw flew through the air and crashed into several other men who were running toward the warehouse.

Preacher wasn't sure how they were going to get through the gates in the stockade wall. As Nighthawk turned and loped toward the corner of the warehouse, Preacher realized going out the gates wasn't the escape route Audie and Nighthawk had planned. He tugged Annie with him and broke into a run following the big warrior.

They rounded the corner and headed for the wall at the back of the compound. Behind them, the shooting was dying away, but confused, angry shouts rose to fill the air in its place. The members of Ozark's gang were figuring out that somebody was trying to help the prisoners escape.

The eastern sky continued to grow brighter. In the increasing light, Preacher spotted a rope hanging over the wall. Nighthawk must have gotten into the compound that way and left the rope there for their escape. Preacher wasn't sure Annie would be able to climb it, though.

He didn't have to worry about that. As they reached the wall, Nighthawk turned to Annie and scooped her up without wasting any time on explanations. She cried out in surprise as he draped her over his left shoulder and clamped that arm around her.

Then he grabbed the rope with his other hand and began walking up the wall, winding the rope around his wrist as he ascended.

When he reached the top, he slung a leg over the wall between two of the sharpened logs, balanced himself, and lowered Annie on the outside. The rope dropped back down to Preacher, who grabbed it and began pulling himself up. Nighthawk disappeared over the wall.

Boot soles slapped the ground as men ran around the warehouse. A voice Preacher recognized as belonging to Mack Ozark bellowed, "There he is! Shoot him! Kill him, you fools!"

The mountain man smiled to himself as he neared the top of the wall. It sounded as if Ozark no longer cared about keeping him alive until he'd found the babies.

Guns began to boom again. Rifle balls thudded into the logs around Preacher, some of them close enough to chew splinters that stung his bare torso as they sprayed in the air. He was close enough to the top to throw a leg over, grab a couple of the sharpened ends, and hold himself away from them as he rolled over the wall.

Suddenly empty air was under him. He dropped straight down and landed on his feet, flexing his knees to take the strain of his weight. He had to take a quick step forward to maintain his balance.

A huge hand gripped his arm to steady him. Preacher glanced over to see Nighthawk standing there. Beyond him was Annie Collins, looking disheveled and confused and frightened, but clearly unharmed.

Preacher straightened, nodded his thanks to Nighthawk, and said, "We'd better get out of here while the gettin's good."

More shouts rose inside the compound.

"They'll be on our trail before long," Preacher added.

Nighthawk nodded and loped into the trees. Preacher grasped Annie's arm again and asked, "Can you keep up?"

"Don't worry about me," she said. "Just take me to my children!"

"You'll be back with 'em before you know it," Preacher said, and hoped that was true. "But if you're havin' any trouble, let me know. Nighthawk can carry you."

"That's his name? Nighthawk?"

"Yep. He's strong as an ox, and your weight wouldn't slow him down none."

"I can make it," Annie said determinedly.

By now they were hurrying through the trees a few yards behind Nighthawk. The gloom was thick under the branches and would be even after the sun came up, but Preacher didn't have any trouble following the big Crow.

From time to time, Nighthawk paused to hold some of the undergrowth back out of the way so Preacher and Annie would have an easier path. They made good time with him breaking trail like that. Ozark's compound fell behind them. But Preacher knew there would be pursuit coming after them. After all the trouble Mack Ozark had gone to recover those infants, he wouldn't give up easily. Preacher might not know yet why they were so important to Ozark, but the man wanted them and would stop at nothing to get his hands on them.

In the end, the only way to prevent Ozark from doing that might be to kill him.

That seemed like a perfectly reasonable enough solution to Preacher, and he'd be glad to take care of it as soon as he got the chance.

CHAPTER 17

The fugitives reached the back of the ridge on which Mack Ozark's compound was located. The terrain sloped up, climbing in a series of steep but not impassible ridges to the thickly wooded mountainsides looming above them.

Preacher glanced back as they started up. It was light enough now for him to see the compound below them. Men were still moving around down there, but he was confident that pursuers were already after him and his companions. The trees and brush hid that pursuit.

He could see beyond the compound to the creek that flowed past it, and on the other side of the stream were the woods where Audie had staged his distraction. They were putting distance between themselves and the little man with each step they took, and that bothered Preacher. He had plenty of confidence in Audie's ability to take care of himself, but he didn't like the idea of Ozark getting his murderous hands on the former professor.

Maybe it wouldn't come to that. Audie was mighty clever when it came to dodging folks who were hunting for him.

Annie had begun to breathe harder. Pulling herself up the slope using bushes and small trees for handholds was difficult work for her. Preacher grasped her arm to steady her and assist her in climbing.

He was starting to feel the effort himself. Normally he would scramble up a slope like this without any trouble, but he had endured quite a bit of punishment in the past twelve hours. Not only that, but the brush clawed at his bare torso as he pushed through it, leaving long, blood-seeping scratches in his flesh.

Annie's dress was getting ripped, as well, and Preacher was sure she was bleeding from scratches, too. But she didn't complain and kept going as best she could.

"Thank you," she said after he helped her over a particularly rugged stretch. "Do you know where we're going?"

"No, but I reckon Audie and Nighthawk had a good plan," he assured her. "We'll find out soon enough."

"Who is Audie?"

"Another friend o' mine. Smartest fella I know, too. He used to be a professor." Preacher grinned. "With you likin' books the way you do, I reckon you and him will get along just fine. He can recite whole plays by that Shakespeare fella, and some o' them ancient Greeks and Romans, too."

"He sounds like an interesting man."

"Oh, you don't know how interestin'."

Preacher chuckled, looking forward to Annie meeting up with Audie. She was in for a surprise, but he hoped it would be a good one.

Ahead of them and farther up the slope, Nighthawk paused. Preacher could tell from the way the Crow warrior cocked his head that Nighthawk was listening to something. Preacher put his keen hearing to work, as well, and picked up the same thing Nighthawk had heard.

Far back down the slope, men called to each other. Ozark's men were searching for them, and if any among the outlaws were good trackers, they wouldn't have much trouble following the trail. It was impossible to struggle through thick brush without leaving signs.

The pursuit wasn't close yet, however, so after a moment Nighthawk grunted and moved on. Preacher and Annie followed.

A few minutes later, Preacher heard a sharp yip, and then a shaggy gray head poked through some nearby bushes. Annie stopped short and gasped in fear.

"A wolf!"

"Nope," Preacher assured her as he stepped between her and the big cur. He was accustomed to that reaction from people when they first laid eyes on his trail partner "That's Dog. He's a good friend."

The fierce-looking creature proved that by rearing up, placing his paws on Preacher's shoulders, and eagerly licking the mountain man's face. Preacher laughed, dug his hands into the thick fur around the big cur's neck, and roughhoused playfully with him for a moment. Dog's tail swept back and forth, wagging enthusiastically.

After a few moments, Preacher told Dog to get down and brought him over to Annie, who still looked frightened but tried to control it.

Preacher performed the introductions. "Dog, this here is Annie. She's a friend. Understand? Friend. She's the ma of Apollo and Artemis." He glanced at Annie. "Probably best to stick to those names with him, since that's what he knows 'em by."

"That . . . that's fine," she said.

"But we'll call 'em by their right names sometimes, too, and he'll get used to it."

"Is he trustworthy around them?"

"Ma'am, he'd protect them young'uns like they was his own pups."

She mustered up a smile and said, "Then I'm glad to be his friend. Is it all right if I . . . if I pet him?"

"Just hold your hand out first and let him get a good sniff of it."

Annie did so, and while Dog was familiarizing himself with her scent, Preacher repeated that she was a friend.

"You can go ahead and pet him now," he told her. Annie stroked Dog's head and rubbed his ears. He licked her hand. Annie smiled.

"He's really rather nice, despite being so fearsome looking, isn't he?" she said.

"He's a pretty good ol' boy," Preacher agreed. "Now that you two are friends, we'd best get movin' again. We don't want to give Ozark's bunch too much of a chance to catch up to us."

A shudder went through Annie. "We certainly don't. Now that I'm away from him, I can't believe I was willing to just stay there and wait for him to do whatever he was going to do. I suppose I was just too beaten down to oppose him."

"Folks can get that way after a bad spell," Preacher said as they began making their way up the slope again. "It ain't anything to worry about."

"I can't imagine you ever giving in to such feelings, though."

Preacher laughed. "I've always done my best to keep busy. When you've got plenty of things to do and just keep on a-goin' straight ahead, it ain't quite as hard to get through the bad times."

"I'll try to remember that."

A short time later, they reached the crest of the first ridge. Preacher felt a surge of relief go through him when he saw who was waiting there for them.

"How'd you manage to get so far ahead of us, you little varmint?" he asked Audie.

The former professor grinned and said, "In some ways, my small stature is an advantage, as I've pointed out many times. I can pass through openings in the brush that you and Nighthawk can't. And believe me, I put that ability to good use, especially when I know there's a gang of killers on my trail."

They paused to talk for a moment, which gave Annie a chance to rest again.

"How'd you manage to make it sound like there was a small army over yonder across the creek?" Preacher asked. "I figure you rigged all the rifles and pistols to fire at once."

"That's exactly what I did," Audie said. "Then I reloaded and fired each of them again. Did it work? Were Ozark's men fooled?"

"For a few minutes, and that's all the time we needed."

"I'll admit, I was very glad to see you—and to meet this lady."

Audie stepped over to Annie, who appeared to be trying not to stare rudely at him. He took her hand and pressed his lips to the back of it. He didn't have to bow to do that, but he made the gesture seem quite courtly and gallant, anyway.

"It's an honor to meet you, Mrs. Collins," he said. "Our young Salish friend speaks highly of you."

"Little Bear is all right?" Annie asked.

"He's fine." Audie pointed up at the next ridge. "He's waiting for us up there with the horses. And Edward and Elizabeth, of course. We arranged a rendezvous with him, and he proceeded to the spot during the night, taking the children with him for their safety. His familiarity with this region is a very good thing."

Annie nodded. "He's such a smart, sweet boy. I'm sorry that he's risking his life working against Mack Ozark, too, but I'm certainly glad to have his help."

Nighthawk grunted, and Audie said, "Absolutely correct, my friend. We need to get moving again. Are you up to climbing some more, Mrs. Collins?"

"I'll climb all the way to heaven if necessary to get back to my children," Annie said.

Sunlight washed over the landscape as the fiery orb rose higher in the sky. The temperature climbed, as well, but a hint of coolness remained in the air, making it easier for the fugitives to climb to the top of the next ridge.

By the time they reached that crest, the outlaws' compound was far below them. When Preacher looked back down there, the men he spotted moving around looked almost like ants.

They hadn't caught sight of the pursuers, so Preacher figured it was unlikely Ozark's men had spotted them. From time to time, they heard a faint shout. The outlaws were still searching for them. They were probably so afraid of Ozark that they would be reluctant to give up.

Preacher hoped to stay so far in front of them that eventually the men would have no choice but to abandon the search. Once that happened, the mountain man and his companions could begin circling back to the south.

In the long run, they needed to get around the compound and head east again. Preacher wanted to get Annie and her young'uns back to civilization, even though that in itself wasn't really a guarantee of their safety.

As they were making their way toward the spot where they were supposed to rendezvous with Little Bear, Audie fell back alongside Preacher, who was bringing up the rear, and asked quietly, "While you were Ozark's prisoner, did you get any idea why recovering those infants is so important to him?"

Preacher shook his head. "Not a clue. Ozark was open enough about wantin' to get 'em back at all costs, but he didn't say a word about why."

"A part of me would really like to know." Audie sighed. "But it's more important that we get them, and their mother, as far away from that madman as possible."

"Damn right," Preacher said with a curt nod of agreement. He looked up ahead to where Nighthawk was still leading the way with Annie following him and Dog striding along beside her. The big cur had adopted the same sort of protective attitude toward the young woman as he had demonstrated toward her children.

They hadn't gone much farther when Nighthawk stopped short, turned toward Preacher and Audie, waved his arm at their surroundings, and said, "Umm!"

Audie hurried forward and asked, "Are you certain this is the spot?"

"Umm!"

Audie turned back to Preacher and Annie.

"This is where we were supposed to meet Little Bear," he explained.

Preacher looked around. He saw two pine trees growing on a nearby knob, and off to the other side was a rough circle of boulders. Those were pretty unmistakable landmarks to somebody who knew the area.

He didn't see any signs of the Flathead youth, Horse, or the other mounts and pack animals. However, Dog would be able to scent them if they had been here.

He was about to order the big cur to hunt when Nighthawk suddenly pounced like a big cat toward a clump of brush. He moved some of it aside with one long arm and reached into the growth with the other.

What he dragged out into the open brought a gasp of shock from Annie.

"That's one of the blankets the babies were wrapped in!" she cried as she rushed forward to grab it out of Nighthawk's hand. She brought the blanket to her face and rubbed it against her cheek as she moaned.

With a flat tone in his voice, Preacher asked, "The young'uns ain't there in the bushes, are they?"

Solemnly, Nighthawk shook his head. He made a curt, slashing gesture to indicate that the babies weren't there.

It would have been a relief if the infants had been found alive, of course, but for a terrible moment, Preacher had expected that their bodies were hidden in the brush.

If they weren't here, at least it meant there was a chance they were alive somewhere else.

But they had been here, and the blanket was proof of that. Preacher hated to take it away from Annie, who seemed to be getting some comfort from it, but he held out his hand and said, "Let me see that for a second, ma'am."

She swallowed and reluctantly handed the blanket to him. Preacher looked at it, briefly noting the beadwork design on it.

He had seen both blankets many times during the past week, since he and his friends had taken custody of the twins at Dutch Charley's, but he hadn't paid much attention to them. The beadwork looked Indian at first glance, but he had soon realized it didn't match the typical designs of any of the tribes he was familiar with.

That didn't matter, so he thought about it only fleetingly now. Instead, he held out the blanket so Dog could sniff it.

"Find the babies, Dog," Preacher ordered. "Find Apollo and Artemis."

Dog didn't really need the blanket; by now he knew the scent of both infants quite well. But sniffing the blanket probably reinforced the scent for him. He whirled around and dashed off, heading north along the ridge crest.

Preacher gave the blanket back to Annie, who clutched it to her chest.

"It's been a hard mornin'," he said. "Are you up to comin' with us while we follow Dog?"

"Don't even think about leaving me behind! Can he really find my children?"

"If any creature on the face o' God's green earth can, it's that shaggy varmint," Preacher assured her.

"Then let's go. We don't want him leaving us too far behind."

"No, ma'am. He won't let that happen. If he finds 'em, he'll double back and fetch us if he has to."

"If he finds them?" Annie repeated.

"Preacher meant when," Audie said. "I concur with his estimation of our canine friend. With Dog on the trail, it's only a matter of time until we find them!"

CHAPTER 18

Time wasn't a luxury they necessarily had plenty of, though. Not only did they need to locate the twins, Little Bear, and the horses, but they had to stay ahead of the pursuit Mack Ozark had sent after them.

Knowing that, Preacher kept the group moving at a fairly fast pace. It helped that they were following the ridge crest now instead of climbing a slope. The crest was rugged in places, but at least it was fairly level and about fifty yards wide. They made good time when they weren't detouring around large boulders or impassable thickets of brush.

Nighthawk loped ahead. His long legs allowed him to stay within sight of Dog. Preacher and Audie were farther back, accompanying Annie.

She tried valiantly to keep up, as she had vowed she would do, but it wasn't long before Preacher could tell she was tiring. She was staggering and her steps became more awkward. She had been through a great deal the past twelve hours, and she wasn't accustomed to so much physical effort.

"Listen, you're gonna have to rest a spell," Preacher told her as they hurried along some twenty-five yards behind Nighthawk.

She shook her head stubbornly and insisted, "I have to find my children."

"We're gonna find 'em, you don't have to worry about that, but if you don't stop and catch your breath, you're liable to fall flat on your face. Might even pass out. You don't want that."

"Why don't Mrs. Collins and I pause for a bit?" Audie suggested. "You can go ahead and join Nighthawk, Preacher. When you've located the twins, one of you can come back to get us, assuming, of course, that we haven't gotten a second wind and caught up by then."

Preacher thought that was pretty unlikely and knew Audie was saying it for Annie's benefit. But if it would get her to agree, that was fine with the mountain man.

Annie kept going for a few more steps but then stopped and heaved a sigh. Preacher could tell from the sound how worn out she was. He and Audie stopped, too.

"I suppose it wouldn't hurt to rest for a few minutes," she said. "But you have to promise that you'll come get us right away if you find the children."

"Sure," Preacher said. "You can count on it."

In truth, he wasn't sure what he'd do when they found the youngsters. That would depend on what the situation was. It might be better for Annie to keep her distance.

No point in explaining that to her now, though. Instead, Preacher patted her shoulder reassuringly, nodded to Audie, and loped after Nighthawk, who hadn't stopped or even slowed down when the others did.

The sun felt good on his bare torso, and so did the cool air. The combination soothed the numerous scratches he had gotten from the brush as they were fleeing. The little wounds were already scabbing over, and he had no trouble ignoring the discomfort from them.

Nighthawk heard him coming and slowed down slightly so that Preacher could catch up. As Preacher drew alongside the big warrior, he said, "Mrs. Collins is gonna rest a short spell, and Audie's stayin' with her. Is Dog still in sight?"

Nighthawk pointed. Preacher spotted Dog about a hundred

yards ahead of them, with his nose to the ground as he followed the top of the ridge.

Suddenly, Dog swerved to the left, which carried him down the western slope. It dropped to a narrow trail, on the far side of which was another slope leading even higher. Dog didn't start up the next ridge, however. He followed the trail between them.

When Preacher and Nighthawk reached the spot where Dog had changed course, they saw the well-worn path leading down from the crest.

"That ain't a game trail," Preacher commented. "Moccasins made that path."

Nighthawk grunted in agreement.

"A Flathead trail," Preacher went on. "Little Bear's people must come through here pretty often. You reckon a huntin' party came along and he went with 'em, figurin' the babies'd be safer that way?"

Nighthawk paused and pointed at something in the trail, but Preacher had already noticed it himself while he was talking. He dropped a knee and touched a finger to a small dark splotch on the dirt. Some of whatever had made it stuck to his fingertip. He tasted it.

"Damn it," Preacher said. "That's blood, all right. That don't have to mean that Little Bear's in trouble, but he sure might be."

Nighthawk nodded gravely.

The two men moved faster now. Audie and Annie were out of sight behind them. Up ahead, Dog turned around and ran toward them for a few seconds and then stopped to look intently at them before whirling around and taking off again.

"He's sure on the trail," Preacher said. "And I got a hunch we may be gettin' close to what we're lookin' for."

They followed the trail between the ridges for another half-mile, though, before Dog ran back to join the two men and stayed with them this time. Knowing they had to be close to their destination, Preacher and Nighthawk slowed and began to use every bit of cover they could find as they followed the trail. They didn't want to stumble upon their quarry without warning.

Up ahead, the trail curved between two large boulders that had rolled down from the higher ridges sometime in the past. They sat on either side of the trail like gate pillars.

Silently, Preacher pointed toward a thick stand of pine trees on the slope to their left, about fifty feet higher than the trail. If they could get up there, they could stay in the cover of the trees as they followed the trail around the bend.

They ought to have a good vantage point to see what was on the other side of the massive rocks, too.

When they felt certain nobody was watching them, Preacher and Nighthawk hurried up the slope into the trees. They stayed in the shadows under the branches and worked their way along parallel to the trail.

The gulch between the ridges curved around and opened up on the other side of the natural rock gateway into a broad, level space in which an Indian camp was located. Preacher estimated there were two dozen tipis visible.

A few women, children, and dogs moved around the dwellings, but he didn't see any warriors.

"Flathead?" he asked Nighthawk as they crouched in the cover provided by the trees.

The big Crow nodded.

"They ought to be friendly, then."

Nighthawk shook his head and pointed.

"Yeah, I see 'em, too," Preacher said. His eyes narrowed as he watched half a dozen warriors emerge from the largest of the lodges, the one that probably belonged to this band's chief.

Four more men came out of the tipi. The first group stopped and one of them spoke animatedly to the four who had followed them out.

Whatever he said provoked an equally passionate response. The two groups stood there facing each other, sharp words flying back and forth. Both sides were angry about something, but at this distance, Preacher couldn't make out what any of them were saying. Then one of the warriors from the second group, an older man from the looks of his gray hair, turned toward the tipi and gestured emphatically. The entrance flap opened, and two more warriors emerged, holding a short, stocky figure between them.

"Little Bear," Preacher breathed. His rugged features tightened into angry lines as he saw the dark smears on the young man's face. That was dried blood. Little Bear had been on the receiving end of some rough treatment.

He was standing up and moving around all right, though, so maybe he wasn't seriously injured.

"Where are the young'uns?" Preacher asked, although he didn't expect an answer from Nighthawk, who wouldn't know the answer to that question any more than Preacher did. "And who roughed up Little Bear?"

The warriors who had brought the young man from the tipi had hold of his arms, one on each side. One of the men let go, and the other shoved Little Bear toward the first group. A couple of them grabbed him as if making him their prisoner again.

"The fellas in that first bunch must be the ones who grabbed him and the twins," Preacher mused. "They brung him back here, but the second bunch don't like what they did and are washin' their hands of the whole deal. Does that seem to be the way it played out to you?"

Nighthawk nodded.

Preacher rubbed his chin and frowned. "But where are the young'uns, and what in blazes do those varmints figure on doin' with Little Bear?"

The argument continued for a moment longer before the group holding Little Bear prisoner turned away and stalked off stiffly, taking him with them. Two warriors flanked him and held his arms, marching him along.

Preacher and Nighthawk watched as the men took Little Bear to one of the other tipis and shoved him inside. Four of them turned to walk away, but two remained just outside the tipi's entrance flap, taking position there with their arms crossed and stern looks on their faces. Preacher knew they were there to stand guard on the prisoner.

But then the hide flap was thrust open again and a woman in a buckskin dress emerged holding something in her arms. She called after the warriors who were walking off.

Nighthawk made a low, rumbling sound in his throat. Preacher said quietly, "Yeah, that's one o' the twins she's holdin'. Can't tell which one at this distance, but you can't miss that blond hair o' theirs shinin' in the sun."

It was difficult enough to tell Edward and Elizabeth apart close up. Not that it mattered which one the Indian woman held, because right behind her came another woman carrying the second twin.

Preacher was relieved at the sight of them. They appeared to be all right. He heard crying coming from both infants, which meant they were unhappy but didn't have to signify anything other than that.

"Leather-lunged little varmints, ain't they?" he asked with a grin.

Nighthawk only grunted, but he looked relieved, as well.

The first woman who had come out of the tipi was arguing with one of the warriors. The man was the same one who'd been talking to the chief. Preacher pegged him as the leader of the bunch that had grabbed Little Bear and the babies.

But the question of why they had brought the three prisoners back here to their village still remained.

Down below, the warrior arguing with the woman raised his arm and pointed at the tipi. The woman said something else, and the warrior poked the air with his finger as he gave her a haughty look and pointed again.

Despite the seriousness of the situation, Preacher chuckled. He had never been married himself, but he had witnessed enough husbands and wives wrangling with each other to know that was what he was watching now. The warrior had dumped the job of caring for the babies on his wife and the other woman, who, quite possibly, was also his wife. And the gals, who went back into the tipi with obvious reluctance, weren't happy about it. Evidently, nobody was very happy with the warrior and his friends. But that didn't mean Preacher and Nighthawk could just march into the village and demand that the prisoners be handed over to them. Even if the other men didn't agree with what had been done, they wouldn't take kindly to high-handed interlopers.

Preacher frowned in thought, tugged on his earlobe, and scraped his thumbnail along his jawline, as he often did without even being aware of it when he was trying to puzzle out a particularly difficult problem.

"If we could afford to wait for nightfall, I reckon we could get in there and free Little Bear and the young'uns without too much trouble," he said. "But if we do that, the men Ozark sent after us will catch up and we'll have to deal with them. We need to get 'em out now."

Nighthawk tapped a fist against his broad chest and then pointed down at the village.

"You're gonna walk in there and distract 'em?" Preacher considered the suggestion and then nodded. "Ain't no bad blood between your people and the Flatheads as far as I know, and you do tend to attract some attention wherever you show up. Yeah, we'll give it a try. Don't reckon we've got any choice."

Quickly, they worked out the details of the plan. Preacher would keep going up the gulch a short distance to reach a spot where he could approach the tipi where the prisoners were being held from directly behind the dwelling.

Meanwhile, Nighthawk would go back the way they had come, inform Audie and Annie of what was going on, and then follow the gulch to walk openly into the village. It wasn't uncommon for members of other tribes to visit a village as long as the tribes weren't at war with each other.

Preacher wasn't sure how he would keep the women in the tipi from raising a ruckus, but he'd have to tangle with that problem when he got to it.

Preacher and Nighthawk split up. As Preacher carefully moved into position, the village settled down after the brief disturbance. Two warriors remained on guard outside the tipi while the other four members of their group, including the leader, drifted off to various other pursuits.

Preacher had plenty of experience sneaking in and out of Indian villages from his many nocturnal forays against the Blackfeet. Those lethal visits had been carried out in the middle of the night, however, not in broad daylight. Preacher had to use every bit of cover he could find as he crept closer to the tipi that was his goal.

Due to the narrowness of the gulch, only about twenty feet separated the base of the ridge from the back of the tipi. Preacher crouched behind a deadfall. Some dry brush had accumulated around the fallen tree and provided even more cover. From here, it would take him mere seconds to reach his destination.

He didn't have to wait long before a surprised shout told him that Nighthawk had been spotted approaching the village. The towering Crow warrior was hard to miss. Carefully, Preacher parted the brush to look back along the trail that followed the bottom of the gulch.

Nighthawk strode along with confidence that bordered on arrogance, as if he had every right to be where he was. His expression was solemn but friendly as he lifted a hand in greeting, palm out in the universal signal that he came in peace.

Several warriors immediately moved to meet him, their attitudes wary, as they would be of any stranger. The gray-haired man

Preacher had taken to be the chief of this band emerged from his tipi and strode forward with a confidence that matched Nighthawk's.

The other warriors waited to allow the chief to take the lead then fell in close behind him, ready for trouble if any should develop. The men weren't armed with bows or lances, but each of them carried a knife or tomahawk, if not both.

The chief spoke first, no doubt welcoming Nighthawk to the village. As usual under such formal circumstances where Indians were concerned, quite a few high-flown words were required to convey a simple greeting.

Nighthawk responded in kind, his deep, booming voice ringing out and filling the gulch. He spoke the Salish tongue well enough to be understood. Notoriously taciturn, this was more words than Nighthawk usually came out with in a month of Sundays.

Preacher smiled. His old friend was doing a fine job of keeping the villagers distracted. Most of the warriors had turned out to take a look at the huge newcomer, and many of the women and kids had straggled up behind the warriors, too.

From where Preacher was, he couldn't see the front of the tipi where Little Bear and the twins were, but he assumed the two guards were still there and hadn't gone to get a better look at the visitor. No matter which tribe they belonged to, warriors didn't take their duties lightly.

As far as Preacher could tell, everyone was looking the other way now. He stepped out from behind the deadfall and brush and darted toward the tipi. Dropping to his knees when he reached it, he took hold of the tanned hide out of which the dwelling was made and lifted it.

No one inside responded. Preacher squirmed his head and shoulders under the hide and looked around. Little Bear sat cross-legged a few feet away, facing away from him. The two infants lay on the ground beside him.

The two women were at the entrance. They must have heard the commotion outside caused by Nighthawk's arrival and had pulled the flap back to see what was going on. Preacher heard them talking to the guards but paid no attention to what they were saying. Preacher pulled the bottom half of his body into the tipi. He lifted himself onto his knees. His left hand went around Little Bear's head and clamped over the young man's mouth so Little Bear couldn't cry out and alert the women. At the same time, Preacher grasped Little Bear's shoulder with his right hand and squeezed reassuringly.

Little Bear jerked in surprise but didn't try to pull away. Preacher was glad the young man had that much self-control. Little Bear's eyes were wide with shock as he looked over at Preacher, but he remained quiet as Preacher took his hand away.

A curt gesture from the mountain man told Little Bear to crawl out under the tipi's rear wall. Little Bear nodded to show that he understood. He gathered up one of the babies in his arms, evidently thinking that Preacher would bring the other infant.

That was what Preacher planned to do, but he had to wait for Little Bear to get out of the tipi first. The young man moved as quietly as he could, but he couldn't help but make some noise as he struggled under the buffalo hide wall.

And that made one of the women glance around. She cried out in alarm when she saw Preacher and leaped toward him, her hands extended with the fingers hooked and ready to claw at his face.

CHAPTER 19

Preacher surged to his feet, grabbed the woman's right wrist, and slung her away from him, sending her rolling across the ground beside the now-cold fire ring in the middle of the tipi.

The other woman shrank back at the sight of the mountain man, giving the two guards room to charge through the entrance. Preacher sprang forward to meet them. If he could dispose of them without too much ruckus, he hoped he and Little Bear could still get away with the twins before the rest of the village knew what was going on.

That hope disappeared as the second woman rushed out and started screaming her head off.

The warrior closest to Preacher tried to tackle him. Preacher twisted aside, and as the man lunged past him, he hammered the edge of his hand against the back of the man's neck. The warrior went down hard, stunned by the blow.

The second guard was armed with a knife, but he didn't draw the weapon, trying to get closer to Preacher and wrestle instead.

However, it was hard to maintain a grip on Preacher's bare torso. He writhed free, got behind the warrior, and clamped his left forearm across the man's neck, anchoring it in place with his right hand gripping his left wrist. Preacher's arm was like a bar of iron cutting off the warrior's breath.

The first guard, still a little disoriented from being knocked down, tried to get back to his feet. He made it as far as his knees.

Without loosening his grip on the second guard's throat, Preacher kicked the first warrior in the face and knocked him sprawling on his back.

Angry shouts sounded from outside. Preacher couldn't tell what was going on, but he was willing to bet that Nighthawk was trying to keep the rest of the warriors occupied. That would be a well-nigh impossible task even for the giant Crow, but Preacher knew Nighthawk would do his best.

Nighthawk would sacrifice his own life if it meant giving Preacher a chance to get away with Little Bear and the babies.

The warrior Preacher was choking suddenly went limp as he passed out from lack of air. Preacher flung him down on top of the other man, who was only half-conscious after being kicked in the face.

The woman Preacher had slung to the other side of the tipi was on her feet again, but she backed away and didn't try to stop the mountain man as he scooped the other crying infant from the ground. Preacher didn't try to get out the back of the tipi; there was no longer any point in stealth.

Instead, he wrapped his left arm around the baby and ducked out through the entrance, shouldering the flap aside as he did so.

He stopped short as he found himself facing a half-circle of warriors. Judging by their fierce expressions, they were all ready to attack, but the gray-haired chief Preacher had noted earlier held them back. His arms were out to the side in a signal for them to wait as he stepped forward toward Preacher and Little Bear, who stood nearby holding the other infant.

Preacher glanced toward the edge of the village where Nighthawk stood, also surrounded by warriors. A couple of men were sprawled on the ground nearby, doubtless where Nighthawk had tossed them, and two more sat shaking their heads as they tried to recover from whatever the big Crow had done to them. Preacher figured they had probably been introduced to Nighthawk's fists.

The chief spoke angrily in the Salish tongue, addressing Preacher. The mountain man made out some of the words, but Little Bear gave him a full translation.

"Red Shirt wants to know why you and Nighthawk have intruded on our village and caused injury to our people."

"He's the chief o' this bunch?" Preacher asked.

"That's right."

"He ain't wearin' a red shirt."

Despite the danger they faced, Little Bear smiled. "He had one, once, and liked the name so it stuck."

"And these are your people? This is your village?"

"It was." A sorrowful note entered the young man's voice. "I have no more living relatives, and I've spent so much time at the compound with Annie, and Annie and Jonathan before that, they don't really consider me one of them anymore. My grandfather and Bluebird and I were all that was left of our family."

The gray-haired chief was regarding Preacher with an unfriendly gaze. Preacher could have responded to Red Shirt's question directly, but Little Bear might be able to phrase things better, he decided.

"Tell him we mean no harm to him or his people, but we only wished to help our friends who are bein' held against their will," Preacher said to the young man. "I reckon that's true, ain't it? You don't want to be here, do you? Those fellas grabbed you and the young'uns and brought you here."

"That's right. It was all Standing Cloud's idea."

One of the warriors stepped forward with a fierce scowl on his face. Preacher recognized him as the one who had been arguing with the chief earlier. From the looks of the angry expression he wore now, he realized that Little Bear was talking about him.

"That's Standing Cloud, eh?" Preacher said. "Not too friendly, is he?"

"Definitely not friendly to me," Little Bear answered under his breath. "He wanted to take Bluebird as his third wife, but she refused. That didn't make him like me any better—not that he had a high opinion of me to start with. I never showed any signs of being a good warrior, and that's all Standing Cloud cares about."

Red Shirt snapped something, no doubt demanding an answer to the question he had asked. Quickly, Little Bear spoke, relaying the message Preacher had given him.

That prompted a half-shouted response from Standing Cloud, who waved an arm and looked like he was about to attack Preacher. Red Shirt spoke sharply and gestured for him to move back.

"Why'd they grab you and the twins to start with?" Preacher asked Little Bear.

"Because Standing Cloud thought it would be a good idea to—"

Before Little Bear could finish, Standing Cloud started haranguing them again, loudly and emphatically, accompanied by more arm waving.

Preacher was surprised when he picked out the name "Ozark" among the warrior's ranting.

"What's his connection to Mack Ozark?" Preacher asked Little Bear while Standing Cloud continued yelling.

"I told you we trade with Ozark. When Standing Cloud found out that Ozark was pursuing us, he got the idea that capturing us and turning us over to Ozark would improve our standing with him, maybe get us better terms when we trade."

"He wanted to curry favor with Ozark, you mean."

Little Bear nodded. "That's it. But Red Shirt thought it wouldn't be a good thing to do and told Standing Cloud he wouldn't have anything to do with it. He said it was dishonorable to use children that way."

"Good man," Preacher said.

"That doesn't mean he's willing to overlook you sneaking into the village and fighting with those men, though. That offended the chief's honor, too."

Standing Cloud finally ran out of steam and stood there glowering at Preacher and Little Bear. Red Shirt didn't look much happier with them.

Preacher said, "Tell the chief that if he'll allow us to leave with the babies, we won't cause any more trouble."

Little Bear translated that proposal.

Red Shirt answered immediately, and as he spoke at length, Standing Cloud began to smile. It was an ugly expression, more of a drawing back of his lips from his teeth rather than an actual smile.

Little Bear swallowed and said, "Red Shirt says that whether he agrees with it or not, since the twins and I are Standing Cloud's prisoners, it's up to him what he does with us. As for you, you gave offense to the entire village, and you can't leave without being punished."

"What's he figure on doin'?" Preacher asked. He was getting a little angry himself.

Standing Cloud jerked a hand toward Preacher and spouted some more words.

"He's asking Red Shirt to turn you over to him, too," Little Bear said.

"Now that just ain't gonna work," Preacher said. "I've got a better idea."

"You'd better let me have it quick, then. I think the chief is seriously considering Standing Cloud's suggestion."

"Let me fight Standin' Cloud. Just him and me, man to man."

Little Bear looked sharply at Preacher, his eyes widening at the audacity of the mountain man's words.

"If I win," Preacher went on, "then I leave here with you and the young'uns, and nobody from the Salish tribe bothers us again. If Standing Cloud wins . . ." Preacher shrugged. "I reckon he can do whatever he wants. I won't be there to stop him 'cause he'll likely have to kill me to beat me."

"I can't challenge him to a . . . a fight to the death like that!"

"Say it any way you want," Preacher told the young man. "As long as I've got a fightin' chance to leave here with you and the twins, I don't care about nothin' else."

Little Bear let out a resigned sigh and then began speaking to Red Shirt. As Standing Cloud listened, his ugly grin widened even more.

When Little Bear finished, Standing Cloud flung both arms out wide and rattled off more words. Preacher only understood what he was saying here and there, but the warrior's contemptuous tone was easy to recognize.

Red Shirt wasn't going to be rushed into a decision, though. He pondered everything that had been said to him as a tense silence settled over the gathering. The other warriors and the women were clearly eager to hear what the chief was going to decide.

Preacher could tell by the looks in their eyes that they liked the idea of him and Standing Cloud battling each other.

None of them would be rooting for him, the mountain man knew. It would be just fine with them if Standing Cloud emerged triumphant.

And it might be even better, as far as they were concerned, if he didn't survive the battle.

Red Shirt raised both hands, drawing out the dramatic moment just a little more. Evidently, he had made up his mind.

He looked at Standing Cloud, looked at Preacher, and then barked a command.

"Fight!" Little Bear cried, but that was unnecessary because Standing Cloud was already charging at Preacher with hate and murder in his eyes.

CHAPTER 20

Preacher sprang forward to meet Standing Cloud's attack. The mountain man had never been one to sit back and let trouble come to him.

He swung his right fist at Standing Cloud's face. The warrior jerked to the side. Preacher's blow scraped his ear. Standing Cloud's momentum carried him forward. His right arm shot out, looped around Preacher's chest, and drove him backward off his feet.

Both men went down hard.

Preacher landed on his back with enough force to knock the breath out of him, but he knew he couldn't allow that to slow him down. He brought his elbow up and drove it into the side of Standing Cloud's head.

A blow like that would have been enough to knock most men out cold, but Standing Cloud must have had a hard head. He just grunted and grappled at Preacher with both hands. Preacher knew his opponent was trying to get a grip on his throat so he could choke the life out of him.

Preacher grabbed Standing Cloud's shoulders and rolled to his left, forcing the warrior to go with him. Standing Cloud wound up on the bottom. Preacher tried to ram his knee into Standing Cloud's groin, but the man writhed aside and avoided it.

Standing Cloud threw his right leg up, hooked it across Preacher's chest, and levered the mountain man off him. Both combatants rolled away from each other to give themselves more room to maneuver as they surged back to their feet.

Indians generally preferred wrestling to fist-fighting, Preacher knew, but Standing Cloud was completely caught up in the heat of battle now and threw wild punches with both fists as he drove in on Preacher.

Preacher gave ground deliberately, drawing the warrior on. He was able to block most of Standing Cloud's blows. He had to just absorb the punishment from the ones that got through. They rocked Preacher but didn't put him down.

When Standing Cloud was out of control and starting to stumble, Preacher ducked under a wild, roundhouse swing and caught hold of the warrior's arm with both hands. He pivoted and heaved, and Standing Cloud lost his balance and footing. He flew through the air and crashed to the ground, landing where several women had to scamper out of the way to avoid being hit.

As Standing Cloud rolled in the dirt, some of the village dogs dashed forward and capered around him, barking wildly in excitement.

That humiliation just infuriated him more. When he came to a stop, he yelled at the dogs to chase them away, then pushed himself to his hands and knees and looked up at Preacher with pure murder on his face.

"You're pretty damn handy when it comes to pushin' around a youngster and a couple o' babies," Preacher said. "How's it feel goin' up against somebody your own size?"

He didn't know if Standing Cloud understood any of those words, but the mountain man's mocking, derisive tone was unmistakable. Standing Cloud let out a furious roar and powered to his feet in another wild charge.

This time, Preacher didn't back off. He met Standing Cloud's attack head-on. He blocked Standing Cloud's first swing with his left arm and hammered a powerful right hook into the warrior's midsection.

That brought Standing Cloud to a sudden stop and left him in position for the left cross Preacher shot to his jaw. Standing Cloud's head jerked to the side, and for a second his eyes went vacant.

Preacher took advantage of that opening to lift his right in an uppercut that exploded under Standing Cloud's chin and lifted the warrior off his feet. Standing Cloud went down hard on his back with his arms and legs splayed out to the sides.

Confident that Standing Cloud was out and wouldn't be getting back up again for a spell, Preacher turned to Red Shirt. The mountain man was breathing a little hard from his efforts, and beads of sweat coated his bare torso even though the morning wasn't really that warm.

He was about to tell Little Bear to remind the chief of their bargain when Red Shirt looked past him and a shout went up from the assembled villagers.

Preacher saw the surprised look on Red Shirt's face and thought, *Aw, hell.* Sure enough, when Preacher turned his head and looked back over his shoulder, he saw Standing Cloud getting up.

The warrior wasn't too steady about it, but he made it to his feet. Blood smeared his mouth where Preacher had hit it with his left.

The other warriors yelled encouragement to Standing Cloud, even the ones who had sided with Red Shirt earlier. None of them were going to root for an outsider over one of their own. Some of the women let out ululating wails of excitement.

Life on the frontier was hard. These people were enjoying this break from their day-to-day routine.

Standing Cloud shook his head back and forth. He was groggy, but as he stood there with his chest heaving, he began to get his senses back. Strength flowed back into his muscles. Preacher could tell that by looking at him.

"We don't have to keep on with this," Preacher said. "I'm willin' to end this if he is. No real harm done on either side. But if we keep fightin', he's liable to get hurt pretty bad." He gestured toward Standing Cloud and added, "You tell him that, Little Bear." Hurriedly, the young man blurted out a translation of what Preacher had said. Even before Little Bear finished speaking, Preacher could tell it wasn't going to do any good. Standing Cloud was so full of rage that he wasn't capable of calling off the fight. He let out a furious bellow and charged again.

Preacher knew Standing Cloud was still dangerous, even in bad shape. The warrior was tall and brawny, probably outweighed the mountain man slightly, and was about equal in reach. If he ever got his hands on his opponent in a grip that Preacher couldn't get out of, or even just landed a lucky punch, the tide of battle could change in a hurry.

Knowing that, Preacher was well aware that he couldn't afford to get careless. He darted aside from Standing Cloud's first lunge, whirled, and was ready when Standing Cloud tried to turn back toward him.

Because of the beating he had taken already, the warrior's movements were lumbering and awkward. Preacher stepped in and hit him with a left jab that rocked Standing Cloud's head back. Standing Cloud's arms came up to guard his face, and Preacher's right sank to the wrist in Standing Cloud's belly. Breath gusted from the warrior's mouth as he doubled over.

Preacher grabbed the back of Standing Cloud's head and forced it down. At the same time, Preacher brought up his right knee. It smashed into Standing Cloud's nose, pulping it.

When Preacher let go of him and stepped back, Standing Cloud fell on his face. He lay there with air wheezing and rattling through his broken nose. He moaned and tried to push himself up, then slumped down again, unable to rise.

This time, the fight really was over.

The shouting stopped abruptly as it became obvious to the onlookers that Standing Cloud couldn't continue. Most of the villagers glared at Preacher, but some of the warriors regarded the mountain man with grudging admiration.

It had been a good fight between two evenly matched opponents, and Preacher had won fair and square.

Red Shirt stared at Preacher for a long moment and then walked over to him. In only slightly halting English, the chief said, "You free to go, white man. Take babies with you."

Preacher nodded toward the stocky young man and asked, "What about Little Bear?"

"He one of us. Whether he stay or go up to him."

Little Bear spoke quickly to the chief in the Salish tongue, then turned to Preacher and said, "I told him I was going with you and the twins. I said I'd been helping take care of them, and I needed to continue with that."

"I appreciate it," Preacher told him. "I know Annie likes havin' you around, and you make it easier for Audie, too. But these are your people, so I reckon we'd understand if you wanted to stay with 'em."

Little Bear sighed. "No, this village will never be home for me again. Not with Bluebird and my grandfather gone. I had hoped that I might be able to follow them someday and be reunited with them."

"I'm sorry that ain't ever gonna happen. But I'm dang sure that by helpin' take care o' those little ones, you're doin' what they would have wanted."

"I think so, too." Little Bear took in a deep breath. "Now we need to find Audie and Annie."

Nighthawk had just caught Preacher's attention and pointed back up the gulch. When Preacher looked in that direction, he saw Audie and Annie riding toward the village on the horses that had disappeared earlier. Preacher's rangy gray stallion was with them, as were the pack animals.

"We don't have to look for 'em," Preacher said. "Here they come now." Dog was with the new arrivals, too, and bounded on ahead to enter the village first. People shied away from the big cur as he ran to Preacher and reared up with his paws on the mountain man's shoulders.

"After Nighthawk and I got caught, you went lookin' for the others and found 'em, didn't you, old son?" Preacher asked as he hugged Dog's thick, shaggy neck and scratched the big cur's ears. "You're a mighty good fella."

Nighthawk loped out to meet Audie and Annie. None of the warriors tried to stop him. He walked back into the village alongside the horse Audie rode.

"Howdy," Preacher called to them as he raised a hand in greeting.

Annie dismounted as soon as they were close. She ran forward and cried, "Edward! Elizabeth!"

The two Indian women now holding the twins pulled back and tightened their grips as if they weren't going to allow Annie to take the babies. But when Red Shirt spoke sharply to them, one of the women gave up her charge to Annie, who took the infant in a frantic hug.

Little Bear took the other baby and held it while Annie finished fussing over the one she held, who turned out to be Edward. Then she and Little Bear exchanged the infants so Annie could be reunited with her daughter.

Preacher wanted to talk to Audie, but at the moment, he was more concerned with Standing Cloud, who had regained his strength and senses and climbed laboriously to his feet. The warrior, whose face was bloody from his broken nose, glared at Preacher for a moment before turning away and trudging off with some of his friends around him.

The mountain man knew he had made a bad enemy there, but Preacher couldn't bring himself to get too worried about it. He'd made lots of bad enemies during his life. Most of them were dead now, but a few weren't. Standing Cloud would just be added to that number.

Preacher and Dog walked over to where Audie had reined in and was sitting his saddle calmly, ignoring all the curious stares the Salish villagers sent his way because of his small size.

"You found the horses, I see," Preacher commented.

"They found us, is more like it," Audie said. "Horse led them to us. They came up out of the brush when we weren't expecting it. A short time later, Dog showed up and acted like you might be in trouble, so I decided we should check." He lowered his voice slightly. "I hated to bring Mrs. Collins along in case there was danger, but with Ozark's men trailing us, I couldn't very well leave her behind, either."

"No, you couldn't," Preacher agreed. "The way it's worked out, this is the best thing all around, I reckon. The Flatheads are gonna let Little Bear and the young'uns go."

"Why did they take them in the first place?"

"That's kind of a long story, and we ain't got time to waste on it right now. How far behind us do you reckon Ozark's men are?"

"Nowhere near far enough," Audie replied. "We need to be on the move again as quickly as possible. Where do you think we should go?"

"Only one good place I can think of," Preacher said. "We're goin' up. We're headin' for the high country."

CHAPTER 21

A few minutes later, the whole group was mounted and heading out of the village. The babies were safely back in the cradleboard slings Audie had rigged for them.

Annie wanted to hold them, but she couldn't do that and control her horse, too, so she had agreed reluctantly to let the twins ride as they had so far.

Nighthawk dropped back to check on the pursuit and find out how far behind them it was. Dog ranged ahead, as usual. Preacher motioned for Little Bear to ride alongside him while Audie and Annie rode a short distance behind with the mount carrying the babies between them.

"Ain't had a chance to ask you until now," Preacher said. "What happened when Standin' Cloud and them other fellas jumped you?"

Little Bear sighed. "I was supposed to be standing guard, but I suppose I didn't do a very good job of it. They were there before I knew it and grabbed me and the twins. They tried to get the horses, too, but that stallion of yours wasn't having any of it. He pulled loose, prodded the others until they broke loose, as well, and then they all stampeded off into the woods. Standing Cloud didn't want to take the time to go after them."

Preacher grinned, patted Horse's shoulder, and said, "Yeah, this ol' boy's a one-man horse unless I tell him it's all right. He don't want nobody else layin' hands on him."

"I suppose he found your scent and followed it." Little Bear frowned. "Can horses do that, like dogs?"

"This one can."

Once they were all back together, Preacher had gotten a spare buckskin shirt from his possibles bag and put it on. He had taken his extra set of revolvers from the bag, too, so a pair of Paterson Colts rested in their familiar holsters again. The Indians had provided a knife and tomahawk to replace the ones the outlaws had taken from him. His hat was lost somewhere back in Mack Ozark's compound, but other than that, Preacher was fully dressed again, and it felt good.

He hoped that by climbing higher in the mountains, they might be able to lose their pursuers. Ozark's men might even give up if the chase was hard enough on them.

However, Preacher didn't expect that to happen. He had a hunch Ozark's men were scared enough of their boss that they would put up with any hardship in order to avoid his wrath.

The ridges continued rising, broken here and there by terrace-like shoulders of level ground. On the steeper slopes, the riders had to dismount and lead the horses. Nighthawk took charge of Annie's horse for her during those difficult stretches while she walked alongside the horse carrying the cradleboards. Preacher knew that not holding her children had to be hard for her, but she didn't complain.

From time to time, he stopped and lingered behind the others to watch their back trail for a few minutes. His keen eyes sought any sign of pursuit. He knew Ozark's men were back there, but he didn't spot them, and neither had Nighthawk earlier when he had checked.

If Preacher couldn't see them, he was confident that they couldn't see him and his companions, either. If he had been alone, he could have given them the slip without much trouble. Even if he'd been traveling with just Audie and Nighthawk, they would have left Ozark's men far behind with no hope of trailing them. But a group this large, including two who were inexperienced when it came to chases like this, couldn't help but leave plenty of signs. They would just have to stay far enough ahead of Ozark's men that eventually the pursuers would be worn out and low on supplies and might finally give up.

The middle of the day came and went. As the afternoon passed, the group had to stop more and more often to rest the horses. During one such halt on one of the narrow terraces, Preacher walked over to where Annie had taken the twins out of their cradleboard slings. She had unwrapped them from their blankets and was checking their diapers. The infants seemed happy, cooing as they waved their arms and legs.

"Those are nice beadwork designs on the blankets," Preacher commented. "I was lookin' at 'em earlier and didn't recognize which tribe did 'em. Did they come from the Flatheads?"

Annie laughed softly and said, "No, Jonathan did the beadwork on these blankets. He did it to pass the time while Ozark was holding him prisoner. I was a little surprised Ozark allowed him to have the supplies, but I suppose he wasn't a totally inhuman monster all the time."

Preacher bent over and fingered one of the blankets.

"Your husband did this, eh?" he said. "Fine work. Did he learn from watchin' the Indians?"

"I think Bluebird may have taught him some of it. They were friends. But Jonathan always had an artistic bent." Annie shook her head. "I know you probably have a hard time believing that a man could have a fine talent like that and still be the leader of a gang of outlaws."

"Oh, I can believe it," Preacher said. "Most folks have a wider range o' things inside 'em than you'd think."

Audie had walked up in time to hear the conversation. He put in, "The French philosopher Blaise Pascal said, 'Human Nature is, in truth, a union of opposites that are not only incongruous but are contrary and conflicting.'"

"Ain't that what I just said?" Preacher asked. He grinned. "Does that make me as smart as that Blazer fella?"

His grin disappeared before Audie could respond as Preacher noticed something else. Leaning forward, he stared at the blankets Annie had spread on the ground next to the twins. He muttered something under his breath.

"What was that, Preacher?" Audie said.

"Well, son of a—" Preacher pointed at the blankets. "Look at that, Audie."

The former professor studied the blankets intently for a moment.

"There's some fine beadwork," he said. "I don't recognize the tribe."

"Jonathan Collins did it."

"Really? It's unusual to see such quality from someone who wasn't raised in the tradition of doing beadwork like that."

"Now look at it this way," Preacher said.

He picked up one of the blankets, turned it ninety degrees, shook it out, and then laid it down flat on the ground so that its bottom overlapped slightly with the top of the other blanket.

"Now what do you see?" he asked.

Audie's eyes widened. "Good heavens! It's a map!"

Annie frowned and said, "Really? I don't see it."

"Them lines there are mountains," Preacher said, pointing out which designs he meant. "And that there's a river."

"I thought they were just pretty designs."

"You got to turn the blankets just right for things to match up, and it helps to be familiar with this country around here."

"Indeed," Audie said. "Now that I know what I'm looking at, I recognize several landmarks." He leaned down and put a finger against some of the beadwork near the top of the lower blanket. "This is approximately where we are right now."

Preacher leaned in from the other side and traced a path on the other blanket with a fingertip.

"Look here. This is a trail o' some sort, and it leads up here to this area that's got several circles o' beads around it."

"Concentric circles like that make it look like a target," Audie said. "That must be a location of some importance. It's so obvious once you realize what you're looking at. How in heaven's name did we miss it until now?"

"The blankets were nearly always wrapped around the young'uns, so you couldn't see the whole thing laid out like that. Anytime they were unwrapped, you were busy messin' with the little ones, changin' diapers or feedin' 'em and such, and you weren't thinkin' about nothin' else. As soon as you finished with what you were doin', you'd wrap the blankets around 'em again, so you still couldn't see it."

Annie still looked a little doubtful, but she said, "I suppose I can make out what you're talking about. But why in the world would Jonathan put a map in beadwork on these blankets?"

"After he decorated 'em, what did he do?"

"He asked me to use them with the children and . . . and to always keep them close by."

Preacher nodded. "He was tryin' to tell you somethin'. He wanted you to keep the young'uns safe, of course, but he wanted you to keep these blankets with 'em and take care o' them, too. Because they show the way to somethin' important."

"But what could it be?" Annie asked.

"I don't know," Preacher replied with a shake of his head. "But there's one way to find out." He knelt beside the blankets and once again put his finger on the concentric circles that marked a location in the mountains north of them. "Whatever it is, it's right there—and that's where we're goin'."

Once the discovery had been made, Preacher called Nighthawk and Little Bear over and showed the blanket map to them, as well.

When Preacher asked Little Bear about the target-like design, the young man shook his head and said he had no idea what it signified.

"I've never been that far northwest of the village," he said. "I don't know what's up there."

"Did your husband ever travel to those parts?" Preacher asked Annie.

"Not that I know of," she said, "but that doesn't really mean anything. Jonathan . . . was gone a lot. I don't know where he was during all those times. It's possible he went to that place, whatever it is."

With Ozark's men likely gaining on them with every minute that passed, they couldn't afford to wait around. As soon as the horses had rested enough, they mounted up again and rode out, but instead of heading up the next ridge, they followed the terrace-like shoulder. It ran north and south, and north was the direction they wanted to go.

By nightfall, they had covered several more miles. Preacher kept the group going even as darkness gathered around them. The pursuers would have to stop for the night because of the possibility of losing the trail, but Preacher and his companions were able to keep moving.

Preacher could steer by the stars winking into existence in the ebony sky above them. There was no chance of them veering off in the wrong direction. Audie and Nighthawk were just as capable of steering by the stars.

Eventually, though, they had to stop. The horses couldn't keep going, and neither could Annie and Little Bear. They weren't used to spending long hours in the saddle as they had today.

Preacher found a good spot to camp up against a bluff. It would be a cold camp, though, since they couldn't risk a fire. They would have to make do with jerky and leftover biscuits for supper.

Edward and Elizabeth each had a few teeth, but they couldn't handle jerky, of course. Audie crumbled one of the biscuits and moistened it to make a sort of mush. It wasn't much of a supper for growing youngsters, but it was the best they could do.

"I wish I could still feed them," Annie commented. "But they were gone long enough that I'm afraid that's not a possibility anymore. My milk has dried up."

Little Bear looked embarrassed at the mention of breast-feeding. He shuffled away from the campfire to tend the horses.

Audie continued using a finger to scoop up some of the mush and put it in the infants' mouths, first one and then the other. Annie said, "Let me help," and sat down cross-legged beside him. Audie had both twins in his lap but shifted one of them over to her, then held the bowl of mush so she could dip her finger into it as well.

The light from the stars was bright enough that Preacher could see the smile on Annie's face as she beamed down at the baby in her lap. He was glad that he and his friends had been able to re-unite them.

Annie had sent the twins away so they would be safe, and now they were back in danger, but the mountain man could tell that she had regretted that decision and was happy to be with her children again.

Now the challenge would be to keep them all safe until they reached someplace where they could be protected against Mack Ozark and his men. Maybe that marked location on the map was just such a place.

Preacher had his doubts about that, however. He was generally familiar with the Bitterroot Mountains and knew there were no settlements in the direction they were traveling unless it was one he had never heard of.

That didn't seem likely. It probably would have been better for them to head south as they fled from Ozark's men. Eventually, they would have reached Santa Fe. The authorities there would have looked after Annie and the little ones.

But it was too late for that now. The way things had worked out, the outlaws were between Preacher's party and any safety they might have found to the south. All they could do now was continue heading north.

Preacher and Nighthawk hunkered on their heels and gnawed on jerky while Audie and Annie fed the babies. Preacher heard Little Bear moving around where Horse and the other mounts and pack animals were picketed. Dog was off hunting somewhere, trying to find a small animal for his supper.

Preacher's head jerked up as he heard a sudden scuffle of feet from somewhere close by. A second later, someone grunted, and he could tell the sound came from the other side of the horses.

Trouble—and that was where Little Bear was!

CHAPTER 22

Preacher sprang to his feet with Nighthawk right beside him. They rushed around the horses and spotted several struggling figures in the shadows.

At that moment, one of the shapes broke free of the others and let out a yell. That had to be Little Bear.

The young man surprised Preacher by whirling around and throwing a punch at the nearest figure. Little Bear was fighting back instead of fleeing.

His attack was awkward, though, and the man easily avoided the blow. He lashed out and his fist connected with Little Bear's face. The stocky young man stumbled backward a couple of steps and fell.

Preacher suspected these intruders were some of Mack Ozark's men. It appeared only a few of them had stumbled upon the camp, but the main party could be nearby.

Because of that possibility, Preacher didn't haul out his Colts and open fire on the men, although he could have and probably would have gunned down all of them if he had.

Instead, he and Nighthawk leaped to the attack, wanting to dispose of these outlaws without creating a lot of commotion and attracting the attention of any other varmints who might be within hearing.

The man who had struck Little Bear followed up on that, rushing after the young man and leaning down to swing a fist at him again.

That fist stopped short and the blow never fell as Preacher met it with the palm of his left hand. The nighttime gloom was too thick for anybody to see very well, but Preacher's eyes were keen enough that he could tell what he was doing.

The attacker grunted in surprise as his fist seemed to run into a rock wall that somehow closed around it and held it in place with inexorable force.

A heartbeat later, Preacher's right fist exploded in the man's face and crushed his nose. The impact drove him backward and he would have fallen if Preacher hadn't still grasped his hand so tightly.

Preacher jerked the man back toward him, and this time he hit the intruder in the belly, hooking his right fist into the man's midsection as hard as he could. When Preacher let go of him and stepped back, the man fell to the ground, gagging and retching.

Meanwhile, Nighthawk had gotten his hands on the other two men. His long, incredibly strong fingers wrapped around their throats as he lifted them until their feet were off the ground and their legs flailed around.

They kicked wildly and pawed at Nighthawk's hands in utter futility for a moment before the giant Crow warrior slammed their heads together.

Preacher winced as he heard the sound of bone shattering. At least one of the men had a broken skull; quite possibly both.

Sometimes, Nighthawk just didn't know his own strength.

When he let go of the men, they fell bonelessly to the ground and sprawled there. Preacher had a hunch both of them were dead, or soon would be.

But the man Preacher had tangled with was still alive. He dropped to one knee beside him, grabbed the man's hair with his left hand, and yanked his head back.

With his right hand, he held the razor-sharp edge of his knife to the drawn-tight skin of the man's throat.

"You know it won't take much effort for me to open up your gullet clean from one side to the other, old son," Preacher said in a quiet voice that conveyed a tone of deadly menace. "Just a leetle pressure on this blade and you'll be spoutin' blood five feet in front of you. If you don't want that to happen, you'll answer my questions mighty quick-like and tell me the truth."

The man couldn't nod or speak with Preacher's knife so tight against his throat like that, but he managed to make a slight noise and lifted both hands, palms out, as if he were surrendering.

Preacher took it to mean that and lessened the pressure on the blade just enough so the man could swallow without cutting his own throat.

"Are you one o' Ozark's men?" Preacher asked, leaning close to the prisoner and keeping his voice down.

"Y-Yeah."

"Were there just three of you in this bunch?"

"Th-That's right. Just me and Dooley and Fred."

"Dooley and Fred are done for, but you're still alive and might stay that way if you cooperate," Preacher said. "How close are the rest?"

"I . . . I don't know. We split up . . . to cover more ground . . ."

"How many followed us from Ozark's compound?"

"Six . . . sixteen men."

"Why are those young'uns so damned important to him?"

Preacher figured there was a good chance the man didn't know the answer to that question, but he didn't see any harm in asking it.

"He . . . he never said. He just told us . . . to bring them back . . . just like they left . . . with their blankets . . . and everything."

Preacher's mouth quirked a little in the darkness. Without knowing it, the outlaw had confirmed Preacher's suspicion.

It wasn't Edward and Elizabeth who were important to Mack

Ozark, although he probably figured it would be a good idea if he had them in his hands to use as possible leverage in the future. And maybe just to get back at Jonathan Collins.

No, it was the blankets that mattered to the boss outlaw, and the map that Collins had concealed in the beadwork was the only reason Preacher could think of for that to be true.

Preacher was sure now the map would lead them to something hidden at the circle-marked location, and if it meant so much to Ozark, chances were it was something valuable. The whole thing was starting to come together in Preacher's head and make sense now.

As Preacher was mulling that over, the prisoner asked haltingly, "Are . . . are you gonna kill me?"

"Well, now, I reckon that'd be the smartest thing to do. Wouldn't take but a second to cut your throat, and then we wouldn't ever have to worry about you no more."

"Don't, mister! Please! You let me go and I'll turn around and head the other way. You'll never see me again, I swear it!"

"Are you tryin' to tell me you're more scared o' me than you are of Mack Ozark?" Preacher asked. "Because I just plumb don't believe that. If I was to let you go, sure enough, as soon as you were well away from here, you'd double-cross us and go runnin' right back to the rest of Ozark's bunch."

"No, sir, I give you my word, I wouldn't! I don't even like most of those fellas who work for him. They're a wicked bunch, mister. They were a bad influence on me after I fell in with 'em. I wish I never had—"

The man fell silent as Preacher took the knife away from his throat. He must have believed that his pleas had convinced Preacher to spare him.

A second later, Preacher turned the knife and slammed the brass pommel at the end of its handle against the man's head. The outlaw jerked and then stilled, knocked unconscious.

Preacher cut some strips off the man's shirt and used them to bind his wrists behind him. He tied the man's feet, as well, and then gagged him.

As Preacher came to his feet, he said to Nighthawk, "Toss this varmint in the brush and leave him. When he comes to, maybe he can thrash around enough that some of his friends will find him. If they don't . . . well, maybe a mountain lion or a bear'll be the one to come across him."

Nighthawk grunted in agreement. That wouldn't be a good way to go—but the man shouldn't have set out to rob and kill folks, and for sure he shouldn't have tried to steal a woman's young'uns away from her.

While Nighthawk was doing that, Preacher went over to Little Bear, who had gotten back to his feet, and asked, "Are you all right, son?"

"Yes, I think so." Little Bear took hold of his chin and worked his jaw back and forth. "He hit me pretty hard, but nothing seems to be broken. And at least they didn't take me completely by surprise this time! I realized they were there before they jumped me, just not in time to yell a warning to you and the others."

"That's all right. You put up a good scrap and raised enough of a ruckus for us to realize that somethin' was goin' on. That's about as good as a yell. Maybe even better, since you didn't know whether more of Ozark's men were close by."

"Are they?"

Preacher said, "That fella couldn't tell me. We have to figure they are. Because of that, we need to light a shuck outta here."

"The horses have barely had time to rest."

"I know, and I don't like it," Preacher said. "But I ain't gonna be easy in mind until we've put some more distance betwixt ourselves and those varmints chasin' us. You go tell Audie and Annie we're gonna be pullin' out soon. I reckon I'll do a mite of scoutin' around before we start."

* * *

When Preacher moved off into the darkness, he let out a low whistle that most people would have believed was the call of a night bird.

But he knew that if Dog heard the summons, the big cur would return as quickly as possible.

Preacher had to whistle twice more before Dog appeared out of the shadows as if by magic. Dog could move through the brush almost as silently as Preacher.

Dropping to a knee beside him, Preacher told Dog to hunt. Dog drifted off into the night. Preacher waited for five minutes, and when Dog returned and didn't seem bothered by anything, the mountain man knew that no enemies were close by.

That was a relief. Preacher headed back to camp with Dog following him.

He found Nighthawk getting the horses ready to ride while Little Bear packed up the camp and Audie and Annie prepared the twins. When the infants were wrapped securely once more in those all-important blankets, they were loaded into the cradleboard slings.

Tired from traveling, they were cranky and wanted to settle down for a night's sleep, but Preacher figured they would quiet down and doze off from the horse's steady movement once they got started.

He hoped so, because he didn't know how far the sound of a crying baby would travel at night, up here in the thin air of the high country.

He swung up into the saddle on Horse's back and waved the party forward. Annie and Little Bear came next, flanking the pack horse carrying the twins in their slings. Audie and Nighthawk brought up the rear.

Audie had been staying close to the babies during the journey, but with pursuit possibly coming up fast behind them, Preacher wanted both of his old friends back there, ready to fight a delaying action if need be.

He had no doubt that both Audie and Nighthawk would sacrifice their lives to protect the infants if things ever came down to that. So would he, and he figured Little Bear would, too.

Those two little ones might not know it, but they had some good folks protecting them.

Preacher told Dog to scout. The hound loped off into the darkness. If he encountered any signs of danger, he would be back to alert the mountain man to its presence.

Despite the urgency of their situation, Preacher had to set a deliberate pace. There were ravines and gullies in these parts, and he didn't want to lead his companions into any of them. Any kind of accident would just slow them down more.

Even without rushing, they made steady progress. It could have been pure bad luck that the small search party had stumbled across them, Preacher reflected, and it was possible none of Ozark's other men were very close behind.

Even knowing that, he would feel better once they had covered more ground.

The stars wheeled through the ebony sky above them as they continued northward. As Preacher had hoped, Edward and Elizabeth fell asleep in their slings and slumbered peacefully. It had to be long after midnight when the mountain man called another halt and told his companions they would stop for a few hours.

Annie and Little Bear were both stumbling with exhaustion when they dismounted and moved away from their horses.

"You two get some sleep," Preacher told them. "We'll look after things."

"What about you, though?" Annie asked. "You must be tired, too."

"Shoot, me and Audie and Nighthawk are used to goin' without sleep durin' times of trouble. And we'll trade off standin' guard, too, so each of us can get a little shut-eye. Don't worry about us."

"Preacher is right, Mrs. Collins," Audie added. "Why, I feel almost as fresh as a daisy."

Nighthawk let out one of his grunts that passed for laughter.

"Yes, I know, none of us are exactly what you'd call fragrant," Audie said. "But you know what I mean."

Annie and Little Bear spread their bedrolls. Audie got the babies from their slings and nestled them next to Annie, between her and the Salish youth. As far as Preacher could tell, the young woman was sound asleep almost as soon as she had closed her eyes.

Audie volunteered for the first watch, Nighthawk for the second, and Preacher would get up early and take the third. It was so late now that none of them would get much sleep, but like all seasoned frontiersmen, they knew how to snatch what moments of rest they could and let that be enough to keep them going.

Preacher seemed to have barely closed his eyes when Nighthawk touched his shoulder and said softly, "Umm."

Preacher sat up, instantly wide awake, and asked in a half-whisper, "Any trouble?"

The Crow warrior shook his head. Preacher stood up while Nighthawk stretched out and closed his eyes.

The eastern sky held just the faintest tinge of gray. The sun would rise in another couple of hours. Preacher figured they would be on the move again before that happened.

A chill had crept into the air. A fire would have felt good, and he would have paid a hefty price for a cup of strong black coffee right now. He didn't want to risk that, however, so he would just have to do without, as would the others.

Later this morning, maybe, if they could find a good spot, they would stop for a little while and fix some breakfast.

He walked back and forth to warm up and stay alert. The night was quiet. Dog padded into camp from somewhere and sat, then lay down and rested his head on his front paws. Some of the horses moved around idly.

Preacher stopped short as the hair on the back of his neck stood up and the skin there prickled. His instincts were trying to tell him that something was wrong.

A second later, Dog lifted his head and growled softly. Whatever it was that Preacher had sensed, Dog was aware of it, too.

Preacher's hands dropped to the butts of the Colts holstered on his hips. He didn't draw the revolvers, but he was ready as he turned slowly. His senses, already on high alert, were especially keen as he searched the gray gloom around him for any sign of danger.

He heard a faint snap, recognized it as the sound of a twig breaking under someone's foot, and whirled in that direction as he pulled iron. His knees bent as he dropped into a crouch and the Colts came up.

A gun roared and muzzle flame spurted from the nearby brush. Preacher felt as much as heard the wind-rip of a rifle ball slicing through the air inches from his head.

A split-second later, before he could return the fire, a horde of howling demons burst out of the fading night shadows and charged into the camp.

CHAPTER 23

Preacher got off a single shot with each Colt before one of the attackers crashed into him and knocked him off his feet. He landed hard on his back with the man's weight on top of him. That knocked the air out of his lungs, but he managed to hang on to the guns in his hands.

The sky had grayed enough for him to see the man's silhouette looming above him. The attacker screeched wordlessly as he raised his right arm. He was holding something, and Preacher felt pretty sure it was a tomahawk.

He rammed the muzzle of the right-hand Colt under the man's chin and thumbed off a shot.

The blast blew off most of the Indian's face and pitched him backward. Without the weight pinning him to the ground, Preacher rolled over and came up on one knee.

The confusion of battle surrounded him. Audie, Nighthawk, and Dog were fighting with the marauders. Preacher couldn't risk a shot with his friends in the line of fire. He pouched the irons as he surged onto his feet and threw himself into the ruckus.

He had a tomahawk, too, tucked behind his belt on the right side, around toward the small of his back. He pulled it free and swung it at the head of a man struggling with Annie as she screamed for help.

The roach of hair sticking up from the man's head, as well as the feather rising above it, told Preacher the attacker was an Indian.

The tomahawk struck the back of the man's head with devastating force, splintering bone and cleaving into the brain. Preacher jerked the weapon loose, grabbed the man's shoulder, and flung him aside. Already dead from the terrific blow, the corpse landed in a limp sprawl.

Preacher got his free arm around Annie and pulled her to him. She continued screaming and fought frantically against his grip for a few seconds. Her struggles subsided as she seemed to realize it was the mountain man who held her.

"Are you all right?" he asked her.

"I'm fine," she answered with hysteria edging into her voice. "The babies! Where are my babies?"

"I'll find 'em," Preacher promised. He pushed Annie against the trunk of a pine tree and told her, "Stay here."

A few yards away, Nighthawk had his hands full as four men attacked him, swinging knives and tomahawks at him. The massive Crow was armed with a knife and a tomahawk himself, along with incredible speed for a man of his size and bulk. He twisted and darted and whirled, parrying and blocking the attacks aimed at him. Metal clashed against metal and sparks flew.

Nighthawk wasn't simply defending himself, either. He seized every opening to carry the attack to his foes. His knife flashed out and buried cold steel in warm flesh. The tomahawk in his hand slashed throats and stove in skulls. The air around him and his opponents was filled with a dark mist as blood sprayed from severed arteries.

It was an awe-inspiring display of speed, skill, and savagery.

Audie was dealing with more than one attacker, too, putting his small size and quickness to good use as he dodged back and forth between them, causing the men to get tangled up with each other.

As one of the Indians lost his balance and started to fall even though he was windmilling his arms in a vain attempt to stay upright, Audie was ready with his knife. The man's throat was cut from side to side by the time he hit the ground.

Audie had to turn his back on the other attacker to accomplish that, however, and that gave the man a chance to grab him from behind. The warrior got both arms around Audie and lifted him into the air as he yipped shrilly in triumph.

Unfortunately, that positioned Audie so that he could kick backward and slam the heel of his boot into his captor's groin. The man's victory cry turned into a howl of agony. He lost his grip on Audie, who twisted as he fell and drove his knife into the man's belly.

Audie's weight dragged the blade down and opened up a gaping vertical wound through which the dying man's guts spilled. Shrieking, he fell to the ground and then pitched forward to spasm a couple of times before lying still in death.

Preacher took in all of that carnage in little more than the blink of an eye. He saw that Little Bear was putting up a fight, too, but the young man was no match for the warrior who had attacked him. Little Bear was on the ground as the enemy knelt on him and raised a knife high to strike.

Almost invisible in the gray light, Dog was just a streak of movement as he came out of nowhere and launched himself at the man about to kill Little Bear.

The big cur crashed into the warrior and knocked him off. Dog's teeth sank into the man's flesh and the powerful jaws clamped down. The warrior died with a hideous gurgle as Dog ripped his throat out.

Little Bear rolled over and tried to get up. Preacher moved in and grasped the young man's arm to lift him to his feet.

"You all right?" the mountain man asked.

"Y-Yes, thanks to Dog."

"Do you know where the babies are?"

"I haven't— No, wait! I think I saw one of the men grab them."

Little Bear pointed. "He was going that way the last I saw of him. Then that other man grabbed me and knocked me down—"

Preacher didn't wait to hear anymore. He ran in the direction Little Bear had pointed, calling over his shoulder, "Dog, hunt! Find the babies!"

Dog flashed past him a second later, running flat out.

Preacher followed, his long legs stretching and his wiry muscles carrying him quickly over the ground. He lost sight of Dog in the shadows that clung to the earth and coiled around the trees. Full daylight was still an hour or more away.

Dog wouldn't be relying solely on his sight, however. His keen sense of smell would be just as important in leading him to his quarry.

Preacher weaved between trees and around clumps of brush. He heard a horse whinny somewhere ahead of him. The attackers must have left their ponies nearby in order to sneak up on the camp on foot. The man who had grabbed the twins was trying to get back to those mounts and escape.

A yell sounded, followed by growls and snarls. Dog had caught up to the man he was after. Preacher ran even faster as a rifle boomed. If that varmint had shot Dog—

Hooves pounded the earth as several ponies burst out from some boulders that formed a rough ring at the base of a slope, having rolled down there in ages past. That would make a good place for early morning skulkers to leave their horses.

Growling still filled the air. Preacher was glad to hear it; the sound meant Dog was still alive.

He ran through a gap between two boulders but hadn't gotten a good look at what was going on before something whistled out of the gloom and struck him across the chest. His feet went out from under him as the impact knocked him backward. His head bounced off the hard ground with enough force to stun him.

Even though his muscles refused to obey his commands for a

moment, his ears still worked. He heard a pair of wailing cries rise and intertwine. The babies!

Edward and Elizabeth were here, and that knowledge was enough to energize Preacher's nerves and muscles. He groaned and rolled onto his side, then pushed himself up to his knees.

No sooner had he done that than he had to fling himself desperately to the side as a huge, speeding shape raced at him, threatening to trample him.

Preacher landed on his shoulder and rolled. The galloping pony barely missed him, passing by so close that Preacher felt it disturb the air around him.

The rider didn't try to wheel the pony around and make another attempt at trampling Preacher. Instead, he kept the animal moving fast, even banging his feet against its flanks to urge more speed out of it.

As Preacher got to his feet, he peered after the racing pony and saw a tall, broad-shouldered man on its back. Something about the warrior was familiar. A name leaped into Preacher's mind.

Standing Cloud!

Preacher had known when he and his companions left the Salish village that Standing Cloud bore a grudge against him. The warrior's eyes had been filled with hatred the last time Preacher saw him.

It came as no real surprise that Standing Cloud might follow them and try to take his revenge.

The yowl of an unhappy baby's cry drifted back to Preacher for a second before the early morning breeze snatched it away. Standing Cloud was getting away with at least one of the infants.

More hoofbeats sounded behind Preacher. He whirled around to meet this potential new threat, but his tension eased slightly when he recognized Little Bear sitting astride one of the horses from their camp.

"Preacher!" the young man called as he reined in and looked around. "Preacher, where are you?"

"Over here!" Preacher responded.

Little Bear kicked his mount into motion and rode swiftly toward the mountain man.

"Did you find the twins?" he asked as he hauled the horse to a stop.

"Standing Cloud got away with at least one of 'em."

"Standing Cloud! He came after us?"

"Yeah, I'm pretty sure it was him I saw gallopin' off. Let me have that horse."

Preacher would have preferred having his own stallion under him, but right now, he would take whatever mount he could get if it meant being able to give chase to Standing Cloud.

Little Bear swung down from the saddle and handed the reins to Preacher. Just as the mountain man took them, more crying came from inside the circle of boulders.

"He only got away with one of the little varmints," Preacher said. "Take care o' the one he left behind."

"Of course!"

Little Bear turned and ran through the gap between the boulders while Preacher practically leaped into the saddle and kicked the horse into a run.

He knew in which direction Standing Cloud had fled, but he could no longer hear the hoofbeats from the man's horse. His only option was to keep going and hope he caught up before anything bad happened to whichever of the twins Standing Cloud had ridden off with.

Eventually it would be light enough for Preacher to pick up the trail, but by that time, Standing Cloud might have too much of a lead.

Preacher's keen eyes searched the gloom ahead of him in the faint hope that he might catch a glimpse of his quarry. When fortune smiled on him, he almost missed it. He saw something from the corner of his right eye and swiveled his head to get a better look.

For a mere split-second, he saw the unmistakable figure of a man on horseback topping a ridge. The man dropped out of sight an instant later, but what Preacher had seen was imprinted on his brain.

He knew it had to be Standing Cloud. Nobody else was likely to be roaming around up here. The renegade warrior was no longer following the level bench but had turned to climb higher in the rugged terrain.

Preacher turned his mount and started up, too.

This ridge rose maybe a hundred feet before dropping off on the other side. Beyond it towered a sheer bluff.

Even in the dim light, Preacher could see well enough to realize that the landscape was vaguely familiar to him. He had been here before, as he had been most places west of the Mississippi, but it had been quite a few years since his last visit.

A memory nagged at the back of his mind. He recalled something about that bluff . . .

Abruptly, he remembered that a trail zigzagged back and forth up the sheer granite and sandstone cliff. It was just a narrow ledge, but it was wide enough for a man on horseback, especially if he dismounted and led the horse.

If Standing Cloud knew about that trail, he might plan on using it to give the slip to any possible pursuit. At this point, Preacher wasn't sure where else he could go.

Armed with that hunch, Preacher stopped trying to watch for any sign of Standing Cloud and just headed for that trail he'd recalled as fast as he could push the horse he was riding. The mount was a good one, strong and determined. He wasn't Horse, but then, Preacher knew better than to expect that.

They topped the ridge, dropped down through a rugged gulch choked with brush. That slowed them down, and the delay gnawed at Preacher's guts. However, all he could do was keep going, and a short time later, they worked their way through the obstacles and reached the bluff.

From there, Preacher followed the base of it until he found the spot where the trail started up. He had relied on his instincts to let him know he was going in the right direction, and they hadn't let him down.

Back to the east, the sky was considerably lighter now. A few streaks of reddish-gold were beginning to be visible in the gray. When Preacher paused at the foot of the trail and looked up, he was able to follow the ledge as it climbed, back and forth, toward the top.

Something moved up there. Preacher looked closer and a moment later, he discerned the figure of a buckskin-clad man leading a dappled Indian pony up the trail.

Standing Cloud hadn't gotten away from him. The warrior was a couple of hundred feet above him—and the thin cries of an unhappy baby told Preacher that Standing Cloud still had the stolen twin with him.

Preacher dismounted, wrapped the horse's reins around his left hand, and started up the ledge after them.

From time to time, Standing Cloud's pony dislodged pebbles that came bouncing down from one level of the trail to the next. A few of them hit Preacher, but none of them were large enough to cause any damage.

He hoped none of them would strike the horse because that might cause the animal to spook, and the ledge wasn't wide enough for that to be safe.

When those rocks stopped falling, Preacher figured that meant Standing Cloud had reached the top. There was no telling where he would go from there.

If he knew Preacher was following him, he might even lie in wait and try to get the drop on the mountain man. Preacher knew he was running a risk by continuing, but there was nothing else he could do.

He heard a scraping sound somewhere above him and paused to lean back and look up.

That was all the warning he had before a rock more than twice as big as a man's head rolled over the brink fifty feet above and plummeted straight at him.

CHAPTER 24

Preacher had only a second to react to the danger hurtling at him. Luckily, his reflexes had been finely honed by decades of surviving a perilous existence.

He flattened himself against the bluff and tightened his grip on the horse's reins. He would let them go and lose the animal if he had to, but he hoped he could keep the horse under control.

The rock shot past them, missing Preacher by no more than a couple of feet. It clipped the edge of the trail and bounded out farther away from the bluff as it continued falling to the ground far below.

"Come on," Preacher grated as he lunged up the trail and dragged the horse after him.

Instinct warned him, made him glance up just in time to see another rock falling toward him. He drove hard along the ledge as he tried to get himself and the horse clear.

They almost made it. The rock, which was only slightly smaller than the first one, struck the horse on the rump. The animal let out a shrill scream of pain and fear and reared up to paw at the air with its front hooves.

"No!" Preacher yelled, but of course it didn't do any good. The horse was badly spooked and its rear legs skittered around on the ledge.

The result was inevitable. Preacher knew that and let go of the reins so that he wouldn't be dragged off the trail when the horse fell. The horse maintained its balance for a moment, but when it tried to drop its front hooves back onto the ledge, the rear ones slid and went out from under it.

Preacher's lips drew back from his teeth in a grimace as the horse fell heavily and landed at the very edge of the trail. Its weight and the flailing legs tipped it over the brink. The horse screamed again as it fell to its death, a disturbingly human sound that came to an abrupt, grim ending.

Preacher was already moving again before the horse hit the ground at the base of the bluff. He charged up the trail, reached the next spot where it turned back on itself, and swung himself around the turn at dangerously high speed. He was sure-footed, though, and kept his balance without any trouble.

Another rock crashed onto the trail ahead of him. Instead of bouncing farther out, this one went up into the air, landed on the ledge again, and began rolling toward him.

Preacher jerked a glance over his shoulder, thinking that maybe he could get back around the turn and let the rock tumble on past him harmlessly. But it was too far away, he saw. He wasn't going to have time for that.

Nor could he hug the cliff face and avoid the rock that way. The trail just wasn't wide enough.

There was only one thing he could do, Preacher realized, and it had to be timed perfectly.

Just before the rock slammed into him, he leaped into the air and pulled up his feet as high as he could.

He cleared the rock by inches, but his feet hit the back of it lightly as he came down, throwing him off-balance just enough to make him sprawl forward on his belly. He scrambled to his feet and continued running up the trail.

Part of him wanted to pull his Colts and blast some shots at the rim to force Standing Cloud away from the edge, but since he didn't know where the baby was, he couldn't risk it.

Standing Cloud had to run out of rocks to toss down at him sooner or later, blast it!

That time might have arrived, because no more rocks plummeted down from the top of the bluff. Preacher kept going until he reached the top of the trail and stepped out onto the bluff, which was relatively level and stretched back a good quarter of a mile before the next slope.

He came to an abrupt halt because Standing Cloud was waiting for him about twenty feet away. The Salish warrior stood there glaring as he held one of the infants against his chest. His left arm was looped around the baby, who fretted and squirmed.

Standing Cloud raised his other hand and held it out toward Preacher.

"Stay where you are," the warrior ordered. "Come closer and I throw child over edge."

"You speak better English than I figured you did," Preacher said.

"Good enough to tell you I kill you."

"You ain't managed to do that so far, old son."

"Drop guns," Standing Cloud ordered.

Preacher shook his head. "I don't reckon I will."

"I throw baby off cliff!"

Preacher had to take a chance. Sometimes that was the only way.

"I don't believe you'll do that," he said, keeping his voice calm and level. "You're smart enough to know that if I don't have to worry about hittin' that kid, I'll fill you so full o' lead that you'd sink all the way to the bottom of the ocean." He laughed. "I don't expect you've ever seen the ocean, but it's mighty deep."

"You not care if I kill baby?" Standing Cloud challenged.

"Oh, I care, all right. That's why you'll be dead half a second later if you do anything to hurt it." Preacher cocked his head a little to the side and added a question. "Is that the boy or the girl you got there?"

Standing Cloud's scowl darkened. "Is little boy."

Preacher had a hunch his question had accomplished its purpose, which was to remind Standing Cloud that he had a human being in his arms, a young, innocent life that deserved a chance to continue.

"Now listen here," the mountain man said, hoping to take advantage of this opportunity. "I don't believe you really want to hurt that young'un. You're a warrior. You don't make war on kids. You might've wanted to give those babies back to Mack Ozark, but that don't mean you wanted any harm to come to them."

"Salish people owe nothing to white woman and her squalling brats!"

"Maybe not," Preacher allowed.

"You and your friends enemies to Salish people."

"Not at all. You could ask Little Bear about that."

Standing Cloud made a face like he had a bad taste in his mouth. "Boy is traitor to his own people!"

"No, he's not, and you know it. He's got good reason for hatin' Ozark." Anger surged up inside Preacher at the insult to Little Bear. "Just because he wants to help Mrs. Collins and those children don't make him a traitor."

"Mack Ozark trades with village. Helps us."

"And that don't make him any less of a monster, either. He's just takin' advantage of you, Standin' Cloud. You figure turnin' Annie and her babies over to him would put him in your debt, but he wouldn't give a damn about that, not really. He'd still just use you for whatever you could do for him. That's what varmints like Ozark do. They use people and then cast 'em aside when they're done with 'em. That's what he did to Jonathan Collins, and he was downright evil about it, too. He made sure Collins suffered the torments o' the damned before he died." Preacher nodded emphatically. "He's liable to do the same thing to the Salish people one o' these days."

Standing Cloud's jaw was a tight, grim line.

"You talk, talk, talk," he said. "I seek vengeance! What would you have us do?"

"Well, that's simple enough," Preacher said. "We fought before. We'll have it out again—and this time it'll be to the death."

Standing Cloud's eyes lit up with anticipation at that idea, but then he became suspicious again almost immediately.

"What I do with baby?"

Preacher looked around, saw a little hummock of ground with grass around it about fifty feet away from the edge. He pointed and said, "Lay the little varmint over there. He ought to be safe enough."

"I set baby down, you shoot me!"

Preacher shook his head. "I give you my word I won't use my guns. We'll settle this however you want. Knives, tomahawks, bare knuckles, you name it."

Standing Cloud frowned narrowly at him and demanded, "Your word?"

"My word," Preacher said.

The warrior glared at him for a few heartbeats longer, then turned and strode over to the hummock. As he placed Edward on the ground, he looked over his shoulder and asked, "Can baby crawl?"

"Yeah, he can, some."

Standing Cloud looked at the brink, back at the baby, and then a second time at the bluff's edge. He shook his head.

"Too close. Dangerous. Baby might crawl off." He picked up the infant again. "Take him over there by trees."

"All right," Preacher agreed. "Reckon that's pretty good thinkin'. And it just goes to prove I was right when I said you don't really want any harm comin' to those little ones."

Standing Cloud glanced back at him. "Maybe I give them to Ozark. Maybe I do not." The warrior's mouth twisted in a snarl. "But either way, I kill you!"

"Fair enough," Preacher said. "You can try."

Standing Cloud carried the infant to the edge of a line of trees and found a good spot to place him on the ground where Edward would be comfortable. The baby had stopped crying and now had his thumb in his mouth, sucking on it furiously.

The little one was hungry, Preacher realized. Maybe he'd have him back with the others soon and Audie and Annie could come up with something to put in the empty little belly.

"Be safe there," Standing Cloud said with a decisive nod as he straightened. He turned and walked back toward Preacher, who was unbuckling his gun belt.

"What do you reckon?" Preacher asked. "What sort o' fight is this gonna be?"

"Knives," Standing Cloud said.

"Knives it is."

Preacher coiled his gun belt and holsters and set them aside. He pulled his tomahawk from behind his belt and dropped it beside the Colts. Then he drew his knife from its sheath just behind his right hip.

He had just raised his eyes to Standing Cloud when the warrior charged at him, knife upraised in his right hand and poised to strike.

CHAPTER 25

However, Standing Cloud had launched his attack too soon and left himself with too much ground to cover before he reached his opponent. Preacher had no trouble whirling aside and getting out of his way.

The mountain man lashed out with the knife in his hand, thinking that he might draw first blood as his enemy's charge missed, but Standing Cloud veered instantly to his right, away from Preacher, when he realized his miscalculation. Preacher's blade missed his left shoulder by inches.

"Too slow, white man," Standing Cloud taunted as he turned to face Preacher again.

"I ain't the one who was lumberin' along like an ox," Preacher shot back. "If you think you're fleet-footed as a deer, old son, you're sadly mistaken."

Standing Cloud snarled and came at him again, moving much more deliberately this time. He waved his knife back and forth in front of him, but Preacher didn't fall for the trick of watching it. He studied Standing Cloud instead, and when he saw the warrior's muscles tense, he was ready.

Standing Cloud leaped at him, drove the knife in low, then whipped it up.

Preacher hadn't fallen for the feint, either. His blade met

Standing Cloud's and turned it aside with a ringing clash of steel against steel.

Preacher sprang back. Frustrated, Standing Cloud thrust again, but he was more careless this time. Preacher not only avoided the strike, but he was also able to land an attack of his own during the split-second when his opponent was off-balance and open.

The razor-sharp edge of Preacher's knife raked across Standing Cloud's forearm. It wasn't a deep wound because Standing Cloud was already pulling away, but it was first blood and Standing Cloud didn't like it.

Bellowing in rage, the warrior came at Preacher again, slashing wildly back and forth. Preacher parried some of the attacks and avoided others.

Then he realized that, whether it was intentional or not, Standing Cloud was forcing him steadily toward the edge of the bluff.

Aware of that potential danger now, Preacher took a step to his right, then another. Standing Cloud lunged to his left and tried to turn Preacher back. The warrior committed himself too much, and Preacher darted even farther in that direction. In order to keep facing him, Standing Cloud had to swing around.

That neat maneuver had taken only seconds, but in that time, Preacher had turned the tables on his opponent.

Now Standing Cloud was the one with his back mostly toward the brink.

If that bothered him, he didn't show it. He attacked as ferociously as ever, and Preacher had his hands full for the next few minutes fending off a series of slashes and thrusts and jabs that were delivered almost too fast for the eye to follow.

Like all battles, the tides of this one ebbed and flowed. Eventually, Standing Cloud began to tire. His movements became just a little slower. It was barely noticeable—but Preacher noticed.

He deliberately made a misstep. Standing Cloud came at him with a burst of renewed energy, but that burned out quickly and left him even more tired than before.

As they fought, they had moved closer and closer to the edge. Now it was only about twenty feet away. Preacher waited until Standing Cloud launched another barely controlled assault and dropped underneath the warrior's blade. He felt the steel brush his hair as it narrowly missed him.

Preacher caught himself on his left hand and left hip and brought his right leg around. It caught Standing Cloud at an angle behind his left knee and swept both legs out from under the warrior. Standing Cloud went down hard, landing on his rump, and the fall caused both his arms to shoot into the air.

Preacher sprang up and kicked with his right foot. It struck the wrist of Standing Cloud's right hand with enough force to make the man lose his grip on his knife. The weapon sailed back away from him, landed near the brink, bounced—and vanished over the edge.

Well, that little move had worked out better than he'd hoped for, Preacher thought. He had figured he might disarm his opponent, but now Standing Cloud's knife was gone, out of his reach for good.

But that surprising outcome had a disadvantage, too, and as Preacher backed off and held his own blade ready, his mouth tightened into a grim line.

Standing Cloud was winded. He sat up and stayed there with his shoulders hunched and his chest heaving for a long moment before climbing wearily to his feet.

"Knife or no knife, this is fight to the death," he said. He raised his hands and beckoned for Preacher to attack him.

"Son of a . . ." the mountain man muttered. He half-turned, drew back his arm, and threw his knife so that the blade buried itself in the earth next to where his gun belt, holstered Colts, and tomahawk lay.

It was a foolish gesture, he knew, but sometimes that was what honor demanded.

Before he could turn back to Standing Cloud, the warrior roared and charged. The brief rest might have done him some good; he was fast enough to tackle Preacher around the waist and drive him to the ground.

Preacher hammered both fists against the sides of Standing Cloud's neck where it met his shoulders. Standing Cloud grunted from the brutal impact, but he didn't let go. In fact, he tightened his grip on Preacher. His arms had shifted upward so they put more pressure on Preacher's lower ribs.

His ribs might crack under that bear hug, Preacher knew. He rolled over a couple of times but couldn't shake Standing Cloud loose. He got his hands on Standing Cloud's face and dug his thumbs at the man's eyes. Standing Cloud jerked his head back and forth to avoid the crippling attack. Preacher couldn't hang on to him.

Balling his right hand into a mallet-like fist, Preacher swung it up and around and brought it down with all his strength on the top of Standing Cloud's head. He struck the warrior like that again and again, as if his fist were a hammer and Standing Cloud's head a nail he was trying to drive into a board.

That constant jarring finally weakened Standing Cloud's hold. Preacher grabbed his arms and pulled them loose. Standing Cloud tried to get another grip on him, but Preacher drove both hands up under the warrior's chin and levered Standing Cloud's head back so far that the man had no choice except to break away from Preacher. Standing Cloud threw himself backward and rolled to put some distance between him and the mountain man.

Preacher was glad for the respite. His ribs twanged and ached from the bear hug as he climbed to his feet. Standing Cloud was a mighty strong varmint.

Standing Cloud made it upright again, too. He stood a dozen feet from Preacher, slowly shaking his head as if it were clogged with cobwebs and he couldn't get them cleared away.

He summoned up enough breath and energy to repeat, "To the death . . . white man . . . That is what you said."

"Unless you want to call it off," Preacher countered, knowing how unlikely it was Standing Cloud would ever accept that.

Another furious charge was the warrior's only answer.

This time, Preacher met the attack head-on. Both of them were too tired and battered for anything fancy now. Instead, they stood there toe to toe, slugging away at each other, brute strength and endurance against brute strength and endurance.

Such an epic contest couldn't last long, despite the almost superhuman abundance of strength and stamina each man possessed. A battle of the titans, Audie might have called it. But sooner or later, one of them would make a mistake.

In this case, it was Preacher.

One of Standing Cloud's roundhouse swings slipped unimpeded through Preacher's defense and exploded on the mountain man's jaw. The punch felt like it was almost strong enough to tear his head off.

His head stayed where it belonged on his shoulders, but suddenly Preacher found himself sailing through the air. He landed on his back with bone-jarring, tooth-rattling force. The world spun crazily around him, whirling not only with dizzying speed but seemingly in the wrong direction. Preacher was a whisker away from losing consciousness.

He clung to awareness grimly, knowing that if he passed out, Standing Cloud would see to it that he never came to.

But that might not matter, because the warrior was coming after him, clearly intent on leaping on top of Preacher and pinning him to the ground.

Once he had done that, he would clamp his hands around the mountain man's throat and choke the life out of him.

Somewhere deep inside him, Preacher found the strength to pull his legs up and then thrust his feet out as Standing Cloud sprang at him. The kick drove into Standing Cloud's belly and doubled him over, but his weight and momentum continued carrying him forward. With a herculean effort, Preacher straightened and lifted his legs and tossed Standing Cloud over and behind him.

Preacher didn't hear the warrior hit the ground.

Even in his somewhat addled state, that didn't seem right to Preacher. He heaved himself onto his stomach and lifted his head to peer toward the spot where Standing Cloud should have landed.

Sometime in the past few seconds, the world's rotation had slowed back to normal and it was turning the right way around now. Preacher blinked, shook his head, and stared at the empty ground where he expected to see Standing Cloud sprawled. With any luck, he would be unconscious.

Instead, there was no sign of the warrior, but Preacher saw that they had been a lot closer to the edge than he realized. The bluff dropped off sheer no more than ten feet away.

Oh, hell, Preacher thought.

Slowly, he pushed himself onto hands and knees and then struggled unsteadily to his feet. He took a few shaky steps before realizing that he probably shouldn't get too close to the edge, as wobbly as he was.

But he had to go close enough to peer over the brink and see Standing Cloud lying face down, fifty feet below at the base of the bluff. The warrior wasn't moving. A small, dark pool spread on the rocky ground around his head.

The way Standing Cloud was lying, he must have seen his death rushing up at him. Although the fall would have lasted only seconds, that was long enough for him to know what was going to happen.

Yet he had made no sound. No scream, no angry yell, nothing. Just silence as his life ended.

Preacher liked to think he had enough self-control that he would have gone out the same way if it had been him.

But he couldn't be sure of that.

He didn't say anything now, no utterances to mark Standing Cloud's passage from this life to the spirit world. The surly varmint wouldn't have appreciated that, and the most he would have said over Preacher's body was a shrill, triumphant yip.

Preacher just turned away from the brink and trudged toward the trees where Standing Cloud had left little Edward Collins.

CHAPTER 26

By the time Preacher rode up to the circle of boulders, mounted on the pony on which Standing Cloud had fled, not only were Little Bear and Elizabeth waiting for him there, but so were Audie, Nighthawk, and Annie Collins.

When Annie saw Preacher riding toward them, she cried out and ran to meet him. Preacher had Edward's blanket-wrapped form nestled in the crook of his left arm. He bent down from the pony's back to hand the infant to his mother.

"Here you go, ma'am," he said. "A mite hungry and annoyed, I expect, but other than that, safe and sound."

"Thank you, thank you!" Annie clutched the little boy in both arms and rocked him back and forth. "Oh, Edward, I was afraid I'd never see you again!"

Little Bear came up alongside the pony and asked, "Standing Cloud?"

Preacher shook his head.

Little Bear sighed. "He despised me, but he was a fine warrior and did many good things for our tribe."

"I'm sure he did." Preacher swung a leg over the pony's back and dropped to the ground. "But he got to thinkin' that he could trust Mack Ozark, and that was a mighty bad mistake."

The warrior Dog had killed still lay within the circle of boulders.

Preacher assumed he was the man Standing Cloud had left behind to watch the horses. On the way back here, he had figured out that it must have been Standing Cloud who hit him, stepping from concealment to do so. More than likely, he had used the horse-holder's empty rifle as a club to wallop the mountain man.

None of those details mattered now. The members of their little group were reunited.

"What about the rest of the bunch that was with Standing Cloud?" Preacher asked.

Nighthawk's emphatic grunt and slashing hand motion provided all the answer he needed.

"They won't bother us anymore," Audie added anyway. He was holding Elizabeth. The little girl was amusing herself by reaching over to tug on Audie's hair where it stuck out under his broad-brimmed hat. "But the possibility of pursuit from Ozark's men remains as likely as ever."

"So we'd better get movin' if we're gonna go on headin' toward that spot on the map Jonathan Collins left."

"Yes, we can still cover more ground today." Audie frowned in thought. "If fortune smiles upon us, we ought to reach that location late tomorrow."

"Let's ride, then," Preacher said.

The strain of everything they had gone through showed plainly on the faces of Annie and Little Bear. Even Audie was starting to look tired, although Nighthawk's features were as stony and expressionless as always. Preacher put his own weariness aside and set a brisk pace during that day's travel.

Nightfall found them camping in a canyon that angled to the northwest, deeper into the mountains. Preacher had recognized the canyon as soon as he saw it, late in the day. He knew it led to a pass that would take them even higher, to the level where they needed to be in order to reach the spot marked on the bead-work map.

During the day, Nighthawk had dropped back several times to

make sure pursuers weren't closing in on them. Each time, he had reported seeing no sign of Ozark's men.

"They're still back there, though," Preacher mused the last time Nighthawk had delivered that information, during a brief stop to rest the horses. "I can feel it in my gut, and in my bones, too."

"Umm," Nighthawk agreed.

Audie was there listening to the conversation while Annie and Little Bear checked on the twins. The former professor said, "Doesn't it seem as if Ozark's minions should have at least made an attempt to catch up to us by now?"

"Seems likely," Preacher said. "But the fact they haven't has set a new thought to percolatin' in my head."

"That perhaps they're not *trying* to catch up?" Audie said. "They might be content to simply follow us instead until they can figure out where we're going. Or, failing that, follow us to our destination, whatever it may be, and make their play against us there."

"That makes sense," Preacher said. "And it sure explains why they haven't jumped us yet."

"So, if that's true, what are we going to do about it?"

Preacher grinned. "Ain't much we can do, as far as I can see. But we can't afford to let our guard down, neither, since we don't know for sure that's what they're plannin'." He lifted his gaze to look toward the higher mountains to the northwest. "We'll keep goin' and play out the hand the way it's dealt."

Their camp that night had an oppressive feeling to it, probably because of the way the canyon walls loomed over them. The thick shadows didn't help.

Preacher was tempted to let them have a fire; if Ozark's men didn't intend to close in until Preacher and his friends reached their destination, then it didn't make any difference if the varmints knew where they were.

But as he had told Audie and Nighthawk, they had no guarantee of that. He'd hate to get this close to where they were going and then make a mistake that would cause them to be captured—or worse.

Despite the gloom, the night passed without incident. Everyone was still tired the next morning, but a little rest was better than none.

Audie approached Preacher that morning and said quietly, "Our supplies are getting low. You and I and Nighthawk can live off the land, of course, but I'm not sure the others can. And since we don't know what we'll find when we get to this place, we're going . . ."

"It's a problem, all right," Preacher allowed. "Chances are, we ain't gonna find a stockpile of supplies."

"I don't see how that's likely."

"There ain't no settlements for a long way, either."

"Ozark's compound is the closest we're going to find in these parts, I'm afraid."

"But there are probably some Indian villages where they'd be friendly to us," Preacher said.

"Friendly, yes, but would they protect us from Ozark and his band of outlaws?"

The mountain man shook his head. "Not likely. They'd figure that was a white man's problem, and it'd be up to us to solve it."

"So, eventually, we're going to have to return to that compound." Audie's voice was grim as he reached that conclusion.

"Yep. But I'm hopin' by then we'll have found somethin' to use as leverage against him. Or there's one other possibility."

Audie looked interested. "What's that?"

"All this time we've been thinkin' that Ozark sent a search party after us because that's what he did when the young'uns disappeared the first time. But he could've come along, too, chasin' us his own self this time instead of leavin' it to others. When we get where we're goin', he could be right behind us, champin' at the bit for a showdown."

"Then, if that's the case . . ."

"I hope it is, because I figure if we kill Mack Ozark, most of our problems go away," Preacher said.

The canyon grew narrower as it climbed higher into the mountains. The babies were unhappy because they hadn't gotten much to eat that morning, and their crying echoed back from the stone walls pressing in from the sides.

Those echoes mixed with each other in a weird melody that reminded Preacher of Wailing Woman Pass, far back to the southeast, where this adventure had gotten started. That seemed like a long time ago, he reflected, as he listened to the eerie sound. More like months than the mere weeks that had passed.

In addition, the slope increased. Eventually, it seemed as if they were traveling up a long, narrow ramp with nothing at the top except a cold, gray mountain towering above them.

"I don't like this," Annie said. "It seems like we're climbing toward . . . death."

From where he rode on the other side of the horse carrying the infants, Audie said, "Think of it as more like we're climbing toward Asgard."

"The realm of the Norse gods?"

Audie smiled. "I thought you might be well read enough to be familiar with the name."

"Yes, I've read about it. I've read Thomas Gray's poem 'The Fatal Sisters' and Laing's translation of Snorri Sturluson's work."

Audie looked at her in surprise. "Those volumes of translation by Samuel Laing are very recent. I believe they only came out last year."

"Yes, they were among the last batch of books Jonanthan brought me before . . . before . . ."

"It's all right," Audie said as her voice trailed off. "I understand.

You know about Asgard, then, and the Rainbow Bridge . . . and Valhalla."

"The hall of the dead," Annie said.

"I prefer to think of it as the place where heroes celebrate glory to the brave."

"Either way," Annie said, "the hammer falls. The ending is written."

Preacher's keen hearing had picked up enough of the conversation to follow it. He hipped around in the saddle and said, "A while back, I met some real Vikings, and they talked about those things all the time. I don't reckon there was a one of 'em who was scared to cross that bridge if it was his time . . . especially if he could cross it with a sword or a battle-axe in his hand."

Nighthawk contributed a grunt.

"Indeed," Audie said. "Your people sing their death songs as they go into battle because they welcome it, if such is the fate the spirits hold for them on that day."

Annie said, "You're talking about warriors. I'm not a warrior, and neither are my children."

"That's why you have us with you," Little Bear told her. "We won't let anything happen to you or the babies."

Preacher hoped that was a promise they would be able to keep.

Before they reached the end of the canyon, the slope became so steep that they had to dismount and lead the horses again. Finally, they made it to the top, and when they did, the view improved slightly. They could see the pass ahead of them, a couple of miles away on the other side of a wooded rise that wasn't nearly as precipitous as the canyon through which they had just traveled.

They stopped for a short time to rest and allow the horses a breather, too. Annie took Edward out of his cradleboard sling and said, "I think I'd like to try feeding them again."

"We'll see if we can find something for them," Audie said.

Annie's face reddened slightly as she said, "No, I mean I want to try, well, feeding them. Myself."

She looked down at her chest.

"Oh!" Audie's face was a little flushed, too. "I didn't think that was possible once you'd stopped, uh, nursing."

"Maybe not, but I'd like to try."

Preacher said, "You can go in that brush over there for some privacy, ma'am. Nobody'll bother you."

"Thank you."

Annie came back a short time later with the little boy, gave him to Audie, and took Elizabeth into the brush. When she returned, Preacher could tell she was upset.

"Didn't have no luck, eh?" he asked.

"No, but that doesn't mean I won't. And at least I tried. That has to count for something."

"Yes, ma'am, it sure does," Preacher agreed.

They had a little of the mush left. Audie split it between the twins. The adults gnawed on strips of jerky. They had only a few of those, but plenty of game roamed these mountains. Preacher could find some fresh meat for them—assuming things didn't take a turn for the worse with Ozark.

Preacher sent Dog ahead to scout before they moved on through the trees. The big cur came back wagging his bushy tail, indicating to Preacher that he hadn't found anything threatening. They all mounted up and moved on.

By midafternoon, they reached the pass. Sheer granite cliffs reared up on both sides, towering a hundred feet or more above the trail, which was no more than twenty feet wide.

Annie shuddered as they rode into the forbidding passage. Preacher understood her discomfort. The air here was cool and clammy. The blue sky was just a narrow line far above them. The place reminded him of a gigantic trap, the jaws of which were poised to slam shut and crush the life out of them.

Because of that, they felt more relief than they might have

otherwise when they emerged once more into the open air. It was only about a mile from one end of the pass to the other and it hadn't taken them long to ride through it, but to Preacher it felt as if they had been in there a long time. More than likely, it had been even more disquieting for the others, especially Annie and Little Bear.

Edward and Elizabeth were fortunate in a way, because they would never remember this or any of the other hardships that had befallen them in their short lives so far.

Preacher, in the lead, reined in at the head of the pass and waited for the others to come up and join him. As they did, Annie said in a hushed voice, "Oh, my. This is lovely."

She was right. The landscape that spread out in front of them was beautiful. There was a gentle slope leading down into a park-like high mountain valley, covered with lush grass and dotted with pine trees.

Beyond the valley, a snow-capped peak rose majestically into the deep blue afternoon sky. White clouds floating in that sky seemed to mirror the snow on the mountain.

"Is this where that map Jonathan left has been leading us?" Annie went on.

"Not quite," Preacher said. He lifted his arm and pointed across the valley at the mountain. "Unless I've gotten mighty turned around, the place we're lookin' for is over yonder some-where, part of the way up that mountain."

Audie reached into one of his saddlebags, brought out a spy-glass, and extended it. He lifted it to his right eye and peered through the lens for a long moment.

Then he handed the spyglass to Preacher and said, "Look about halfway up, where those outcroppings resemble a human face."

Preacher studied the distant slope with his naked eyes for a few seconds to orient himself to what Audie was talking about, then raised the spyglass and used it to take a better look.

The spot was easy enough to see, especially through the glass.

Rocks jutting out from the slope looked like eyes, a nose, and a jagged-toothed mouth. Some clumps of brush even formed eyebrows. It was only a rough resemblance, but close enough to attract attention.

Preacher could tell that the whole thing was completely natural; nobody had done anything to increase the similarity to a face. It was just one of those striking coincidences that could be found in nature more often than most folks would expect.

But something about it seemed off to Preacher, so he looked closer. A few more moments of keen study told him that his first assumption was a mistake.

"I thought that dark spot under the rock that makes the nose was just a shadow," Preacher said as he passed the spyglass back to Audie. "But it ain't."

"It's not?" Eagerly, Audie looked through the lens again. "What is it?"

"It's the mouth of a cave," Preacher said.

"Good heavens, you're right!" Audie lowered the glass. "Do you think that's the spot Jonathan Collins marked on that makeshift map?"

"I got a mighty powerful hunch that it is," Preacher said. He nodded toward the slope across the valley. "And whatever it is that he wanted somebody to find, it's right over yonder in that cave."

CHAPTER 27

They took advantage of the opportunity to rest the horses again for a few minutes before starting across the valley toward the snow-capped mountain.

While they were doing that, Preacher asked Annie, "Your husband never said anything to you about stashin' anything in a cave?"

The young woman shook her head. "No, not that I recall. What could it possibly be?"

Audie said, "The most likely answer is obvious. He could have hidden some of the gang's loot there. Or was it always share and share alike as soon as the men returned to the compound, or even before?"

He looked concerned and put a hand on Annie's arm as he added, "I know these are uncomfortable questions for you to consider. I'm sorry."

Annie shook her head and said, "No, I'm fully aware that Jonathan was an outlaw. It won't do any of us any good for me to deny that or try to ignore it. If we're going to get through this, we have to be able to speak plainly."

She looked back and forth between Audie and Preacher and went on, "Jonathan never divided up the spoils from a raid until everyone was back at the compound. And he was solely responsible for that division." She swallowed. "So it's possible that he could have been, well, less than totally truthful about how much was taken."

"Did he ever go off on his own without any of the other men?" Audie wanted to know.

Annie nodded. "He did. He always said that he could think better in the wilderness by himself, and that was where he planned the gang's next moves."

Audie looked at Preacher and said, "That could have been when he visited that cave and hid part of the loot in it."

The mountain man nodded.

"The other fellas were never suspicious of him?" Preacher asked Annie.

"Some of them were." Annie made a face. "In fact, that was how Mack Ozark was able to generate the resentful feelings against him. Ozark hinted numerous times that Jonathan wasn't being completely fair with them. Most of the men didn't go along with that—they liked Jonathan and respected his leadership—but enough of them felt that way, obviously, and eventually that led to his downfall."

"So if Jonathan was keeping more than his share," Audie mused, "there could be a considerable amount of money and other valuables hidden up there."

"There could be a small fortune," Annie admitted.

Preacher said, "That sounds like somethin' Ozark would want to get his hands on. If he had any idea that your husband had hidden a clue to the location in that map, it'd make those blankets important enough for Ozark to want 'em back. He made it seem like he was more interested in the young'uns, though, because he didn't want the others knowin' about that cache." The mountain man nodded slowly. "It sure seems like we might be onto somethin'. There ain't but one way to find out, though."

"Umm," Nighthawk said.

"You're right, my friend," Audie said. "We have to go up there to that cave and find out."

The horses had rested long enough while they were talking. They mounted up again and Preacher led the way down the slope into the beautiful valley.

Audie moved up alongside him and said quietly, "A man could settle down in a place like this and spend the rest of his days just enjoying all the splendor around him."

"I reckon so, but it could get a mite lonesome after a while if he was here all by his own self."

"Yes, to be truly happy, most men need a . . . companion."

"Like a wife," Preacher said with a grin.

"Well, yes, I suppose that would be the best arrangement."

"A fella would have to have somebody he could get along with, though. Somebody he had somethin' in common with. Like, say, if he was an hombre who enjoys readin' books, it'd probably be a good idea if the gal he got hitched to liked that, too."

Audie looked over at Preacher with a frown and said, "That's just common sense. What are you—" He stopped short, and his eyes widened. He glanced back over his shoulder. "What are you suggesting? Surely you don't think that I should—I mean—with Mrs. Collins?"

"She's a widow woman," Preacher pointed out. "She's young enough, though, that she's likely to want to find another husband one o' these days. You and her seem to enjoy talkin' to each other and spendin' time in each other's company, and you been workin' side by side with her takin' care of those infants. You're a mite attached to them, too."

"Everything you say is true, Preacher, but for heaven's sake, I'm much too old for her!"

"She might think of it more like you bein' seasoned and experienced. Some gals like it when the fella they're with is older and wiser."

"That's crazy," Audie muttered. He glanced back over his shoulder to where Annie was riding next to the horse carrying the twins, with Little Bear flanking the mount on the other side.

"You haven't indulged in any wild speculation like this with Mrs. Collins, I hope."

"Wouldn't figure it was my place to do that. But you and me are old pards, so I didn't think it'd hurt to say somethin'." Preacher chuckled. "For one thing, even though you're the smartest fella I've ever knowed, or will know, you can be downright dumb now and then. You ain't even noticed the way Annie looks at you when she thinks you're not payin' attention, have you?"

"What are you talking about? There's been nothing of the sort to see."

Preacher nodded and said, "All right, you just go on tellin' yourself that if you want to. I done my part. Anything else is up to you, old son."

"Old is right," Audie muttered. "It would never work out, not in a million years."

Preacher didn't think his friend sounded totally convinced of what he was saying, though.

Nothing more was brought up about the subject as they crossed the valley. From the way Dog romped ahead of them, acting almost as playful as a puppy as he spooked rabbits out of their hiding places but didn't bother to chase them, Preacher knew nothing threatening lurked here.

At one point, they came across half a dozen moose. The ungainly creatures loped off at the sight of humans and horses. Dog started to chase them, but Preacher called him back.

"Leave them moose be," he told the hound. "They didn't do nothin' to you."

Dog just grinned, his tongue lolling from his mouth, and bounded off again to see what else he could find.

By the time they reached the far side of the valley, Preacher judged that it was too late in the day to start the climb to the cave, which was not visible from where they were now. They would be able to go part of the way on horseback, but some of the ascent would have to be on foot.

"We'll get a good start first thing in the mornin'," he told the others.

Annie asked, "Won't that just give Ozark's men more time to catch up to us?"

"Yeah, but it can't be helped. That looks like a pretty hard climb in stretches, and we don't want to be tryin' it in the dark. We might be halfway up when night falls, and then we'd have to wait until mornin' before movin' on. We'll be a heap more comfortable here."

"I'm not sure I care about comfort anymore," Annie said. "I just want this to be over."

"I reckon that's what all of us want, ma'am."

Annie didn't put up any argument after that. Instead, she and Audie got busy tending to the babies while Nighthawk and Little Bear saw to the horses.

Preacher studied the slope rising in front of them, his eyes searching for the best path to take them up to the cave he had spotted. He mapped it out in his mind and memorized all the landmarks he could find, because he knew things might look different the next day when they were actually on the mountainside.

As usual, Preacher, Audie, and Nighthawk took turns standing guard that night. By now, Preacher was convinced that Mack Ozark was waiting for them to do the work, to lead him to whatever it was Jonathan Collins had hidden. He wasn't expecting any trouble just yet, and that was how the night went—quiet and peaceful.

In the morning, they broke camp and started climbing toward the cave. Preacher estimated it would take them at least half the day to reach it.

The first part of the ascent was easy. The slope was gentle enough that the horses could handle it with riders in the saddles.

The trees grew close together and the riders had to weave back and forth, finding the easiest routes. But they made steady progress.

The tree line extended more than halfway up the mountainside. Before they reached that point, the riders had to dismount and lead the horses yet again. It seemed to Preacher that they'd had to do that a lot during this journey—and they weren't even in the highest part of the Rockies.

Late in the morning, the trees and undergrowth thinned out and then stopped. Preacher called a halt. The people and the horses were all winded and needed a breather.

The tree line was important for another reason. Above this spot, the mountainside was bare rock and even more rugged. Preacher gathered the others around him and announced, "Nighthawk and I are the only ones goin' on up. The rest of you will wait here for us."

"If my husband hid something up there in that cave, I have a right to know what it is," Annie objected.

Preacher nodded. "Yes, ma'am, you sure do, and we'll tell you what we find, you can bet a hat on that. But gettin' up there is liable to be a rough go, and after comin' all this way, we don't want you fallin' and gettin' hurt now."

"I understand that, but I hate being left out of the discovery."

"You won't be, in the long run," Preacher assured her.

Audie said, "I suppose you don't want me coming along for the same reason. You don't think I'm up to the task, physically."

Nighthawk grunted, frowned, and shook his head.

"The big fella's right," Preacher said. "It ain't that at all, Audie. I don't want to go off and leave Miz Collins, Little Bear, and the twins down here without anybody to look after 'em. Dog's stayin' behind, too—"

The big cur whined.

"You ain't a mountain goat, so there ain't no use you complainin'," Preacher told him. "Anyway, as I was sayin', Dog's stayin' here, too, and I figure between the two o' you, you'll be a match for any trouble that rears its ugly head."

Audie sighed and nodded. "As usual, what you say makes sense, Preacher. I'll stay here with the others, of course, just as you suggest. But I expect the two of you to be careful up there."

"Ain't we always?"

Audie just rolled his eyes at that. Even as a rhetorical question, it wasn't worthy of a response.

Preacher used his knife to cut one of their last strips of jerky in two and gnawed on half of the tough meat while he gave the other half to Nighthawk. They washed it down with swigs from their canteens and then, their meager meal finished, they started up toward the cave without looking back.

Preacher could feel the eyes of the others on him and the giant Crow warrior, though, as they pulled themselves up the steep, rocky slope.

Some stretches were easy enough that they could walk, but most of the time they climbed by using footholds and handholds. The mountainside wasn't sheer, but it was steep enough that they were nearly always leaning forward and clinging to whatever grip they could find.

They rose slowly but steadily, and Preacher knew that if he looked back over his shoulder, he would see the landscape falling away in dramatic but dizzying fashion.

For that reason, he didn't look back. He was about as unbothered by heights as they came, but why risk making his head spin?

Time didn't mean much where they were. If it hadn't been for gradual, subtle changes in the light splashing over the peak, Preacher wouldn't have known that it was passing.

They reached an area that was almost straight up and down, and the rock was as flat as it could be with no little knobs or anything else to offer handholds and footholds. They would have to work their way to the side and look for a path around that obstacle. A ledge a few inches wide meandered off to the right.

Preacher nodded toward it and said, "Reckon that way's about as good as any."

"Umm," Nighthawk said.

They set out, Preacher going first. It was easier for his lean body to cling to the rock face. Nighthawk's massive bulk made it more difficult for him.

After a few feet, Preacher said, "I think you're gonna have to go back down to where this ledge starts and wait there. You can't make it, old son."

Nighthawk didn't say anything, but the stubborn look that came over his face spoke volumes. Preacher tried not to sigh. It was his friend's choice to make. They pressed on, and somehow Nighthawk managed to stick to the ledge, which angled gradually upward.

Finally, the ledge widened out a lot, and there was plenty of room for the two men to sit down and rest for a few minutes. Preacher's muscles were trembling from the strain, and so were Nighthawk's.

Preacher tugged at his earlobe and scraped a thumbnail along his jaw as he thought. He said, "If Collins hid a bunch of loot up there in that cave, how in blazes did he get it up there? There's got to be another trail that we ain't found yet. He didn't bring it up the way we've come, that's for sure. That ledge'd give a mountain goat the fantods!"

Nighthawk nodded solemnly.

With their iron constitutions, both men recovered quickly and resumed the climb. The going was easier now. They were past the worst of it, Preacher realized.

In early afternoon, they pulled themselves up and over a slightly rounded edge of rock and rolled onto a flat area in front of the cave's entrance. The opening in the rock wall was an irregular arch eight feet tall at its highest and perhaps twenty feet wide. Sunlight illuminated the first few feet of the cave, but beyond that, darkness hung down like a curtain.

Directly above the cave mouth was the prominent outthrust of rock that from a distance resembled a nose. It would be easy to overlook the cave, as Preacher and Audie had done at first even with the spyglass, because the rock above it did cast an obscuring shadow.

Preacher and Nighthawk rested again for a moment before Preacher climbed to his feet. Nighthawk took another deep breath and then stood up, as well.

"We should've brought somethin' to make a torch," Preacher said, "but I didn't think of it. Not sure we could've carried much while we were climbin' up here, anyway. I almost felt like tossin' these guns o' mine away a time or two." He grinned. "Almost."

Both men had keen eyes that would adjust to the shadows inside the cave. They moved forward and approached the opening warily. Up here on the side of the mountain, it was unlikely a bear or any other varmint would be holed up in there, but it never hurt to be careful.

Preacher had his left hand extended in front of him and his right hand resting on the butt of the Colt on that side as he moved into the cave. Nighthawk was close behind him. Preacher hadn't gone very far when he began to be able to make out shapes looming ahead of them.

Just as he suspected, there was nothing living in this cave, although the stacks of burlap-wrapped bundles they found looked vaguely like some sort of hunched over beast. Preacher took hold of one of the bundles and hefted it.

"A mite on the heavy side," he said. "Looks like there's a dozen or more of 'em, too. Let's take this one back to some better light so we can get a good look at it."

The thing didn't look like much, Preacher thought as he laid it on the ground in the cave entrance. A little more than two feet long, a foot and a half wide, maybe a foot deep. Wrapped tightly in burlap that was tied in place with sturdy twine. Preacher knelt next to the bundle, pulled his knife, worked the tip under one of those bindings, and cut the twine.

He pulled back the burlap to reveal smaller bundles wrapped in oilcloth. About twenty of them, Preacher estimated, packed in so tightly that they had formed an almost solid block. They were wedged in together so securely that he let out a grunt of effort as he pulled one of them free.

The slight shifting of its contents as he held it and the faint clinking he heard gave him a pretty good idea what he and Night-hawk had discovered. But he wanted to be sure, so he unwrapped the oilcloth and then opened the drawstring of the soft leather pouch he found inside.

Upending it, Preacher poured out a glittering cascade of gold coins that made a nice-sized pile on the cave floor.

CHAPTER 28

Neither Preacher nor Nighthawk were money-hungry by nature. As long as they had enough funds to allow them to live the sort of life they wanted to lead, they were content.

But there was something about the sight of a pile of gold, Preacher supposed, that made any man's insides do a little flip-flop.

It wasn't greed, exactly, but he felt the urge to pick up a handful of those coins and rattle them around in his palm and let them dribble through his fingers.

Nighthawk appeared to be feeling that impulse less than Preacher was, but even so, his dark eyes were focused raptly on the money.

And there was more of it where that come from, Preacher thought. A lot more of it.

"If all those bundles are full o' pouches like this, there's a fortune here, like Annie said." Preacher began scooping up the coins he had dumped out and replacing them in the bag. "Thousands o' dollars, for sure. Jonathan Collins must've held back a lot from his men. I reckon it ain't surprisin' that Ozark and some o' the others turned against him sooner or later." Preacher shook his head. "There just ain't no honor among thieves, as the old sayin' goes."

He closed the bag's drawstring and wedged it back into the

bundle with the others, then wrapped the burlap around it again and retied the twine.

He wasn't sure how they were going to get the money back down to the spot where they'd left the others. In fact, they might have to leave it here for now, and if that turned out to be the case, it would be better if the coins were protected from the elements.

Nighthawk picked up the bundle and put it back on the stack. He turned to Preacher with a puzzled frown on his face.

"You're thinkin' about what we're gonna do with all that loot, ain't you?" the mountain man asked. "It don't belong to us. Annie might make a claim on it, since she was married to Collins, but when you come right down to it, that money belongs to all the folks Jonathan Collins and his gang stole it from. Problem is, how in blazes would you ever find out who all those folks are? A bunch of 'em are probably dead. We ain't got no way of findin' their heirs, or the ones who are still alive, for that matter. We may have to let Audie figure out this one."

The two men walked back out onto the open area in front of the cave and began to look around. Now that Preacher knew what was hidden in there, he was certain Jonathan Collins hadn't brought it up that ledge.

He supposed it was possible Collins had tied a long rope to each bundle, carried the rope up, and then hauled the bundles up one at a time by hand, but that would have been backbreaking work. Preacher's gut told him they needed to be looking for a simpler explanation . . .

He was looking up at the "nose" directly above the cave when something caught his attention. He pointed and said to Nighthawk, "Look up yonder. See those places on the front of that outcroppin' where it looks like somethin' has rubbed against it?"

Nighthawk studied the rock for a moment and then nodded. Without saying anything, he moved over to the right of the cave mouth and began climbing higher, using little crevices in the rock to hold on to as he lifted himself.

Preacher followed. They climbed around the outcropping, and once they were above it, it was Nighthawk's turn to point.

A trail rose in the other direction, angling up between the "nose" and the "right eye." Because it was inclined slightly from the outer edge down to the rock face, it was all but invisible from below unless somebody knew it was there.

The trail was wide enough for a horse to travel on it as it curved around the bulging slope of the mountainside. It would be a little tricky because it wasn't level, but a sure-footed mount could manage it, especially if the rider got down and led the horse. Preacher spotted some droppings that confirmed an animal had been up here.

"That's the back door," he said excitedly, "and gettin' here that way looks to be a lot easier than comin' up the way we did. That trail must wind around the mountain and come out down yonder somewhere. Collins must've used it to bring that loot up here on pack horses. Lowerin' the bundles with ropes from here down to that open space in front of the cave would be a whole heap easier than haulin' it up. The ropes are what made those marks on the rock. Blast it! Why didn't he mark this trail on his dang map?"

Nighthawk shrugged.

"Yeah, I reckon he wanted to keep one thing back so anybody who got hold o' them blankets couldn't just waltz up here and clean out the place," Preacher said. "I wonder if he figured on tellin' his wife about the trail and just never got the chance before he died. Seems like that might've been the way it was. Likely we'll never know for sure."

Nighthawk pointed down the mountain.

"Yeah, we'll go back down this way and let the others know what we found." Preacher chuckled. "At least it ought to be easier goin' down than comin' up, and it'll give us a chance to scout that trail."

Nighthawk started to nod in agreement, but then both men

jerked to attention as the sound of a gunshot cracked through the thin high country air.

No more shots blasted from below, but that wasn't necessarily a good thing. In fact, it made a cold finger rake along Preacher's spine.

Without a word, he started across the rock outcropping toward the hidden trail he and Nighthawk had discovered. Going back down the way they had come would take too long, and besides, while they were working their slow, torturous way along that ledge, they would be perfect targets for any riflemen down below.

Nighthawk was right on the mountain man's heels, but both of them came to an abrupt halt as a harsh voice floated up to them.

"Preacher! Hello, up there! You hear me, Preacher?"

That was Mack Ozark shouting at them. Preacher recognized the outlaw leader's grating tones. He had already decided there was a good chance Ozark was with the party pursuing them, but he had hoped that wouldn't turn out to be the case. Ozark probably wouldn't be as easy to outsmart as his henchmen might have been.

He was also the most ruthless member of the gang. Preacher and his companions couldn't expect even a shred of mercy from him.

Preacher and Nighthawk looked at each other. Preacher could tell the big Crow warrior was leaving it up to him whether or not to respond to Ozark's call.

Keeping his voice low, Preacher said to Nighthawk, "Ozark don't know about that other trail. You take it and get back down there. Work your way around if you can and come in behind 'em. You might get a chance to jump some of them. Hold off, though, if there are too many. It won't do us no good in the long run for you to get yourself killed."

A stubbornly determined light burned in the warrior's eyes, but he nodded in agreement with Preacher's words. He might not like it, but he would do what the mountain man said.

"I'll stay here and stall the no-good son of a buck," Preacher went on. "If Ozark leaves with the others as prisoners, you follow 'em. I'll pick up your trail and catch up as soon as I can."

Nighthawk nodded again.

"Good luck," Preacher concluded.

Nighthawk picked his way nimbly across the top of the "nose" and then followed the trail as it curved around the mountainside. The giant warrior had just gone out of Preacher's sight when Ozark shouted again from below.

"I don't have all the patience in the world! If you're up there, Preacher, you'd damned well better answer me. Your friends are all right for the moment, but there's no guarantee they'll stay that way!"

"You'd best not hurt any o' those folks, Ozark!" Preacher called. "If you do, I swear I'll make it my life's work to see that you pay for it!"

"Your life won't last very much longer if you don't act reasonable and cooperate with me! Hell, now that I know where this place is, I don't really need you or the others anymore. I can just kill them and leave you and that big redskin up there to starve to death!"

Preacher felt that icy finger go up and down his spine again. Ozark was right—at least as far as the boss outlaw knew. Preacher could escape from here anytime he wanted to, but for the moment, he wanted to keep Ozark occupied.

"Before we make any deals, I want proof those folks are alive. You let my friend Audie sing out!"

"You mean the sawed-off little runt?" Ozark laughed. "Sure. Go ahead, runt."

"I'm not hurt, Preacher." That was Audie's voice, all right, but not surprisingly, some strain could be heard in it. "They knocked me around a little, but nothing serious." He paused. "What about Nighthawk? He's not hurt, is he?"

Preacher smiled faintly as he lowered his voice to a rumble and called, "Umm!"

Ozark and the others would never know the difference, but Audie would realize that was Preacher imitating the massive warrior—and Audie was smart enough to make an educated guess that his old friends might have set some sort of plan in motion. He would play along for now.

Preacher switched back to his regular voice and said, "How about you, Miz Collins? Are you all right?"

"I'm not hurt at all, Preacher," Annie replied. "Just frightened for the sake of my children."

That prompted Ozark to say, "I'm not going to hurt those kids. Damn it, when I sent men to look for them in the first place, didn't I give orders that they were to be brought back unharmed?"

Annie responded to that, but voices carried in this thin air. Preacher could still hear her coldly angry words even though she was talking to Ozark.

"You didn't really care what happened to Edward and Elizabeth," she accused. "You just wanted those blankets they had with them."

"No point in denying it now," Ozark said. "Even so, I told my men to be careful of the infants."

Preacher cupped his hands around his mouth and shouted, "Little Bear! Are you down there?"

"Blast it!" Ozark burst out. "Are you going to insist on talking to the babies, too?"

"I reckon they're all right," Preacher said. "I want to hear from Little Bear, though."

After a moment, the Salish youth called, "I'm fine, Preacher. Like Audie, they roughed me up a little, but no real harm done."

"Put up a fight, did you, son?"

"Well, I tried."

"Proud of you. But for now, don't cause any more ruckus. I got to talk to Ozark. We got some dealin' to do."

That brought an unpleasant laugh from the outlaw. "If you think you can make some sort of deal with me, you're very much mistaken, Preacher. The stakes are high, and you don't have any cards to play."

"That's where you're dead wrong, mister! There ain't no stakes!"

For several heartbeats, no response came from below. Then Ozark broke the silence by demanding, "What are you talking about?"

"There's nothin' up here. This danged old cave we found is empty!"

CHAPTER 29

The lie came to Preacher out of thin air, but it was a good bluff and would keep Ozark distracted for a while longer, giving Nighthawk more of a chance to scout the situation.

For a long moment, Ozark didn't respond. Then he shouted angrily, "That's a damned lie! That cave's full of money! Jonathan Collins admitted that to me himself. He admitted he'd been stealing from his own men for years and squirreling the loot away in some hiding place!"

"Maybe he did," Preacher said. "I don't know about that. But if he did, then he cached it somewhere else, because there ain't a blasted thing up here except dust and the bones o' some little critter that crawled in here and died!"

He smiled. That business about the bones was a nice touch, he told himself. Just a little detail to make what he was saying seem more real.

Ozark wasn't convinced, however. He bellowed, "He boasted to me that he'd left his wife a map leading to that hidden fortune! He said he made it himself. I didn't figure out until after he was dead and those Indians had run off with the babies that he was talking about the beadwork on those blankets. That was the only thing he made that could've been a map."

The outlaw let out a cackling laugh and went on, "And you

led us right to the place, just like I thought you might! Face it, Preacher—I beat you!"

"I don't know what you think you won."

"You and the Indian come on down from there," Ozark said, putting his gloating aside. "Don't give me any more trouble, and I'll let Annie and the little ones live. I give you my word on that. Hell, I'll even let this Flathead kid go back to his people. You won't get a better deal than that."

"You didn't say nothin' about what'll happen to me and Audie and Nighthawk."

"Oh, you three? You'll die! That's unfortunate for you and your friends, but I've heard too much about you to leave you alive, Preacher. I don't plan on spending the rest of my life looking over my shoulder for you!"

Preacher muttered, "And that's exactly what you'd be doin', old son. After what happened to Bluebird and her grandpa, you got it comin'."

He didn't yell that loud enough for Ozark to hear. Instead, he allowed the silence to drag out, giving Nighthawk more time to get down off the mountainside.

Also, he knew his lack of a response would get on Ozark's nerves, and sure enough, a few minutes later the outlaw shouted, "What's it going to be, mountain man? Are you coming down—or do I kill the Flathead boy?"

Preacher heard the genuine threat in Ozark's voice and had no doubt the outlaw would go through with it. Little Bear's life meant nothing to a man like Mack Ozark. Less than nothing.

"All right, hold on, damn it!" Preacher shouted. "I'm comin' down!"

The thought of working his way back along that ledge, leaving himself wide open for any of the gang who wanted to take pot-shots at him, was unnerving. But there was nothing else Preacher could do. He had to hope that Mack Ozark wanted to kill him face-to-face and would allow him to climb all the way back down to the camp instead of letting the other outlaws blaze away at him.

"The big Indian has to come down, too!" Ozark called. "I want to see both of you!"

Preacher made a face. He shouted, "Nighthawk ain't here! He headed on up the mountain to try to get away! Damned redskin! You wouldn't think somebody as big as him would cut and run like that!"

It pained him to say such things about Nighthawk, but he had to account for the warrior's absence somehow. Ozark might accept the story, or he might not, but there was nothing else Preacher could do.

"Damn you!" Ozark roared. "You're lying again! This is some sort of low-down trick!"

"No, it ain't!" Preacher said. "Listen, I'm comin' down like you wanted! Don't—"

He didn't get a chance to finish that plea. Down below, a man yelled in alarm, and a second later, gun-thunder from half a dozen weapons pealed out and rolled over the landscape.

Preacher bit back a curse, dashed across the outcropping heedless of any danger, and pounded up the trail that was hidden from the sight of those below. They might be able to catch a glimpse of him moving, but that was all.

He didn't know where the trail led, but even though it rose slightly as it curved around the mountain, he was confident that eventually it would take him back to the lower levels. Following it had to be faster and less risky than going back down that narrow ledge.

Unfortunately, no matter how much faster this way was, he was going to be too late, he realized. Already, the gunfire was beginning to die away. The fight, such as it was, would soon be over.

Nighthawk must have made a move against the gang. Either that, or else they had discovered him watching them and opened fire on him. Any hopes of taking Ozark and his men by surprise were gone.

That thought, added to the ominous silence coming from below, made Preacher jerk to a sudden stop. He stood there, breathing a little hard from emotion rather than exertion, and cudgeled his brain into working.

Whatever had happened down there, it was over, and there wasn't a blasted thing he could do about it.

If he was going to fight back against Ozark, he would have to come up with a different way of doing it.

He looked up at the higher slopes. A number of boulders perched there. With a plan forming quickly in his mind, he went back to the rock outcropping and knelt there with one knee on top of the "nose."

"Preacher!" Mack Ozark shouted. "Preacher, where the devil are you?"

"What happened down there?" Preacher yelled back. "What was all that shootin' about?"

"I think you know good and well what it was! That tame giant Indian of yours tried to sneak up on us!"

Preacher's jaw tightened. He hated hearing his old friend referred to in such an undignified manner and knew it would annoy Nighthawk, too. But the current state of the big Crow's health was more important.

"What did you do to him?" Preacher demanded. "Is he all right?"

"He got a rifle ball through the arm, but he'll live. Not for long, though, if you don't come down here like I told you to. And like you already agreed to."

"The hell with you!" Preacher yelled. "I ain't surrenderin' after all. You let my friends go and light a shuck out o' here, or I'm gonna rain down an avalanche on all of you!"

"You crazy fool! If you start an avalanche, it'll wipe out these innocent people, too."

"You mean those innocent people you keep threatenin' to kill? If I can't save 'em, I sure as blazes ain't gonna let you get away with everything you've done!"

Audie's voice drifted up from below. "Go ahead and do it, Preacher!" he urged. "Dying will be worth it if we can take this outlaw scum with us!"

"Umm!" Nighthawk added, confirming Ozark's claim that the massive warrior was still alive.

The two of them wouldn't believe for a second that Preacher meant to kill them in an avalanche. They would know he was up to something else.

But Annie didn't know him that well and must have accepted the threat as a genuine one. She surprised Preacher by crying out, "Go ahead, Preacher! I'd rather die with my children than be separated from them again!"

Hearing her vehement response might have unnerved Ozark a little, if a man such as him was capable of feeling such an emotion. He shouted, "Now, hold on, damn it! Don't do anything foolish, Preacher!"

"If we're all gonna die anyway, what does it matter?" Preacher let out a ringing, gleeful cackle of laughter that echoed from the stony slopes. "Like Audie said, dyin's worth it if I can take a skunk like you with me!"

A moment later, Preacher heard Ozark shouting at his men, although he couldn't make out the words. A minute or two after that, the sound of hoofbeats came to his ears.

They were pulling back, Preacher knew. Trying to get out of the path of that avalanche he had threatened.

And they would be taking the prisoners with them, Preacher knew. Ozark wouldn't give up on the chance of putting his hands on that hidden loot, and he wouldn't throw away any possible leverage he might be able to use in achieving that goal.

The outlaw chief had to have the last word. He yelled up at

Preacher, "You'll never get down off this mountain alive! We'll be waiting for you!"

"Wait and be damned!" Preacher gave another of those maniacal laughs. "You'll never get what's in that cave, either! It'll be buried in that rockslide!"

While Ozark bellowed curses, Preacher turned and began scrambling higher on the slope. He went past a dozen large boulders and countless smaller ones until he reached the one he wanted.

He turned and put his shoulder against it, shoved as hard as he could. The boulder didn't budge.

Preacher gritted his teeth and tried again. The boulder remained as motionless as ever. Preacher braced his back against another rock, lifted his right leg, and rested the sole of his boot against the boulder he had selected as the most promising for his purpose. When he was positioned the way he wanted, he placed his left foot against the boulder, too.

Then he began to push with both legs, summoning up all the strength from deep inside him that he possibly could.

Beads of sweat popped out on his forehead. The pounding of blood inside his skull made it difficult for him to hear the fading rataplan of horses' hooves as the outlaws beat a hasty retreat. Preacher clenched his jaw so tightly it seemed as if his teeth were about to crack.

The boulder shifted.

It only moved a fraction of an inch at first, but when Preacher took a deep breath, set himself, and pushed again, the huge rock tilted forward and slid a couple of inches with a loud grating sound. Preacher threw his powerful muscles into another effort.

This time, the boulder tipped even more, and then suddenly it was gone as its weight shifted and it began to roll down the slope. The change was so swift that it dumped Preacher on the ground where the big rock had been sitting only a second earlier.

He started to slide after it but caught himself. From where he was, he watched as the boulder began to roll faster. It bounced in the air a little whenever it hit a rough spot, and that just increased its speed.

A heartbeat later, it crashed into another boulder, and the impact was enough to knock that one loose and start it rolling, too.

Within moments, a full-scale avalanche was crashing down the mountainside as more and more boulders began tumbling from their perches.

Preacher knew that Ozark, his men, and the prisoners had had time to descend far enough through the trees that they would be safe. The boulders might smash through the pines right at the tree line, but the growth was thick enough to slow and then stop the avalanche.

He had to pray that his hunch was right and Ozark had taken the captives with him. If Preacher had been even indirectly responsible for the deaths of his old friends, as well as an innocent young woman and babies and the Indian youth . . .

It was the worst thing he could think of. The guilt would be pure-dee hell. And even though he would take revenge on Mack Ozark, an ocean of outlaw blood wouldn't be enough to put things right.

Preacher shoved those grim thoughts out of his mind for now and forced himself to approach the situation with a practical attitude. The huge rumble from the avalanche was dying away now, but billowing, swirling, blinding clouds of dust still rose from lower down on the slopes.

Preacher plunged into that dust and began making his way back to the cave where Jonathan Collins had hidden his ill-gotten gains.

Even though he had threatened to cover up the cave with the rockslide, Preacher hadn't known if that was actually what would happen. When he reached the spot, he saw that the "nose" in the telltale face was still mostly intact, although one of the falling boulders had knocked a chunk off the front of it.

Smaller rocks and masses of dirt that had been dragged down with the tumbling boulders had piled up on the level ground in front of the cave mouth, forming a barrier that effectively closed it off.

It wasn't permanently buried, though; a crew of men with picks and shovels could clear off enough of it to gain access to the cave in a day or two of work.

Preacher figured Ozark would send somebody up to check on that. He would be long gone by the time that happened, though. He clambered over some rocks and found the other trail leading up. It was damaged in places but still passable.

Preacher got out of there in a hurry. He needed to find Ozark's bunch and make sure the prisoners were still with them.

Then he could start making plans to rescue those captives and settle the score with Mack Ozark.

CHAPTER 30

After a hundred yards, the back-door trail, as Preacher thought of it, made a sharp turn and entered a narrow crevice that cut through the side of the mountain and sloped down gradually rather than up.

It looked like some giant had taken a knife and started to carve a slice off the mountain as if it were a towering rock cake, then changed his mind for some reason before the slice was cut all the way off.

The passage was narrow but still wide enough for a pack horse to get through it. Once a man started leading that pack horse through the crevice, though, there would be no turning back. It wasn't wide enough for that.

Jonathan Collins had probably never had to deal with that problem. He had just forged straight on through to the cave, unloaded however many bundles of loot his pack animal was carrying, and returned to the compound a couple of days away on the creek.

As Preacher hurried along, he wondered what Collins had planned to do in the long run, if Ozark hadn't overthrown him and taken command of the gang. Would Collins eventually have taken Annie and the twins and disappeared, retreating to the valley below where the loot was hidden and living there for the rest of their lives?

Surely not, the mountain man decided with a little shake of his head. There was nothing in the valley that the hidden loot could buy. Why go to the trouble of stealing a bunch of money from his own men just to live a primitive existence in a high mountain valley?

No, he must have planned to strike out for the coast, taking one or two of the bundles with him so he'd have enough capital to set his family up in a new life there. Then he could return to the cache whenever he needed to in the future and pick up more of the loot.

He must have known that the men he'd double-crossed might try to hunt him down. Maybe he'd been arrogant enough to believe he could stay one step ahead of them for however long it took before they gave up.

Mack Ozark never would have given up, Preacher knew after having met the man. Jonathan Collins may well have been aware of that, too. In which case, he would have made sure to kill Ozark before he took off for the tall and uncut . . .

All that was moot, as Audie would say. Things hadn't worked out that way. Collins was dead, Ozark was alive, and Collins's wife and children were his prisoners.

At least, Preacher hoped that was the case.

The crevice ran for a mile or so and finally opened onto a ledge that Preacher was able to follow all the way back down to the tree line. He was well to the south of the spot where the avalanche had rumbled down the mountain.

He headed back in that direction, sticking to the trees and underbrush so he could use them for cover. He was eager to find Ozark's bunch. Until he saw the prisoners with his own eyes, the uncertainty over their fate would gnaw at his guts.

Without warning, something exploded out of the brush in front of him. Preacher's hands dropped to the guns on his hips, but before he could draw them, he recognized the big, shaggy form charging toward him.

A second later, Dog had reared up, rested his paws on Preacher's shoulders, and was rasping his tongue over the mountain man's beard-stubbled face.

"Take it easy, old son," Preacher said with a grin. Dog was wagging his bushy tail so hard his entire back half was wiggling. Preacher hugged the thick neck and went on, "I'm mighty glad to see you, too."

He enjoyed the reunion with the big cur for a moment longer and then asked, "Where's Audie? Where's Nighthawk?"

Dog dropped his paws to the ground, darted a few steps away, then stopped and looked back at Preacher as he whined.

"You can take me to 'em? I figured you could. Find Audie! Find Nighthawk!"

Dog let out a quiet bark and then whirled away into the woods. Preacher loped after him, warmed by a deep sense of relief that at least one of his trail partners had escaped from the avalanche.

A short time later, he paused to listen intently and made out the sound of numerous hoofbeats in the distance. It was possible someone else was riding through this valley, maybe an Indian hunting party or a group of fur trappers, but Preacher knew that wasn't likely.

His gut told him that was Ozark's bunch he heard, and the prisoners, as well, he hoped.

Dog trotted back to him and whined as if to confirm the mountain man's hunch.

"You follow them, Dog," he told the big cur. "But don't let 'em see you. I'd just as soon those varmints don't know you're still alive. I'll try to keep up, but if I can't, you come back and find me."

Dog looked at him for a moment, communicating almost as clearly as if he'd been human. Then, with a sweep of his tail, he whirled and dashed off through the woods.

Preacher set out at a steady trot after Dog, both of them heading in the same direction as the horses Preacher had heard.

His muscles were like cords of metal cable and could maintain that pace for hours if need be.

Less than an hour had passed, though, when he caught a whiff of woodsmoke coming from somewhere in front of him. Ozark and his men must have retreated well away from the mountainside, just in case any more rocks started falling, and now they were making camp.

Ozark didn't intend to go any farther, Preacher thought. The boss outlaw wanted to stay close to that cave full of stolen loot.

That indicated Ozark hadn't bought Preacher's story about the cave being empty. Well, he'd never actually expected that gambit to be successful. It had distracted Ozark for a few minutes, and that was the most Preacher could have hoped for.

He stopped and waited where he was, knowing that Dog would return and lead him right to the outlaws' camp. He could have found it anyway, of course, by following the smoke, but it never hurt to simplify things.

Besides, he didn't want to take a chance on stumbling right into that bunch of killers. Stealth was the most important consideration at the moment.

After five minutes, Dog pushed through the brush and came up to Preacher. The mountain man scratched his ears and said, "Found 'em, did you? Good job, you hairy old son. Take me to Audie and Nighthawk."

The two of them drifted noiselessly through the undergrowth like phantoms. The woodsmoke smell grew stronger. After a while, Preacher began to hear voices as the outlaws talked among themselves. He was even able to pick out Mack Ozark's harsh tones.

Dog went to his belly and began crawling through the brush. Preacher did likewise. The outlaws' voices grew louder. Preacher stopped when he heard a man say, "—do next, Mack?"

Preacher was mighty interested in the answer to that question his own self.

"Half of you are going to stay here and guard these prisoners,"

Ozark replied. "The others are coming with me back to that cave. All those boulders will have stopped falling and rolling by now. I want to find out how much trouble we're going to have getting in there to retrieve that money."

"You think all that loot Collins stole from us is really squirreled away in there?"

"I don't have any doubt that it is," Ozark declared. "Collins wouldn't have boasted to me about it if he wasn't telling the truth. Preacher lied about the cave being empty. I'm sure of it."

"You reckon that crazy mountain man's still alive?" another man asked.

"I'm hopin' he got caught in his own damn avalanche!" a third man put in.

Ozark said, "There's certainly a chance that's true. But even if he's still alive and tries anything, he won't stand a chance against six of us."

Preacher heard a laugh and recognized it. Audie said, "You just keep telling yourself that, Ozark—right up until the moment Preacher kills you."

The former professor's words were followed a moment later by the sharp sound of an open palm striking flesh. Preacher tensed and Dog growled softly. Audie had gotten himself a wallop from Ozark or one of the other outlaws.

"You're in no position to be mouthing off, runt," Ozark said. "In fact, the only reason you're still alive is because I might need you if I have to bargain again with your unwashed friend. But remember, I have other prisoners. Not all of you have to stay alive."

After that, Ozark picked the men who would go back to the avalanche site with him. The names meant nothing to Preacher. He didn't care who stayed and who went with Ozark.

He could kill them just as well whether he knew their names or anything else about them. He knew all he needed to know.

They were outlaws, with plenty of blood on their hands. Death was all they had coming.

Preacher and Dog waited while Ozark and the men going with him mounted up again. They rode out, heading back across the valley toward the mountain where the cave was located.

Preacher waited until they were well gone and then edged closer to the camp. He parted some brush and peered through the gap at a roughly circular clearing about forty feet across. The small fire he had smelled burned in the center of it.

He knew Audie was alive because he had heard his friend's voice, but a surge of relief went through him when he saw Night-hawk, as well, sitting on the ground next to the diminutive former professor. Nighthawk's wrists and ankles had rope wrapped around them and were tied tightly. Another rope encircled his torso, pinning his arms to his sides.

The outlaws weren't taking any chances with the giant Crow warrior. They had already suffered too many broken necks and stove-in skulls in their previous clashes with him.

Audie was also tied, hands and feet, but didn't have the extra rope around him.

Preacher shifted slightly to get a better view of the rest of the clearing. He spotted Annie and Little Bear sitting on the opposite side of the fire from Audie and Nighthawk. Neither was tied; each held one of the twins.

An outlaw stood close behind them, though, with a rifle in the crook of his arm. Obviously, Ozark had appointed him to guard these two prisoners.

Audie and Nighthawk had guards, as well—two of them. Each of those outlaws held two pistols. Their thumbs were looped over the hammers, ready to cock and fire instantly. They probably had orders to shoot the prisoners without hesitation if any trouble broke out.

Preacher knew that from where he was, he could kill both of those guards with a single shot each, before they had a chance to hurt Audie and Nighthawk.

But could he then swing around and drill the man standing

guard over Annie and Little Bear before the outlaw could get a shot off?

It was likely, Preacher thought, even probable—but he couldn't guarantee that outcome, and he hated to risk the prisoners' lives on such a chance.

Not only that, but two more members of Ozark's gang were still here, one of them kneeling by the fire and putting a pot of coffee on to boil while the other roamed around over by where the horses were picketed, looking around as if he were keeping an eye open for any potential trouble.

Either of those men could open fire on the prisoners at a second's notice.

Hoping that he could gun down all of them in time to save his friends was just too much of a risk, Preacher decided. Besides, an outburst of gunfire could be heard across the valley and would alert Mack Ozark that something was wrong.

He needed to deal with those guards, Preacher told himself, but it would be a whole heap better if he could do it quietly.

Putting his head close to the big cur's ear, Preacher whispered, "Dog, go around yonder and make some noise in the brush." He motioned toward the area on the other side of the horses. "See if you can get that fella's attention and make him come lookin' for you."

Another hand gesture reinforced the order. Dog crawled away through the brush. Preacher could count on his shaggy trail partner to follow orders.

Preacher crawled the other way, toward the side of the camp where Audie and Nighthawk were sitting.

The brush grew fairly close behind them, close enough for Preacher to reach the two guards in one long step. He would cause some noise when he made his move; there was no avoiding that. That would give them some warning, so he would have to strike quickly.

When he was in position, he found a tiny opening in the brush through which he could watch the camp. The man at the fire had the coffeepot sitting at the edge of the flames. He straightened to his feet, but he still stood beside the fire with his hands on his hips, looking pleased with himself.

The outlaw over by the horses was still there, holding himself tense and alert as he looked around. Preacher was glad to see that his own gray stallion was among the picketed animals, as were the other mounts and pack animals from his party.

The sentry suddenly jerked his head a little to the right and leaned forward to peer intently into the trees and brush on that side of the camp.

The man at the fire noticed that reaction and asked, "Something wrong, Moran?"

"I thought I heard something out there," the outlaw called Moran answered.

"Probably just some varmint."

"Yeah, that's what I'm worried about. A two-legged varmint."

The man standing behind Annie and Little Bear said, "Go take a look, but be careful. Mack will kill us if anything happens to these prisoners. He wants that money Collins stole so bad it's got him half-loco."

"He's already half-loco," the man at the fire said. "That's why I don't ever want to get him mad."

"Then you shouldn't be sayin' things like that, Calder. If Mack ever found out about it—"

The man at the fire, Calder, looked worried as he interrupted, "You fellas aren't gonna say anything to him, are you?"

"Just go on and take a look, Moran. I don't trust that damn mountain man not to be sneakin' up on us."

Preacher smiled faintly to himself at that comment. The outlaw had it figured out; he just didn't know it. And Preacher was on the other side of the camp from where they were worried about.

Holding his rifle at the ready, Moran pushed into the brush. It closed behind him. Preacher could still see a little movement through the branches.

He heard a startled curse erupt from the searcher, followed instantly by a savage growl. Moran yelled but thankfully didn't get a shot off as the snarling and growling grew louder.

The two outlaws standing behind Audie and Nighthawk stiffened. One of them exclaimed, "What the hell!"

That exclamation, along with the commotion in the woods, helped mask the sound as Preacher surged smoothly to his feet and stepped out of the brush. In the same swift, efficient manner, he drew his knife and tomahawk.

The knife plunged into the back of the outlaw on his right, directly into the man's heart. He died so quickly that the pair of pistols in his hands slipped unfired from suddenly nerveless fingers and fell to the ground at his feet.

Preacher struck simultaneously with the tomahawk in his left hand, chopping down on the back of the other guard's head. The man's hat was nowhere near enough to blunt the powerful blow. Bone shattered as the tomahawk drove through the man's skull and into his brain.

Instantly, Preacher jerked the weapon back. This man didn't drop his pistols as he fell. His hands clamped around them in his death spasm. One of them went off, but the man's own body muffled the blast to a certain extent as he folded over the weapons.

As the outlaw was falling, Preacher's arm flashed back and then forward. The tomahawk spun across the clearing, above the campfire, and struck the forehead of the outlaw behind Annie and Little Bear in a perfect throw.

That man died as quickly as the others, dropping his rifle and falling backward awkwardly, but the one beside the fire was still alive and clawed at a pistol thrust into his waistband as he whirled toward Preacher.

Even though Nighthawk was trussed up like a pig on its way to market, the warrior's enormous strength enabled him to lever himself to his feet. He threw himself forward, a human battering ram, and crashed into Calder's legs. With no chance to brace himself, the impact drove the outlaw off his feet. He sprawled on his back in the flames.

Screaming and thrashing as his clothes caught on fire, Calder forgot all about trying to pull his gun. Preacher stepped around Audie. Two long strides brought him to the fire, where he leaned over and drove his knife into Calder's chest, putting the man out of his misery. Calder arched his back and then sagged as death claimed him.

The sickening smell of burned meat filled the air. To keep it from getting worse, Preacher took hold of an ankle and dragged the corpse out of the flames.

"I knew you'd be showing up soon, Preacher," Audie said. "It was just a matter of when."

Preacher grunted and wiped his knife blade on what was left of the dead man's shirt. Nighthawk had wound up lying on the ground after he'd knocked Calder into the fire. He had rolled onto his side to put himself farther from the flames.

Preacher bent to saw the knife blade against the big warrior's bonds.

"Are all of you all right?" he asked as he was doing that. "Miz Collins? Little Bear?"

"Ozark didn't hurt me or the twins," Annie said, "but those outlaws were awfully rough with Little Bear and your friends."

"I'm fine," Little Bear insisted. His face was bruised, and Preacher saw a little dried blood on it from some scrapes, but the young man wasn't badly hurt.

The same was true of Audie and Nighthawk. "Those scoundrels would have to do a lot worse to inflict any real damage on us," Audie said. "Are all of them dead? What about the man who went into the woods?"

Dog chose that moment to arrive in camp with blood on his muzzle, wearing a satisfied expression. Preacher chuckled and said, "Yeah, I reckon it's a safe bet all the varmints are done for, includin' that other fella."

He looked across the valley toward the mountain and added, "But Ozark and the rest of them no-good killers are still up yonder, and pretty soon it's gonna be their turn."

CHAPTER 31

After freeing Nighthawk, Preacher cut the bonds off Audie's wrists and ankles. Audie joined Nighthawk in rubbing circulation back in their hands and stomping around to get the blood flowing in their feet again.

"You're not going to ask me to stay behind again when you go after Ozark, are you?" Audie asked Preacher.

"Somebody needs to stay here with Miz Collins and Little Bear and the young'uns," Preacher pointed out.

Audie grimaced. "I know, I know. And from a practical standpoint, it makes the most sense for me to do it. I'm fully aware of that, but it doesn't mean I have to like it."

"No, it sure don't," Preacher agreed.

Audie nodded and said, "All right. I understand. If you two don't come back—not that I believe there's any chance in the world of that happening—I'll get our friends back to safety."

"I know that. Wouldn't feel near as comfortable goin' after Ozark if I didn't."

Little Bear surprised the mountain man by saying, "I wish you'd let me come with you. I wouldn't mind a chance at evening the score with some of those outlaws."

"Sorry, son." Preacher clapped a hand on the young man's shoulder. "I know you got the heart of a lot bigger bear, but the rest of you has got to grow into it. I want to make sure you get the chance to do that."

"Thank you, Preacher." Little Bear squared his shoulders. "I'll help protect Annie and the twins, too, if I need to."

"I know you will."

For now, Audie, Annie, Little Bear, and the infants would remain here at the camp. If enough time passed, though, they would need to flee just in case Ozark might be on his way back.

Preacher and Nighthawk dragged the bodies of the dead outlaws into the woods, well away from the fire. Annie didn't need to have those bloody carcasses around while she and the others waited, and they might attract predators, too.

Audie found some tin cups among the gear that had belonged to the dead men and poured coffee into them. Preacher sipped the strong black brew and nodded in satisfaction.

"This is just what we needed before settin' out after Ozark," he said. "It'll sure fortify us, ain't that right, Nighthawk?"

The warrior grunted and nodded. His years of traveling with Audie had given him an appreciation for coffee that some of his fellow Crow didn't possess.

The two of them didn't linger long. Before they left, however, Annie came over to Preacher and said quietly, "You just risk your life for us over and over, Preacher. Why do my children and I matter so much to you?"

"Well, it's the right thing to do, I reckon. A long time ago, I ran into a fella from Tennessee by the name of Crockett. He had a habit of sayin', 'Be sure you're right, then go ahead.' I was already tryin' to live by that sentiment before I met him, but he did a pretty good job of puttin' it into words."

Annie said, "Are you talking about David Crockett? The famous frontiersman who was killed down in Texas fighting the Mexican army?"

"Yes'm, that was him. To tell you the truth, I'm a mite surprised those boys of Santa Anna's ever managed to kill him. He went down fightin', too, I ain't got no doubt about that. Anybody who says different is just a dadblasted liar."

"I'm sure it would have been the same with you, if you had been there at the Alamo."

Preacher didn't say anything in response to that. His involvement with the Texas Revolution was a story for another time and place.

Impulsively, Annie gave him a hug.

"Please be safe and come back to us," she said as she stepped back.

"I sure intend to," Preacher pledged.

He wasn't sure he liked the look he saw in her eyes, as if she might be feeling things she shouldn't feel for a rough-as-a-cob rascal nearly old enough to be her pa, especially when he believed that Audie would be a much more suitable match for her.

But that was something for another time and place, too.

He and Nighthawk mounted up and rode toward the mountain with Dog trotting before them. None of them looked back at the camp. Their attention was focused on the task ahead.

They had to put an end to the threat of Mack Ozark, and that meant killing him. Nothing else would ever stop the outlaw from coming after them.

They might not have to kill all the other remaining members of Ozark's gang. It was possible some of them might give up and try to put some distance between themselves and Preacher if Ozark was dead.

But it would be simpler and safer in the long run to go ahead and send all of them across the divide, so that was Preacher's plan for now.

It was midafternoon by the time Preacher and Nighthawk approached the area where the avalanche had swept down the mountainside and into the trees. That was the closest spot to the cave, so Preacher figured that was where Mack Ozark would try to reach Jonathan Collins's hiding place, even though the climb would be tougher now.

Looking up at the rocky slope from where they were hidden in the trees, however, Preacher saw that the ascent would be possible. Maybe, despite what he had thought, even easier than it had been before the avalanche, since the boulders had scraped a possible path in places where the slope had been almost sheer when Preacher and Nighthawk climbed it.

Preacher grunted at the irony of it. He had started the avalanche hoping to drive Ozark away, and in the end, he might have made it easier for the man to lay his hands on the hidden treasure he sought.

It didn't matter, Preacher told himself. Mack Ozark wasn't going to live to spend any of that ill-gotten loot.

Preacher and Nighthawk had dismounted as they approached the tree line, and they went ahead on foot with Dog. As they neared the place where Ozark's men had dismounted, they heard the outlaws' horses moving around. Voices drifted to Preacher's ears as the men talked.

He didn't hear Ozark's gravelly tones. Had the gang's leader already started up to have a look at the cave? If so, then Ozark hadn't taken all of his men with him because some of them were still down here.

That would be an opportunity he and Nighthawk couldn't afford to pass up, Preacher thought.

Silently, he signaled to Nighthawk, indicating what the giant warrior should do. Nighthawk nodded in understanding and moved off through the brush with astonishing stealth for a man of his great size.

Preacher went the other way. They closed in from opposite directions on the spot where Ozark's men waited.

Preacher pressed his back against a pine tree's thick trunk, taking as much advantage of the cover as he could. He edged an eye around the trunk for a good look-see so he could take stock of the situation.

His hunch had been right. Ozark wasn't there. He counted four outlaws standing around holding the reins of the horses that had brought them here, along with those of two other mounts. Ozark had brought five men with him, Preacher recalled. Six horses meant that he had taken one man up to the cave with him.

This was a good chance for Preacher and Nighthawk to even the odds against them.

Suddenly, the outlaws jumped and exclaimed in surprise as several rocks the size of a man's head came tumbling down the slope. That set off a miniature avalanche as the rocks started more dirt and gravel sliding. It didn't amount to much, though, as was obvious when the dust that had billowed up momentarily dissipated.

"Damn, that just about scared me right outta my boots," one of the men said. "I thought for a second the whole side o' the mountain was about to come down on us."

"Probably the boss and Truett are diggin' up there around the cave and started those rocks rollin'," another outlaw said. He handed his horse's reins to one of the other men, stepped forward, cupped his hands around his mouth, and shouted up the slope, "Hey, boss, are you all right up there?"

"The entrance to the cave is blocked!" Ozark called back down. "But we can get in there with a little work! We're going to need some picks and shovels!"

Preacher had thought the same thing earlier. Ozark had confirmed it. What Preacher and Nighthawk had to do now was make sure none of the outlaws got a chance to dig out the entrance to the cave.

He knew Nighthawk would be watching from the other side of the open space where the four outlaws waited. The big warrior would follow Preacher's lead.

It would be nice to take Ozark by surprise, Preacher mused. He knew that back-door trail was still intact enough to use. If he could get up there and deal with Ozark and the other man while Nighthawk handled the outlaws down here . . . That meant Nighthawk would be facing four-to-one odds, but if anybody could tackle such a battle, it was the giant Crow.

Besides, he could leave Dog down here to give Nighthawk a hand—or a paw, so to speak.

Preacher let out the soft coo of a bird that sounded absolutely real. One of the outlaws turned his head to listen but then ignored it, and none of the others even appeared to notice.

Nighthawk heard the summons, though, and a few minutes later the warrior appeared in the brush beside Preacher almost as if by magic.

In the faintest of whispers that couldn't be heard more than a couple of feet away, Preacher explained his plan to his old friend. Nighthawk listened solemnly and then nodded to show that he understood and agreed.

"You'll know when you and Dog need to make your move," the mountain man concluded. "I reckon you'll be able to hear the ruckus up yonder."

For a second, Nighthawk almost smiled. Almost.

His huge hand fell on Preacher's shoulder and squeezed lightly for a second. The two men nodded to each other.

Preacher whispered briefly to Dog, who whined softly. Preacher knew that meant Dog wanted to come with him. His voice was firm as he said, "Stay. Help Nighthawk."

Dog licked his hand in affirmation. Preacher rubbed the animal's ears and then set out to circle around to the foot of the back-door trail.

When he was far enough away from the spot where the four outlaws waited for Ozark, he stood up and moved faster. After Preacher had been over some ground, even if it was only once, he had no trouble retracing his steps. He knew exactly where he was going and the fastest way to get there.

Because of that, it didn't take him long to reach his destination.

He followed the trail up the mountainside to the point where it entered the long, narrow cleft.

As he started along that gloomy passage, he drew his Colts. If Ozark or that other outlaw happened to come this direction, he would be a perfect target in the confined space with no place to take cover. If they opened fire on him, all he could do was blaze away in return and pray for a miracle.

But luck was with him and the trail remained empty as it climbed toward the cave. When Preacher came closer, he heard Ozark and Truett talking, their voices interspersed with the clatter of rocks.

The two outlaws were digging at the barrier left behind by the avalanche, using bare hands to pick up smaller rocks and toss them aside. That was probably what they had been doing when they started the little rockslide earlier.

The sounds paused, and the other man said, "I don't think we can get through this way, Mack."

"No, I already said we're going to need tools," Ozark replied. "But until we get them, we might as well clear away what we can. Just think, Ed—there's a fortune in there waiting for us, only a few feet away."

The avarice was so fervent in Ozark's voice that he sounded like a man worshipping something he regarded as holy.

Which, when it came to money, might just be true in Ozark's case.

The outlaws went back to work as Preacher edged closer. His hands were wrapped tightly around the gun butts. When he reached the end of the cleft, he stepped out into the open and narrowed his eyes against the bright sunshine.

What was left of the rock outcropping that formed the "nose" blocked him from sight of the two outlaws. But if he couldn't see them, they couldn't see him, either. He began moving down the trail toward them.

Preacher placed each foot carefully, not wanting to dislodge any small rocks that might tumble down and alert Ozark and Truett that someone was nearby. He was especially cautious when he had to step over small gaps in the trail caused by the avalanche or move around piles of rubble it had left behind. Thankfully, he was sure-footed and had good balance.

He was almost to the outcropping when he heard Ozark say, "We've cleared away enough for now. I'm not sure we could do much more, anyway. We'll get a dozen men up here in a day or two, and it won't take them long to finish the job."

Preacher intended to finish his job right now. With his hands clamped tightly on the revolvers, he slid down the last bit of slope and landed on the level space in front of the cave. Ozark and the other outlaw heard his boots hit the ground and jerked around toward him, but by the time they turned, Preacher had the Colts aimed squarely at them.

"Best not move, gents," the mountain man drawled, "because it'd be a plumb pleasure to fill both you varmints with lead."

CHAPTER 32

Despite giving them that warning, Preacher didn't expect the men to surrender, and sure enough, they didn't.

The outlaw called Truett still held a good-sized slab of stone he hadn't thrown aside, and with a sudden grunt of effort, he heaved it at Preacher as hard as he could.

Preacher triggered both Colts, but Truett's tactic proved surprisingly effective. Both bullets struck the rock slab and whined off harmlessly. Preacher had to duck to the side to avoid being struck and possibly knocked off the rim. The brink was dangerously close to his boot heels.

Truett had followed the rock when he threw it. He was right behind it, and Preacher didn't have time to brace himself before the outlaw tackled him.

For a second as he fell, Preacher thought they were both going over the edge. But they landed right next to it, saving them from a fatal fall—for the moment.

Preacher was on the bottom. Truett tried to ram an elbow into the mountain man's stomach and a knee into his groin at the same time. Preacher writhed out of the way of the knee, but the elbow dug into his belly and made air gust from his mouth.

At the same time, he swung the right-hand pistol and crashed it against Truett's head. Preacher felt bone shatter under the powerful blow. Truett's eyes widened in shock as he loomed over Preacher. Blood welled from his nose and ears. He collapsed on top of the mountain man.

Spasms shook Truett's body as death claimed him. That made it difficult for Preacher to get hold of him as he tried to roll the outlaw's body off.

While Preacher had his hands full with that, Mack Ozark rushed him. Preacher heard the boss outlaw's hurried footsteps pounding on the rock and twisted his left wrist to squeeze off a shot in his direction.

However, from that awkward position the bullet flew wide, and the next instant Ozark's boot heel slammed down hard on Preacher's wrist. The vicious blow caused Preacher to grimace. His hand opened involuntarily, and the gun skidded away.

He finally got his right leg free from Truett's deadweight and twisted onto his left side so he could kick Ozark in the left thigh. That knocked the outlaw back several steps and gave Preacher time to finally shove the dead Truett away from him. Truett toppled over the edge and tumbled down the slope, arms and legs flopping lifelessly.

Preacher rolled away from the brink and came up on his knees just in time to see that Ozark had picked up one of the rocks that had been thrown away from the pile in front of the cave. He heaved it at Preacher, who once again had to dive to the side to avoid being struck and carried over the edge.

He wasn't able to avoid the rock entirely, though. It struck his right shoulder with enough force to make that arm go numb. He knew the other Colt slipped from his fingers because he saw it hit the ground, but he couldn't feel it.

Now he didn't have either revolver, but Ozark didn't reach for his own gun. Instead, he bull-rushed Preacher, clearly intent on forcing the mountain man over the edge.

Preacher scrambled to his feet to meet the charge. Ozark wasn't expecting that and couldn't check his attack in time to stop.

Preacher's right arm was still numb, but he whipped a punch with his left that landed solidly on Ozark's jaw and jolted the outlaw's head to the side. His momentum carried him into Preacher and the two of them grappled, swaying and circling, no more than a step or two from falling.

Preacher got his left foot behind Ozark's right knee and jerked that leg out from under the man. Ozark went over backward, but he hung on to Preacher and dragged the mountain man down with him. They rolled away from the brink toward the cave mouth.

Ozark got a hand under Preacher's chin and levered his head backward. Preacher had to let go. They broke apart and surged upright with about ten feet separating them. Even though the fight had been short, it had been so intense that both men were breathing hard.

Preacher heard shouts and gunfire from down along the tree line, punctuated by fierce snarls and howls of pain. Nighthawk and Dog had gone to work on the rest of the outlaws when they heard the commotion up here. Preacher wished fleetingly that he knew how they were doing, but he didn't have time to wonder about that right now.

Not with a maddened killer like Mack Ozark facing him.

Ozark might have been trying to give himself a moment to catch his breath as he said, "You're a damn fool, Preacher. We both know there's a fortune in there." A sly look appeared on his face. "Why don't you come in on it with me?"

"Because I ain't a no-good thief and killer," Preacher shot back at him. "Besides, I wouldn't trust you as far as I can throw you. You'd double-cross me without thinkin' twice about it."

An ugly grin stretched across Ozark's face. "Yeah, you're right, I probably would," he admitted. "You know, you're pretty hard to kill. I think this time I'm going to get my hands around your throat and choke the life out of you myself, just to be sure you're finally dead."

"Come on and try," Preacher invited. "Even if you do it, I got friends down there. Nighthawk and Dog'll take care o' you."

"Even if they defeat my men, I'm not worried about them. I'll just kill them, too. You see, Preacher"—and the grin got even uglier—"nothing can stop me. I won't allow that to happen. I always get what I want, and I just kill anybody who gets in my way. Man, woman, child, it doesn't matter. I just kill them. I always have."

Rage at such callous, casual evil welled up inside Preacher and boiled over. He reached back, plucked the tomahawk from behind his belt, and threw it in a continuation of the same motion. He felt no more compunction striking like that than he would have felt about killing a snake.

Ozark was worse than a snake because he had a human intelligence, warped and perverted though it might be. Maybe he'd been trying to goad Preacher into making that move. He was ready and darted aside. His hand flashed up and caught the tomahawk as it spun through the air.

Then, almost too fast to see, he whipped it back at the mountain man.

Preacher's reflexes were just as fast. He leaped to the side and landed running. That lunge brought him to Ozark. Preacher's right arm was working again. He swung that fist at Ozark's face, and the outlaw had to jerk away from the punch. Preacher tackled him.

They reeled back against the pile of rocks in front of the cave. Preacher got his shoulder against Ozark's chest and rammed him into the rocks as hard as he could. Ozark finally showed some pain as his back struck against the rough stones.

Preacher lifted a knee into Ozark's belly. He was fighting with a seldom-seen desperation now. The two of them were evenly matched, but Preacher had suffered a lot more punishment over the past days. Ozark was fresher, maybe even stronger. Plus, he had an incredible amount of arrogance fueling him.

But Preacher had an indefinable something that had carried

him through decades of danger and uncountable adventures. Audie might call it a refusal to be defeated. Maybe it was just plain old muleheadedness. But Preacher had no give-up in him, and no back-up, either. He fought until a normal man would have given up—and then he fought some more.

Ozark tried to throw punches at him to fend him off, but those blows were steadily getting weaker now. Preacher grabbed the front of Ozark's shirt, jerked him away from the rocks, and slammed him against them again. And again.

Somewhere close by, above Preacher's head, stone rasped against stone.

Ozark looked up, and for the first time, the confidence in his eyes disappeared and fear replaced it. Preacher knew the reaction was genuine. He glanced up, as well, and saw that one of the slabs of rock about ten feet above them in the pile was balanced delicately on some smaller rocks—and was leaning toward them. The slab was the size of a man's torso and probably weighed a thousand pounds or more.

"No!" Ozark shrieked.

Preacher pulled him forward and then hammered him against the pile again. The big rock tipped and fell. Preacher let go and flung himself backward. Ozark's scream was cut short by the huge crash as the stone slab came down on him.

Preacher had lost his balance and fallen as he got out of the way. He lay there where he was and looked at Mack Ozark, who was pinned to the pile by the rock. Ozark's body was visible only up to his upper chest. The rest of his torso and his head were underneath the slab. His arms and legs jerked and flailed for a couple of heartbeats, then sagged and hung loose and still. A crimson trickle began to run out from under the stone.

Mack Ozark had died less than twenty feet from the fortune in hidden loot he had wanted so badly.

Wearily, Preacher pushed himself to his feet. He went over to the edge and peered down at the tree line a couple of hundred feet below. The shooting and yelling had stopped down there, and as Preacher stepped into view, Nighthawk and Dog came out into the open where he could see them. The giant Crow lifted an arm over his head and waved to let Preacher know that everything was under control down there.

A wave of relief went through the mountain man. He returned the wave and then started looking for his Colts and tomahawk. He wanted to retrieve the weapons before climbing down to rejoin his friends.

He didn't even glance at Ozark's body again. The outlaw was dead, a richly deserved fate. That death wouldn't bring back any of the innocent people Ozark had slaughtered during his bloody-handed career as an outlaw—but at least he would never take another life.

Sometimes that had to be enough. Preacher picked up the revolvers, pouched the irons, tucked away the tomahawk, and started down to where Nighthawk and Dog waited for him.

St. Louis, six weeks later

The sun was barely up and mist still hung over the great river as Preacher and Nighthawk led their horses out of the livery stable where the animals had been kept the past few days. Dog was with them and looked as eager to be back on the trail as the big gray stallion was.

They found Audie waiting for them, standing in the hard-packed dirt street with his arms crossed over his chest and a frown on his face, the same stern look that had struck fear into the hearts of countless students during his university career.

"So the two of you were just going to sneak off and head for the high country without bidding anyone farewell, is that it?"

Nighthawk just looked uncomfortable. Preacher said, "We told you we were gonna be ridin' out today. You won't have no trouble findin' us when you get back out there to the mountains. We'll be somewhere around Dutch Charley's. If we ain't there, he'll know where we are."

"It's going to take quite a while to accompany Annie back to Illinois and see to it that she's settled in a new life," Audie pointed out. "I don't expect you two footloose rapscallions to sit around and do nothing while you wait for me."

"I didn't say we were gonna do nothin'. We'll trap a mite, maybe do some fishin'. I don't really care as long as no trouble crops up." Preacher sighed. "It seems like I never can get out o' the shadow of some ruckus for very long."

Audie nodded. "That does seem to be your destiny. And Nighthawk here isn't much better at avoiding trouble."

"Umm," the giant Crow said.

"I know, I know, it's not your fault. Someone always drags you into it." Audie nodded toward Preacher. "And he's worse about that than anyone else."

"Hey, now, I'm a peaceable man—"

Dog barked. Preacher looked around to see Annie Collins and Little Bear hurrying toward them in the dawn light.

Annie rushed up to Preacher and hugged him. "Don't go back to the mountains," she said. "Come with us to Illinois."

With Audie's help and advice, she was going to found a school there, using the money they had brought back from the cave. They would never be able to find everyone the gang had robbed over the years, but at least that would be doing something worthwhile with the money.

The outlaw compound had been empty when they got back to it. They had gotten word from some of the Salish that Mack Ozark was dead and so were all the men he had taken with him after the hidden loot. A hunting party from Red Shirt's village had witnessed the battles from a distance and returned with the news.

In return for the lion's share of the supplies left at the village, Red Shirt had provided men to help Preacher and Nighthawk dig out the cave and recover the money. Preacher had a hunch the chief was a little embarrassed about cooperating with Ozark in the past, but the man hadn't had much choice about that. He'd wanted to protect his people, and Preacher couldn't fault him for that.

"Civilization?" Preacher said now in response to Annie's invitation to accompany her to Illinois. He made a face. "St. Louis is too civilized for my taste. I ain't sure I could breathe the air back yonder in Illinois anymore." He patted her shoulder. "But don't you worry. Audie'll take good care o' you and the young'uns. Where are the young'uns, for that matter?"

"They're asleep at the hotel. The proprietor's wife is looking after them. We had to come and say goodbye, at least."

Little Bear stepped up and said, "That's right. And you don't have to worry, either, Preacher. I'll help Audie make sure the journey goes smoothly."

"I know you will," Preacher said. "Are you comin' back to the mountains?"

"I don't know yet. Maybe someday. I suppose that will depend on how things are in Illinois. I told you, I never really fit in on the frontier. But . . . I'm an Indian. I may not be welcome back east, either."

Annie said, "You'll be fine wherever you go, Little Bear. You're a fine, intelligent young man. I'm proud to call you my friend."

"Thank you," he said softly. "And I'm very happy to have you as my friend."

Annie moved over beside Audie and rested a hand on his shoulder. Little Bear stood on the former professor's other side. All three of them lifted hands in farewell as Preacher and Nighthawk swung into their saddles and turned the horses west, leading a couple of pack animals behind them.

"This is the first time you and the little fella been apart in a good long while, ain't it?" Preacher asked as they rode away.

Nighthawk's massive shoulders rose and fell.

"You know, there's a chance he might not come back to the

mountains," Preacher mused. "He's a mighty good fit with Annie, if the two of 'em could ever open their eyes and realize it."

Nighthawk grunted.

"You're probably right. Audie's got too much o' the wild frontier in him to stay away permanent-like." Preacher chuckled. "Just like you and me. We ain't fit company for civilized human bein's no more!"

He looked back over his shoulder, something he hadn't done too often in his life. He'd always been more focused on where he was going rather than where he had been.

But sometimes there were moments . . . moments when it was all right to think about all the places he had been and all the things he had done . . . and lurking in the back of his mind, dreams of all the adventures yet to come.

He looked—but only for a moment—at the three people waving goodbye, and then he turned his eyes westward again, toward the high country. Dog was bounding ahead as usual, full of energy and enthusiasm, and a grin creased the mountain man's rugged face.

"Let's go home," Preacher said.

Visit our website at
KensingtonBooks.com
to sign up for our newsletters, read
more from your favorite authors, see
books by series, view reading group
guides, and more!

BOOK CLUB
BETWEEN THE CHAPTERS

Become a Part of Our
Between the Chapters Book Club
Community and Join the Conversation

Betweenthechapters.net